NO ANGEL

Sally could hardly breathe as she let herself and the two women into the cottage. She couldn't remember ever being so excited. Her panties were already drenched with her own juices, her nipples taut and prominent. She trotted up the stairs to the bedroom, Liz and Ros behind her. Her heart was pounding.

'Well, here we are,' Liz said, once Sally had closed the bedroom door and the three of them stood facing each other. 'I hardly know where to start.' Her voice was urgent with desire.

NO ANGEL

MARIAN MALONE

First published in 1999 by
Sapphire
an imprint of Virgin Publishing Ltd
Thames Wharf Studios,
Rainville Road, London W6 9HA

Copyright © Marian Malone 1999

The right of Marian Malone to be identified as the Author of this
Work has been asserted by her in accordance with the Copyright,
Designs and Patents Act 1988.

ISBN 0 352 33462 2

Cover photograph by Steve Diet Goedde

Typeset by SetSystems Ltd, Saffron Walden, Essex
Printed and bound in Great Britain by Mackays of Chatham PLC

This book is sold subject to the condition that it shall not, by way of
trade or otherwise, be lent, resold, hired out or otherwise circulated
without the publisher's prior written consent in any form of binding or
cover other than that in which it is published and without a similar
condition, including this condition, being imposed on the subsequent
purchaser.

ONE

Sally Avery decided that she could put it off no longer: she had to make a start. If she only managed to write a paragraph, it would be a beginning. She forced herself to get her notes down and spread them out on her desk.

It was hopeless. She didn't even know where to begin. The sheer volume of research material she'd accumulated for the book was overwhelming. She didn't know how to organise it, let alone transform it into a finished work. She sat at her desk, staring at the boxes full of papers and documents. Where should she begin?

It was no good. Her muscles were knotted with tension, her shoulders hunched and her fists clenched. She lowered her shoulders and uncurled her fingers. She took a series of deep breaths. Relax, Sally, she told herself. But her stomach was still twisted with tension, her mind still racing.

She'd try to break the job down into smaller, more manageable tasks. She tried to focus on specific jobs that needed to be done. She could transcribe her taped interviews, perhaps – or get things into chronological order. Or she could organise her illustrations. But somehow none of it was working.

No matter how hard she tried, all she saw were the blank pages she needed to fill with 80,000 words. Words that needed to be produced from the jumble of the papers before her. Her heart palpitated; her hands were cold and clammy. Blood pounded in her ears.

She was panicking. She pulled off her reading glasses and threw them down on the desk. She couldn't do it. She turned off her desk lamp and walked out of the office, closing the door behind her.

Listlessly, she wandered into her bedroom and lay down on her bed. At this rate, she'd never get it done. She felt swamped. And it had been the same every time she had tried to make a start on the book over the last few months. She gazed up at her ceiling, concentrating on the whiteness and evenness of its surface. She tried to empty her mind, to replace the maelstrom of doubts and anxieties with the blank whiteness of the ceiling. As she relaxed back into the duvet, her muscles gradually softened and her breathing slowed.

She lay there for ten minutes or so, letting the tension drain from her body and mind. At last she felt calmer. She'd have lunch now, she thought. As she sat up, she spotted the copy of *Diva* she had been reading in bed last night. She picked it up. The magazine was open at the classified section and she glanced through the small ads, looking for an item she had spotted the previous evening. There it was: a discreet advertisement for a lesbian fetish club. She was curious. She was very curious.

Although she'd never admitted it to anyone, the notion of letting go sexually and submitting to someone else seemed highly erotic. Her sexual fantasies had always been explicit and specialised. Although she had never so much as dabbled in the leather scene, in her fantasy life she was a veteran. Her dreams were filled with images of latex-clad doms training gorgeous, submissive slaves for a life of pleasure. From the safety of her bedroom, she indulged her fascination with bondage, punishment and obedience.

Recently, she had plucked up the courage to seek out books on the subject and visit a few fetish websites. As a result, she'd learnt a lot about herself and her sexual nature and was beginning to think about putting her fantasies into practice. She'd even written a couple of erotic stories about them. She looked down at the magazine in her hand. She noticed that the address of the London fetish club was in the same street of her favourite second-hand bookshop. Did she dare? It was only about ten minutes away by car and her curiosity was definitely piqued. If she didn't like it, she could always leave. Why not? She had nothing to lose.

Later that night, Sally was sitting on a high bar stool, sipping a glass of wine. The leather club was really just one big room, with a small bar in one corner and a dozen or so tables scattered around. There was a small dance floor – they even had a disco-style glitter ball, Sally noted with amusement – and a makeshift stage in one corner. The walls were decorated with fetish photos, some of which she recognised as being the work of Robert Mapplethorpe. There were also photos of James Dean, Montgomery Clift and Marlon Brando in his handsome, dangerous prime.

Knots of women sat at tables, or stood near the bar. Some of them were dressed in the exotic garb that Sally's imagination expected. Leather, rubber and studs were everywhere. But most of her fellow customers were dressed pretty much as she was, in casual clothes or jeans.

So far it was OK. Nothing had happened to make her feel out of her depth. She just sat quietly on her stool, drinking it all in. But she was unbelievably excited. Just being in the same room with people who not only shared her interests but actually participated in the kind of activities she hardly dared dream about made her feel wicked. And she liked the feeling. She could get used to it.

There was something happening to her left. She turned her head to look. A group was forming around two women who had recently come into the bar. One of them was clearly the other's mistress. She looked haughty and imperious as her slave stood obediently with her head bowed. Sally couldn't hear what they were saying. What was going on? Was it OK to look? Or would it be considered spying? Though that was silly, she realised. Anything that went on in the public glare of the bar was fair game. They probably even wanted spectators. It probably turned them on to know people were looking.

She held her breath as she watched the scene unfolding only feet away. She took another sip of her drink and crossed her legs, never taking her eyes off the two women in front of her.

The dark-haired woman was kneeling, looking up at the other woman, whose blonde hair spread out over her shoulders. The one on her knees had her hands cuffed behind her back and a leather collar encircled her delicate neck. Her companion wore a supple rubber dress, the corset bodice emphasising her full breasts. She stood looking down at the slave, smiled, then stroked her slave's cheek with the tip of the riding crop she held.

'Honour your mistress,' she commanded.

Instantly, the kneeling woman leant forward and began licking her mistress's shoes. Her back trembled with the strain of maintaining the position with her hands cuffed, yet the expression on her face was one of delight. She smeared her tongue over every millimetre of the blonde woman's black stiletto boots, seemingly eager to please. Her round backside was high in the air, her PVC mini-skirt stretched taut across her cheeks. From where Sally sat, she could see the slave's buttocks, peeking out from underneath the skirt; her black G-string emphasised the pout of her pussy lips. Sally wriggled in her seat. The movement created a delightful friction. She could feel the smooth plastic of the stool rubbing her pussy through her panties and moisture spreading between her legs. She looked around the dim room, hoping her arousal wasn't obvious to everybody.

She hadn't known what to expect when she'd finally summoned up the courage to visit a fetish club, but the evening had certainly proved interesting so far. She wriggled in her chair, enjoying the sensation of her wet pussy rubbing against the hard seat. The slave was licking her mistress's ankles now, sucking and kissing the white flesh. The dominant woman looked down impassively, occasionally swishing her riding crop and flicking her slave's raised buttocks with it. They were light strokes, intended to arouse rather than hurt. The submissive girl reacted strongly to the strokes, her entire body trembling in obvious pleasure. If only that were her, thought Sally. She could imagine the sensation of the crop on her own bottom, smell the leather of the mistress's boots, taste her skin . . .

The blonde woman took a step back, causing the slave to fall forward unsteadily. Without her hands to support her, she struggled to raise herself up and sit on her heels.

'I didn't give you permission to stop, Slave.' The mistress's imperious tone made Sally tingle. How *she* longed to be given orders and forced to obey. The slave shuffled forward on her knees and leant down to start licking the dominant's feet again.

'You clearly need a lesson in obedience,' the mistress declared. 'You will be punished.'

Sally's eyes widened. She could hardly believe that she was going to witness the gorgeous brunette being punished. She hoped that the blonde would decide to use the riding crop on her slave. She longed to witness the crop slicing through the air. She could imagine the sound it would make as it made contact with the girl's creamy buttocks. She visualised the slave's body trembling as the crop struck her.

Please whip her, she thought to herself and then blushed –

ashamed of herself for wishing another person harm. But the slave wanted it, didn't she? Surely that made it OK?

The blonde woman raised her arm high above her head. She swished the crop several times through the air. The sound of it made moisture gush between Sally's legs. The slave trembled, expecting to be hit. The mistress was just teasing her, Sally thought, guessing that anticipation would heighten the experience for the waiting girl. The slave never lifted her head from the floor. She went on licking her mistress's stiletto boots. The mistress leant forward and pulled her slave's skirt up over her hips, exposing her round cheeks to everyone in the club. Sally drew in a long breath. The woman's arse was as perfect as she had imagined. Beautifully rounded and creamily smooth – Sally couldn't wait to see the imprint of the whip on those cheeks.

Swish! The dominant struck her slave across the left buttock. She traced the tip of the crop along the cleft of the girl's bottom and up her spine, then brought it down across her left buttock. Narrow red stripes glowed against the pale flesh. Sally's knickers were drenched. She leant forward to get a better view. How she envied the slave. If only she had the nerve she would step forward and take her place. She wanted to experience the humiliation of a public beating, to serve a mistress while everyone watched. She ached to feel the kiss of the crop.

The blonde woman slapped her submissive on the buttocks until they were scarlet – a mass of bright stripes which seemed to make them glow. Sally imagined that the slave would be feeling highly aroused, that the redness of her arse would make her skin tingly and sensitive. Her pussy underneath her G-string would be dripping with juice, the hard knob of her clit aching to be touched. Sally wondered if the mistress would permit the girl to climax later. Perhaps that would be the slave's reward for an evening of obedience.

She closed her eyes and imagined the two women lying on a disordered bed, wrapped around each other in a frenzied sixty-nine, mouths clamped over each other's cunts. Yes, that was how she would want her mistress to treat her. She watched the two women again. The blonde girl wielded the whip with an economy of movement that made Sally realise how fit and athletic she was. Her arms were muscular, her biceps clearly visible. In spite of her ample breasts, she had no spare fat on her body. She was streamlined and lean. Perfect, Sally thought.

By contrast, the slave was ripe and voluptuous, her breasts spilling over the cups of her PVC top. Her eyes were closed, a rapturous expression on her face as she kissed her lover's feet.

Finally, the punishment was over.

'Enough,' the blonde said tenderly, bending to help her slave up.

'Thank you, mistress,' said the slave quietly, once she was on her feet again.

Sally was turned on all the way home in the car. She could hardly believe what she had just witnessed. To think she had almost chickened out of visiting the club. At the door, she had almost turned around and walked away. Thank God she hadn't. She had finally done it: she'd seen it for herself. She'd seen real people acting out a scene she had only dreamt about. And she knew it was what she wanted.

Her heart was pounding in her chest. She wanted to experience it for herself. She wanted to submit herself to another's will and allow herself to be completely and utterly dominated. If only it had been her tonight, cuffed and half-naked and being punished in public. Her clit throbbed; she reached down and stroked it lightly through her wet underwear. The sensation took the edge off her arousal and seemed to soothe her. If only she were brave enough. If only she could really do it.

She pulled into her drive and gathered up her things. She locked the car and was inside in seconds. She ran up the stairs and let herself into her flat. The moment the front door was locked behind her, she began tearing off her clothes. By the time she reached her bedroom she was naked. She threw herself down on the duvet and parted her legs.

Make it last, she thought. Don't waste it. She ran her nails up and down her torso, barely touching. She kneaded her small, firm breasts. She brushed the tips of her nipples, flicked them with a fingernail; they hardened under her touch. Finally, when she could stand it no longer, she gripped her nipples and squeezed them hard. It felt incredible – almost hurting her, but not quite. Pinching her sensitive nipples until they nearly hurt somehow seemed to intensify the pleasurable sensations she experienced. She didn't understand it – she didn't try to – but she knew that riding the edge of pain gave her exquisite pleasure. She squeezed her nipples again, rolled them and pulled them. Then she spread her legs wider and began to touch herself.

At first the strokes were light and brief, the merest brush of her fingers against the sensitive flesh of her clit; she traced the outline of her labia with her hand, gently teasing the moist slit. A damp patch was forming on the duvet underneath her. She dipped her fingers into her honeyed cleft and teased her hard clit with a fingertip. Both hands were between her legs now. She stretched her lips apart, exposing the tiny nub of her clitoris. She circled it with a finger, not quite touching it – coaxing incredible sensations from it. Tingles of pleasure spread through her belly in a warm glow. As her arousal grew, she touched her clit more directly, increasing her pressure and speed.

Her thoughts kept returning to the club. In her mind's eye, she was kneeling bound at the feet of the haughty, beautiful mistress. She imagined the dominant forcing her head down, pulling her tight skirt up to reveal her naked arse. Fantasising like this always increased her pleasure, but this was the first time she had ever witnessed such a scene first hand. The memory had her almost wild with desire. Her fingers were working overtime between her legs.

Sally was concentrating now, her hair wild and her breasts glistening with sweat. Her breathing was thready and fast. She pictured the mistress lashing her upturned arse with the crop, imagined the stroke of the whip on her buttocks. Images of spanking and submission whirled through her mind, arousing her more than she would have believed possible. She could hear a faint squelching noise as her fingers alternately circled her clit and dipped into her tight hole. The air in the room was heavy with the perfume of sex and sweat. She breathed in deeply, trying to drink in the scent.

She began moaning gently. Her body was taut now, her head against the pillow and her back arched. Her breasts were thrust forward, their strawberry-pink nipples erect and prominent. Tension grew in her belly. Her legs were taut and trembling, her torso shiny with perspiration. As she imagined the mistress delivering her final, blistering blow of the crop, her entire body began to quiver and her pussy pulsed around her thrusting fingers. An incredible orgasm overwhelmed her. In her mind's eye, the rubber-clad woman had knelt beside her and kissed her on the lips. A breath hissed between Sally's lips, followed by deep moans. Waves of pleasure spiralled out from her groin and coursed through her body.

Gradually, her breathing returned to normal and her body stopped trembling. She closed her eyes, a sense of warm bliss overwhelming her. She felt relaxed and content. Realising she was about to nod off, she climbed under the covers and was quickly asleep.

Late the next morning, Sally was at her desk. She stretched her shoulders, stiff from long hours in front of the computer. She scrolled back to the beginning of the article she had just finished writing and checked it for mistakes. Satisfied that the text was OK, she turned on her laser printer and flipped up its lid to make sure it was loaded with paper. Once the machine began to spew out the neatly typed pages, she went into the kitchen to make coffee, looking around the room as she waited for the kettle to boil. The walls could do with a new coat of paint, she thought. She had bought the flat three years ago with the money her grandmother had left her. She had decorated it herself, spending hours choosing colour schemes and fabrics. Sunny colours and bright furnishings emphasised the light and huge pot-plants gave the place a tropical air.

As a freelance journalist, she wrote a weekly column in a local newspaper and occasionally got an article into one of the nationals, and she'd had a couple of short stories accepted recently – dark, erotic stories that had excited her as much as she hoped they would excite her readers. Her book *Secrets of the Sea* – about a Cornish fishing village which believed its fisherman were protected by a paranormal entity – had been a huge success and her publishers had quickly commissioned another. But although she had researched her subject and outlined the book, she'd somehow found it impossible to write.

Not that she had writer's block: she didn't believe in it and, besides, she had no problems writing articles and stories. Just the book. She somehow just kept procrastinating, and putting it off and making excuses not to begin on it. After the success of *Secrets of the Sea*, she'd been terrified that anything she wrote would be an anticlimax. Gradually, her mild anxiety about living up to her first book had developed almost into a phobia. She only had to think about taking down her dusty research notes from the top shelf and she went all sweaty and weak. Yesterday's episode had been typical.

She carried her coffee and the biscuit tin into the living room and threw herself down on the sofa. She rummaged under the cushions for the remote control, then switched on the TV and settled down to watch the afternoon chat shows. Cagney, the friendlier of her two ginger cats, leapt onto her lap and settled down regally. The more independent Lacey snoozed on an armchair nearby.

Surfing between channels, she found her mind wandering back to the club. Last night's experience had proved to be a revelation. She went all tingly just thinking about it. She shifted in her seat and pulled her jeans away from her crotch.

She yearned for a relationship in which her body, even her orgasm, belonged to the other person. She dreamt about handing over responsibility for her sexual needs to her lover. A relationship in which she had no choice but to submit to whatever her partner demanded of her. At heart she was a subbie, searching for her mistress.

Her best friend Katie had always been active in the Brighton lesbian leather scene and had more than once invited her along. But something always held Sally back. She was both compelled and alienated by the thought of submission. She sensed that there was a bottomless well of erotic pleasure to be tapped into, if only she could submit to a dominant partner. Yet, at the same time, she feared the loss of control which was an inevitable part of the process.

In fact, Sally thought ruefully, she had started to believe that this need to retain control of herself and her life was holding her back professionally as well as sexually. She experienced an almost obsessive need to organise and assess every aspect of her routine. Even the most mundane tasks had to be accomplished in the most efficient and practical way. Her cupboards and drawers were neat and tidy. She did her housework meticulously and had a rota for each domestic task. Even her spice rack was organised alphabetically.

Try as she might, she hadn't been able to apply this system to her work. The task before her seemed far too huge for her to control. And Sally needed to be in control. Although journalism and her erotic short stories gave her a measure of financial security, it didn't seem to help her overcome the problems she was facing with her scholarly writing. Maybe if she could free herself from her compulsion and give herself up to the experience of life, she would be truly free. Free not only to enjoy her work and life, but free to explore her sexual nature and express herself fully.

If only she could let go of the need to control the uncontrollable, she'd be able to get on with the book. She just needed to make a start and the rest would be easy.

She thought about the scene she had witnessed last night and wished it had been her being dominated. Just thinking about being restrained made her feel horny. She wondered if she dared buy herself some chains and restraints and have a go at tying herself up. Would it be as exciting as if someone else had bound her? She was not sure, but just visualising it was making her very wet.

Raising her bottom off the sofa, she slid down the zip of her jeans, slipped her hand inside and cupped her mound. It was hot inside her underwear and, as her fingers brushed against her swollen labia, she felt a tremor of pleasure. Trailing a finger along her slit, she spread the slippery juices over her lips. She lay back and began to rub herself in long, slow strokes. She teased her clit, then slid her fingers downwards to push against her hole. After half a dozen strokes, she was breathing heavily and unconsciously spreading her legs even further apart. She began alternately circling her clit and thrusting two juice-moistened fingers deep into her pussy.

With her free hand, she lifted the front of her T-shirt and pulled her bra up and over her breasts, releasing them. On contact with the cool air, her nipples peaked and contracted. She pinched and stretched them with her right hand, her left still working rhythmically between her legs. Heat rose through her body, colouring her face. Her head fell back against the cushions; her breathing quickened. Her fingers wriggled expertly inside her jeans. Her clit tightened and hardened; her fanny began to contract and pulsate. She moaned softly.

Across the hall in her office, the telephone bell began to ring, its insistent peal breaking through her consciousness.

'Damn!' she said aloud, and got up. She ran across the

landing, adjusting her clothing as she went. Her office phone was vital for faxes and the Internet, as well as phone calls. It was part of her business and she didn't dare ignore it. Had it been her private telephone, which rang in the flat rather than the office, she would have let it ring.

'Sally Avery,' she panted her usual greeting as she answered the phone.

'Sally, it's Margaret...' Her heart sank as she heard the familiar, yet not entirely welcome voice of her editor. She hadn't realised that it was that time of the month again. Margaret had a diary note to ring Sally every month to ask about the progress of *House of Spirits* and she never missed the call. She'd even telephoned from the airport once, *en route* for her annual holiday in the Algarve. Does the bloody woman never have a day off? Sally wondered.

Usually, the two women indulged in a sort of verbal ritual dance. Sally issued assurances that she was working on the project and that the delay was a temporary one, and Margaret made sympathetic noises and tentatively asked for a revised delivery date. Of course, Sally had to become more inventive and stretch her imagination to come up with convincing reasons for her lack of progress. Her dancing partner had become more inventive too, trying to pin Sally down and asking to see work in progress. But today Margaret interrupted her before she could begin her usual routine of parry and defence.

'You've probably read that Eden's has been taken over, Sally,' she began. Sally hadn't heard, but she didn't interrupt. 'We've got a new managing director and he's keen to change direction. He's going to honour all projects we're already committed to, but he wants them actioned quickly. He wants all of our old list published by the end of next year. That means that you've got six months to finish *Spirits*.'

Sally was horrified. She couldn't meet the deadline: yet she knew she must. As she tried to come up with something coherent, the editor went on: 'I'm sorry, Sally, but I've been told that unless you can submit three chapters to me by the end of the month, we're dropping the option. And, of course, that would mean you'd have to pay back the advance.'

'You'll have them,' Sally said. 'I promise. They'll be with you by the first of September.'

She'd just have to put her mind to it. She'd spent the advance long ago and she didn't have enough savings to repay it. If Eden's dropped the option, it could mean a court case – one she knew she would lose. So she bit her lip, hid her doubts and assured her editor that she'd meet her obligations.

Three chapters in less than a month. She had to come up with 15,000 words or so when she hadn't the slightest idea where to start. How could she do it? How could she even begin to think about doing it?

Sally felt sick with worry, her stomach tightening into a knot. As always, in times of difficulty, she thought instantly of Katie. At the very least, talking to her friend would calm her down. Katie would no doubt offer her sound, practical advice and her soothing, comforting tones were just what Sally needed.

With shaking hands, she punched the familiar number into her office phone and waited for it to ring.

'Kate Elliot.'

Sally sighed gently. The sound of her friend's voice had already calmed her nerves. 'Katie, it's Sally,' she said quickly. 'I've got a problem: I need your help.'

'Tell me about it, Angel. Just let me get comfortable, first; I was in the middle of something.'

'Am I interrupting? Is this a bad time?' Sally queried anxiously.

'Not at all,' Katie reassured her. 'You're a welcome diversion. Marking exam papers isn't my idea of fun. What's happened? You sound really upset.'

'I am. I've just had a call from Margaret. I assumed it was just her usual monthly duty call, but she said that Eden's has been taken over and they want to get all their current commitments out of the way. Either I deliver three chapters of *Spirits* by next month or I have to pay back the advance.'

'Ouch,' said Katie softly. 'And, of course, you've spent it.'

'Ages ago. And there's not enough in my savings to cover it. Apart from that, I want to write the thing. I think it's a brilliant idea; I've done all the research and I don't want to waste all the hard work I've already done. I just don't know where to start . . .' Sally's voice tailed off.

'But you can do it. You know you can. It's almost become a phobia, hasn't it? You've become so convinced that you can't do it, you're afraid even to begin. You just need to get focused and cut down on distractions. I've had an idea,' Katie said. 'You can stay in our holiday cottage. Helen and Stuart have gone to the Caribbean this year, so it's empty. Just bring all your research and your laptop. We can discuss things and, once you've decided where to start, I'm sure you'll find the rest straightforward. Plus you can have a break from London. You're not writing anything else at the moment, so you'll have no distractions and, as a bonus, we can spend a bit of time together. You can do it, Sally: you just need a bit of a kick up the arse.'

'You've always been good at giving me a boot in the right direction when I've needed it,' Sally said, smiling.

'That's because things are much clearer when you aren't involved in them and bogged down by the endless possibilities. You know where to find the key to the cottage, don't you?' As ever, Katie was practical and modest. How typical of her to underplay her contribution, Sally thought. It was part of the reason that she was so fond of Katie. In many ways, Katie was her rock, providing stability and continuity when she needed it but never being clingy or demanding.

'Yes, I know where the key is, thanks,' she replied. 'I can stop at the supermarket on the way and stock up on necessities.'

'No, don't worry about that. I'll do it. I'll fill up the fridge and make sure there's loo paper and everything. You just concentrate on organising the stuff you need for your work and get yourself there.

'Katie, you're wonderful,' Sally said. 'I can't thank you enough.'

'Nonsense,' said Katie, brushing away the compliment. 'You'd do the same for me. Shall I assume you'll be arriving tomorrow?'

'Yes. Sometime in the afternoon. Thanks again. You're an angel.'

'Stop it,' her friend replied, laughing. 'It'll go to my head. See you tomorrow.'

As she moved around the flat, packing files and tapes into a large cardboard box, Sally felt relieved. Katie was right: away from London and other demands on her time, she'd be able to concentrate on the book. It was just a question of organisation and perspective. If she kept calm and focused, she could easily write fifteen thousand words before the deadline. Katie's practical presence would provide the atmosphere she needed to get down to some serious work.

Typical Katie, she thought, to come to her rescue again. Katie, who'd taken Sally into her home and given her the domestic security Sally had needed to finish her degree. Initially, Sally had been friends with Katie's sister Helen, but once she had been introduced to Katie, the two of them had quickly hit it off. Katie had always been an eager, affectionate but undemanding lover and a loyal and supportive friend. In fact, Katie had always been a haven of peace, security and good sense. She'd been there in bad times and good. Sally knew that no matter how chaotic, overwhelming or insoluble her life seemed, Katie would be there to steer her in the right direction. She had a way of making suggestions and giving advice that almost made it seem as if she were merely helping her to organise her own thoughts. When Sally arrived at the solution she had been so elegantly directed towards, Katie would merely smile enigmatically. 'I knew you'd work it out in the end,' she would say quietly and heap praises on her friend for managing to find the answer to such a difficult problem.

Sally smiled as she remembered how she'd faced a similar crisis of anxiety during her finals at university. She'd been a committed and hard-working student, attending every lecture and turning in her assignments on time. But when she'd started to revise for her finals, the sheer volume of information had overwhelmed her. She'd become bogged down in the detail, unable to distinguish the essential material from the irrelevant.

Katie had come to her rescue, helped her to organise her time and her notes and to break down the information into topics and subtopics. She'd also taught Sally some memory techniques and introduced her to meditation. Once Sally had managed to conquer her anxieties and become more confident about her knowledge of her subject, things hadn't seemed so unmanageable. Thanks to Katie's support and guidance, she'd got an excellent degree. Katie was a good friend.

The other good thing about Katie, Sally mused as she packed, was how compatible they were in bed. They'd been lovers, on and off, since Sally had become Katie and Helen's lodger, after a disastrous row with her landlord. Katie hadn't been Sally's first lover, but she had been the first with any real experience. Sally remembered how she'd laughed when she'd discovered that the older woman was a headmistress at a select girls' boarding school. But Katie didn't live up to the stereotype at all. Far from being repressed, frumpy and inhibited, she was confident, outgoing and stylish. Although she dressed very professionally, as her working life demanded, there was always something elegant and sensual about her clothes. She was drawn to opulent fabrics and soft textures.

Katie had little time for convention. None of the wealthy parents who sent their daughters to the school would have suspected that her respectable suit covered several tattoos. Or that a thick silver ring passed through each nipple and lay flat against the dark circles of her areolae. Her hair was sleek and as dark and rich as an autumn conker. Her body was curvaceous and firm, kept toned by daily visits to the gym and regular swimming.

It was their love of swimming, in fact, which had first brought them together and it was then that she first discovered that the older woman's nipples were pierced. Soon after she had bumped into Katie at the local pool, and they'd taken to going together. It wasn't long before she began to wonder if her friend wasn't showing just a little bit too much interest in watching her change in and out of her costume. One day, buoyed up by the adrenaline of her post-swim high, she plucked up the courage to ask, 'Katie, I was wondering . . . I apologise in advance if I'm wrong, but it occurred to me – I mean, I just thought – is it possible that you might be gay?' She silently cursed herself for her incoherence.

Katie gave her wet hair a final rub and lowered her towel. She didn't answer at first, just looked Sally directly and brazenly in the eyes. Sally began to wonder if she had made a terrible mistake and had offended and hurt her friend. Gradually, however, the older woman began to smile and Sally was reassured.

'I was beginning to think you'd never notice. I've been trying to get you to notice me for so long that I'd almost considered taking out an ad in the *Brighton Evening Argus*. "Katie Elliot would like to announce to Sally Avery that she is gay."'

'Gay and interested?' Sally enquired, still uncertain of her welcome.

'Definitely interested,' her friend replied. 'Interested as hell.' They'd dried, dressed and walked the half a mile home in record time. And they'd talked all the way. About their lives, their families, how they'd first come to realise that they were gay. About everything. When they'd reached the flat, there had been nothing left to say. Katie had simply led Sally by the hand up the stairs and into her bedroom and made love to her. There was no other word to describe it. Before that, Sally had sex with women, but this was different. Katie had woken her up to the possibilities of how one woman could pleasure another – and it had been an education.

First Katie had slowly undressed her, pausing to caress and kiss every inch of skin as she uncovered it. By the time Sally was naked, she was already dizzy with desire. Then they had reversed the process and Sally had gradually stripped her friend, making sure to fondle and taste Katie's golden skin at every stage. Both naked, they had relaxed back on the king-size bed and embraced. Pressing her body against her lover and enfolding her in her arms, Katie had kissed her. A long, slow, delicious, deep kiss that Sally had seemed to feel all over her body. Her toes had tingled, she had felt goosepimples rising, and every pore in her skin had become extra sensitive. It had seemed as though Katie was taking possession of her; yet there had been a gentleness, a sense of submission in the kiss which had made it both tender and passionate.

Gentle hands had roamed all over her body, stroking, cupping, and squeezing. Lips had brushed her ear-lobes, the nape of her neck, the base of her throat. Sally had buried her face in her friend's silky hair and drunk in the scent. She had traced her fingers up and down Katie's spine, using her long nails to tease and tickle. Katie's mouth had been on her throat, her teeth gently nibbling the sensitised flesh, her tongue tracing the contours. A hand had found Sally's right nipple, brushed it lightly, began to rub harder, then to squeeze.

'You like that?' Katie had murmured, raising her head slightly. Without waiting for an answer, she had slithered down the bed slightly and taken Sally's hard, reddened nipple between her lips. At first she had sucked gently, occasionally flicking the hardened point with her tongue. Then she had gradually increased the pressure and begun to nibble and bite. A red flush had spread over the chest and throat of the woman under her and Katie had slid her left hand over the rounded belly and rested it on Sally's mound.

Sally had unconsciously arched her spine and thrown back her head. Her eyes had been closed and she had breathed quickly and audibly, her lips parted. Her friend had moved her attentions to the other nipple and slipped her warm hand lower, until she could feel the heat between Sally's legs. She had traced one finger along the moistening slit, then made light, circular motions over Sally's hard clit, all the time kissing and nibbling the engorged nipple in her mouth. Sally had responded by moving her hips up and down, rubbing her swollen pussy against Katie's hand.

She had been moaning, gasping and mumbling, her pelvis moving rhythmically against her friend's invading fingers. Sally's blonde hair had been slick with sweat. Beads of perspiration had glistened on her upper lip, caught in the dim light from the bedside lamp. Katie had slowly slid two fingers inside her friend's slippery pussy and continued to circle her swollen clit with her thumb. Sally's hip movements had become frenzied, her panting louder. Her cunt had contracted around Katie's fingers and gripped them.

In a single fluid movement, the older woman had slithered down the bed and positioned herself between Sally's parted thighs. Using her right hand to part the plump lips, she had licked her friend's hot pussy, flicking her tongue over the hard bud. She had licked and lapped at the sweet, wet slit, while moving her fingers inside Sally's moist opening. Sensing that her lover was close to orgasm, she had sucked hard on the stiff nub of Sally's clit. Sally's pussy had pulsated and throbbed around Katie's fingers and her body became rigid. She had been moaning, gasping, almost crying, almost laughing, hardly knowing what she was doing. She had been beyond reason, beyond logic, lost in the sensations of the moment, aware only of the growing ecstasy between her legs.

She had been so wet and slippery that Katie had had difficulty keeping her mouth in position. Rubbing her face in the fragrant juices, Katie had locked her mouth over her lover's clit and sucked hard. With her left hand, she had rhythmically finger-fucked her friend, feeling every twitch and spasm of her pussy. Sally had been virtually screaming: then, with an enormous cry, she had come. Come like she never had before and thought she never would again: but fortunately Katie had seen to it that she did. Often. Naturally, Sally also returned the favour as frequently as possible. After that first time together, they had joked that the sex had been so good that the rest of Brighton had needed a cigarette after it.

Getting the opportunity to spend time with Katie would be a definite bonus.

TWO

Sally was wide awake the moment the alarm went off. She felt rested and far more alive than she had in longer than she could remember. She hummed softly as she moved quickly around the flat, watering plants and feeding her cats. By ten, she had everything packed and the car loaded. Her downstairs neighbours had even agreed to come in once a day to take care of Cagney and Lacey.

Around lunchtime, she found herself on the outskirts of Tunbridge Wells and stopped for something to eat. She parked the car in a side street, tucked the morning paper under her arm and dawdled through the town, stretching her legs. In the Pantiles, she found a wine bar she liked the look of and went in. Inside, she was pleased to discover that there was a large patio garden at the rear of the wine bar. Sally picked her way between the tables and chairs and seated herself beside a large bay shrub. She picked a leaf and broke it, releasing its scent. An efficient, friendly waitress took her order and brought her a glass of wine.

While she waited for her food, she enjoyed the warmth and examined her surroundings. A profusion of plant life grew around the patio in terracotta pots. The sun illuminated the brick paving, giving the courtyard a sort of pinkish glow which reminded her of the Mediterranean. She felt relaxed and calm, almost as if she was on holiday.

She was really looking forward to seeing Katie. She frowned, trying to remember the last time she had had sex with anyone. It must be three or four months, now, and that would have been with Katie, too. She hadn't had a girlfriend for a couple of years. There had been a couple of one-night stands since then, but nobody regular. Apart from Katie.

She smiled as her reminiscence began to veer towards the erotic. She thought of her friend's athletic, firm body and how, when they first became lovers, she had enjoyed sucking on those pierced nipples. How Katie had shivered and moaned when she took the ring between her teeth and gently pulled on it. She felt her own nipples peak at the remembered sensation. Yes, she was looking forward to seeing Katie.

The arrival of the waitress with her lunch jolted her from her reverie. She ate it quickly while scanning the newspaper and within half an hour she was back on the road and heading for the south coast. Away from the motorway, the journey was peaceful and pretty. The countryside, green and hilly, seemed to typify England in the summer. Fields of ripening corn danced in the breeze. Cows and sheep grazed in the fields as she passed by. As she neared Brighton, she saw hang gliders, swooping and hovering in the air, the sun glinting on their fragile wings. She felt the cares of the city drop from her, and she made a mental note to thank Katie for offering her the cottage. It would be just the lifeline she needed.

By mid-afternoon, she had reached the outskirts of Hailsham Edge and had to stop in a layby to check the exact location of the cottage on her map. Satisfied that she was heading in the right direction, she drove in to the village and had soon parked outside the cottage. Built of grey stone, like most of the buildings in the village, it was small and functional. At the back, a single-storey extension housed the kitchen and bathroom. A hundred years ago, the people who lived in the cottage had drawn water from a cold pump outside and used a privy at the end of the garden. Built as housing for workers on the nearby estate, the cottages were now so expensive that only the wealthy could afford them. People who lived and worked in London kept many of them as weekend and holiday cottages. Katie had inherited hers from her grandmother and had renovated it, keeping it as an investment and a source of rental income.

She left her bags and boxes on the doorstep and took the side path round to the back of the cottage. She lifted the latch on the small potting shed which was built against one of the garden walls and scrabbled in a box under the rough table, where she knew she would find the key. She let herself in the back door and walked through the kitchen and the small living room and opened the front door. Struggling with her luggage, bringing all the bags and heavy cartons of research material and books into the house, left her panting and sweating. She closed the front door and began stripping off her clothes, leaving a trail of discarded garments across the living room floor. Once she was naked, she grabbed the suitcase containing her clothes and toiletries and headed upstairs.

'What took you so long?' a voice asked playfully as she opened the bedroom door.

For a brief moment she wondered who the voice could belong to. But almost immediately, she realised it was Katie. She was pleased and surprised to see her friend lying naked on the bed. As always, the sight of the thick silver hoops which decorated Katie's nipples sent her pulse racing.

'I see you're ready for me, too,' Katie quipped playfully, indicating Sally's nakedness. 'If I didn't know better, I'd swear you knew I was coming.'

'I was hot. I wore myself out carrying in all the luggage. I was heading for the shower, just bringing these upstairs first. I could have done with a hand, actually, if I'd known you were here,' she explained breathlessly, sitting on the bed beside her friend.

'Sorry, but I wanted it to be a surprise. It would have spoilt it if I'd come down and helped you with your luggage.' Katie sat up and grasped Sally's slim shoulders and gave her a long gentle kiss of welcome. Sally responded enthusiastically. She leant down and planted a gentle kiss on the small Celtic tattoo which adorned Katie's right shoulder.

'Did you say you were headed for the shower? I'll race you,' Katie announced, leaping off the bed and bounding down the stairs towards the bathroom at the rear of the small house. By the time Sally reached the bathroom, Katie was already in the shower, the steamy water pounding loudly against the tiles. Sally opened the glazed door and climbed into the cubicle.

Katie pulled Sally towards her and began soaping her body with a large sponge. She began a slow, erotic massage of Sally's wet skin. The sensation of the rough sponge moving over her flesh made Sally shiver with pleasure. She braced herself against the tiled walls of the cubicle with her hands and gave herself up to the sensual massage. She gasped as her friend soaped her breasts, the coarse sponge producing an exquisite sensation in her nipples, causing them to stand out. Katie continued to tease Sally's nipples for several minutes. They reddened and stiffened as the older woman stroked the sensitive buds. Katie slid the sponge down the centre of Sally's chest and over her curved belly and began to soap between her legs. She rubbed the sponge over her lover's mound and lowered her head and took an aroused nipple into her mouth.

'Ugh! Soap,' she exclaimed, instantly spitting it out. 'Let me rinse you down.' Katie took the showerhead down from its bracket and let fresh water pour down Sally's chest, washing the soap away.

'That's better,' she said, replacing the showerhead. 'Now, where was I?' She bent her head and sucked one of Sally's hard nipples. She drew it into her mouth and nibbled on it, gently at first, then harder.

Sally began to moan softly. 'Nobody knows my body like you do,' she whispered huskily. 'You know just what I want.'

'I'm glad I haven't lost my touch,' replied Katie, smiling. Her hand was still working between Sally's legs. The coarse surface of the sponge felt divine against Sally's sensitive flesh. Katie moved the sponge over her friend's swollen lips, along the slit and back along the crack of her bottom. The soap made Sally's skin slippery and mingled with her own wetness. Tingles of ecstasy coursed through her body as her lover continued to mouth each nipple alternately. Her pussy throbbed with pleasure as the slick material glided over her engorged flesh.

Katie began to concentrate on Sally's clit, gently skimming the sponge over the hard bud.

Sally's legs were trembling now. Her breathing was ragged now, shallow and fast. Her cheeks and chest were flushed red and filmed with sweat, glowing in the light from the overhead lamp. In front of her, Katie stood directly under the showerhead, the gushing water making her luscious body gleam. Her nipple rings glittered in the light. Katie resoaped the sponge and returned her attentions to her lover's pussy. She slithered it along the length of Sally's quim, over her hole and up between her buttocks. She teased Sally's arsehole for a moment then began to circle her hard clit. The sensitive nub twitched and swelled under her touch. Gradually increasing in speed and pressure, she continued to massage the aroused button. She leant forward and kissed Sally's wet mouth, nibbled on her lower lip, explored the warm depths with her tongue. Then she licked her partner's neck, behind her ear-lobe, moving down to the hot flesh of her throat. Just above the collarbone, she used her teeth to nip and nibble, biting harder as Sally's excitement grew.

Hot steam filled the small cubicle, falling water drummed loudly against the hard tiles. Tension built between Sally's legs.

Her wet pussy throbbed, sending shivers of pleasure all over her body. She arched her back. Katie's lips slid over her neck and moved lower, seeking a nipple. The muscles in Sally's legs trembled and twitched. Every nerve ending in her body seemed hyper-sensitive. Heat formed in the base of her belly; her vaginal muscles began to contract and pulsate. She pumped her hips, rubbing her cunt rhythmically against Katie's hand. She was on the edge now, riding the waves of joy, waiting for the moment that would tip her over into orgasm. Pinpoints of pleasure spread out from her nipples, her groin. Her eyes were closed, lips drawn back. Short breaths hissed between her closed teeth.

She gasped as a slippery finger found her anus and snaked inside, claiming it. Triggered by this invasion, surges of ecstasy began to spread out from her groin and surge through her body. Unconscious moans and sobs of joy escaped from her, the sound filling the small bathroom. Her engorged quim throbbed, her tight arsehole contracting around Katie's wriggling finger. Rapture coursed through Sally's womb and left her quivering.

'God, that was good,' she whispered to Katie, when it was over. 'I can hardly stand up, my legs are trembling so much.'

'Let me help you, then,' said her friend, smiling. She wrapped her arms around Sally's still shaking body and held her tightly to her own chest. Slippery naked breasts slid against each other and Sally could feel her lover's nipple rings pressing into her flesh. They kissed gently and Katie held her, lovingly stroking her wet hair, until she had calmed down.

'Let's get out of here, before we drown,' announced Katie eventually, turning off the water.

'Good idea,' her friend replied, stepping out of the shower and grabbing a towel. She passed the towel to Katie and took another for herself from the rack. They dried each other, giggling and joking.

'I owe you one,' said Sally, combing her hair. 'Fancy collecting it now?'

Katie raised an eyebrow and smiled wickedly. 'I shouldn't,' she replied. 'I have things to do. But it's a very tempting offer. You're having dinner with me tonight at the school. I need to start cooking . . .' She paused and traced the outline of Sally's lips with a finger.

'Just a quickie?' suggested Sally hopefully.

'Why don't you give me something on account and I'll collect the balance later?' Katie said.

'Now that is an offer I can't refuse.'

Katie dropped her wet towel in the laundry basket and slipped quickly through the bathroom door and dashed upstairs. A moment later, Sally arrived in the bedroom to find her friend spread seductively on top of the duvet.

'Where shall I start?' Sally asked, laughing. 'I feel as though I'm at a banquet and everything's so delicious that I don't know where to begin.'

'Well, you could start at the top and work down,' suggested her friend.

'Or I could get straight to the point,' said Sally,

She climbed onto the bed and nestled down between her lover's spread legs. She stroked Katie's muscular thighs appreciatively.

'So beautiful,' she mumbled. For a long moment, she did nothing, just looked at the dark-fringed pussy only inches away from her face. She drank in the scent of it, musk mixed with the clean smell of soap. Using a fingertip, she gently traced the length of Katie's slit, the lightest of touches, barely making contact. With her thumbs, she parted the plump labia. Moisture glistened there, betraying her friend's arousal. The swollen bud of Katie's clitoris stood out prominently, invitingly. Sally shuffled a little higher up the bed and brought her mouth close to the ripe, red fruit and extended her tongue. Gently, she licked the fleshy outer lips, up one side and down the other. She dabbed her eager tongue into the moisture pooling at Katie's opening and circled it there, swirling and probing. Her tongue flicked and quivered, darted and grazed, covering every millimetre of her partner's gorgeous fanny.

Katie's legs were spread wide, offering her hot cleft to the questing mouth. Her hands gripped the brass poles of the antique bed so hard her knuckles were white. She took short, shallow breaths as the heat between her legs grew. She bit her lip. Sally knew her tongue was teasing Katie, tantalising her. Arousing her beyond endurance, yet offering no fulfilment. Soon it would be time for the feathery caresses to give way to deeper, stronger strokes: but she was enjoying deliberately tormenting Katie, withholding satisfaction so that when it finally came, it would be all the more sweet.

Katie thrashed her head from side to side against the rumpled pillow, her frustration almost unbearable, and Sally looked up from between Katie's taut legs. She smiled. 'OK,' she said. 'I know you can't wait any longer.' She fastened her hot mouth over her lover's swollen cunt. She sucked hard on the reddened nub, squeezing it between her lips. She massaged the opening with her thumbs and began to lick, deep and rhythmically. She moved her tongue in firm, long strokes over the sensitive bud. Her mouth slid easily over the slippery flesh: it tasted sweet yet salty. She relished the flavour and the sensation of her lips gliding easily over the hot, juicy pussy. Expertly, she tongued her lover's clitoris, sucking, licking, pulling, nibbling. Bringing her closer and closer to the brink of climax.

Katie's hips moved rhythmically and urgently; her open cunt pressed against the hungry mouth. Using her thumbs, Sally gently kneaded around her lover's opening, stretching it wide. Juice gathered there and dribbled down between the buttocks, anointing her rear hole. Katie moaned.

Sally slid her head lower and licked along Katie's arse-crack, lapping up the wetness. She circled Katie's puckered opening, nibbling gently at the crinkled flesh. Her hot mouth explored her partner's behind, her tongue squirming into the tight sphincter. She moved upwards to lap at the other moist entrance, stabbing and probing. She slid two fingers into Katie's pussy, simultaneously penetrating Katie's bottom with her thumb.

She concentrated on the clit, now, alternately licking and sucking: long, strong strokes which brought her friend ever nearer to ecstasy. Tense muscles gripped her fingers, drawing them in as she lavished attention on Katie's swollen nub. Rhythmically, she mouthed the engorged flesh, keeping time with her playmate's urgent thrusting.

Katie sobbed, gripping the bedposts tighter. Sally felt the other woman's pussy begin to throb and pulsate around her probing fingers. With her free hand, she reached up and tugged hard on one of her lover's nipple rings, extending and stretching the sensitive teat. Katie's muscular legs tensed and trembled; her bottom lifting off the bed. She ground her crotch against Sally's mouth, and Sally continued to suck and lick as her friend orgasmed loudly, teasing the sensitive pearl until Katie pulled away. She nibbled Katie's inner thigh, making the older woman laugh and squirm.

'I always get so sensitive after I've come, I can't bear to be touched. It tickles,' said Katie lazily.

'I know,' Sally replied, crawling up the bed on hands and knees. She lay down beside her friend and kissed her gently and pushed the damp hair from her face. 'I think it's sweet.'

The two women embraced, wrapping their arms tightly around each other and rocking for a few moments. It felt good, Sally thought. She'd forgotten how much she enjoyed sex with Katie: how natural, good and uncomplicated it felt. Nothing demanded or given, other than honest lust and affection. She wondered if she'd ever find this comfortable openness with someone else. She hoped so.

'I've missed you, Katie,' she said. 'Being with you always makes me feel so good.'

'That's because we're just good friends,' Katie explained. 'Very special friends, but still just friends. There's no pressure and no complications. It's easier. When you fall in love with someone, that's when it gets complicated.'

'You're right,' Sally reflected. 'Love scares me to death.'

'Me, too,' volunteered her friend. 'Terrifies me, in fact.' She hesitated, then went on uncertainly. 'I think I might be falling in love with someone, actually. Half the time, I'm neurotic with anxiety.'

'Do tell,' said Sally. 'Who? Where did you meet her? Do I know her? What does she do for a living? Is she in love with you?'

'Sometimes I think you're my mother, not my best friend,' joked Katie. 'Her name's Jo. She's a student, or at least she will be in the autumn, when term starts. You don't know her.' She paused, suddenly embarrassed and uncertain. 'She's one of my students,' she went on quietly. 'At least, she *was*; she left school in June. We didn't get together until after the end of term but I feel a bit awkward about it.'

'Why?' Sally reassured her. 'She's over the age of consent. She isn't a pupil any more, so you haven't done anything wrong.'

'I know, but I still feel awkward about it. That and the age difference. She's only eighteen – nineteen next month.'

'It's how you feel about her that's important, not what it says on your birth certificate or what anyone else thinks. If you think you love her, that's all that matters,' said Sally calmly.

'You're right, I know you are,' Katie responded. 'It's just that I've never felt like this before and I'm not sure whether I like it or not.' She blushed, her olive skin taking on a crimson hue. 'Anyway,' she went on, 'you'll meet her this evening. She's coming to dinner. Come over at eight. OK?'

'I can hardly wait.'

After Katie had left, Sally decided to do a couple of hours' work. She felt motivated, excited even. She unpacked her research material and organised everything on the small dining room table. She managed to find a power point for her laptop and checked her e-mail before getting down to work. There were only some technical queries from the magazine which had commissioned her latest article. She dealt with them quickly and settled down to work on *House of Spirits*.

She searched through the files of paper and reference material and quickly divided it into chronological order. She noticed with relief that the familiar tightness in the chest she associated with trying to work on the book was absent. Ages ago, she had written a synopsis for the book and she turned to this, making sure that she had the relevant information relating to each chapter. It all seemed quite straightforward: she wondered why she'd found it so difficult to start on it. She even found a rough draft of her prologue and read through it quickly. Satisfied that she was familiar with all the material, she fetched a long, cool drink, settled down in front of her keyboard, and began to write.

In spite of her fears, the words seemed to flow quite fluently. Thoughts formed on the page logically and clearly. Now and then, she paused to look up a quote or check a fact, but most of the time she tapped away quietly at the computer keys. She became absorbed in her work, typing quickly – her fingers were scarcely able to keep up with the sentences that formed in her mind. As she worked, she began to visualise the book she was writing.

Words tumbled from her fingers, weaving elegant patterns and rhythms in her brain. Her screen filled with paragraph after paragraph of eloquent prose. She marvelled at the ease with which she wrote. Her former fears seemed to evaporate as the letters appeared on her monitor and she relaxed into a natural easy rhythm. Perhaps her anxieties about starting the book had blinded her to how much work she had already done, how well prepared she actually was. To her surprise, she found that ideas flowed naturally into each other, each thought leading logically onto the next. She was excited, rapt; her mind focused on the task in hand.

Finally she began to tire; her back ached. She stretched languidly, then kneaded the muscles of her lower spine with one hand, pulled off her reading glasses and tossed them on to the crowded table. She saved her work, copied it onto a floppy disk and turned off her laptop, closing the lid. Glancing at the clock, she was surprised to see that it was almost seven o'clock. Just time to get changed and drive over to Katie's school.

She trotted up the narrow stairs and into the bedroom, glad that she had decided to unpack her clothes before she settled down to work. She stripped off her shorts and vest and selected a pair of loose blue trousers and a matching silk top. The sleeveless blouse was cool yet elegant. When she'd finished making up her face, highlighting her eyes with smoky grey shadow, she put her make-up bag into her handbag and headed for the car, leaving her mobile phone lying on a small table in the living room.

'I am here to get away from distractions, after all,' she said aloud.

THREE

Cuckmere Manor School was about five miles away on the outskirts of Arlington. The building itself had been an old manor house; its grey stone façade nestled amongst rolling green parkland. Katie's flat was at the top of the main building. Sally left the car in the small car park and rang the bell to her friend's flat.

'Is that you, Sally?' Katie's voice asked over the intercom.

Sally confirmed that it was and the electronically controlled door clicked open. Katie was waiting for her at the top of the stairs with a welcoming glass of red wine.

'Did you manage to get any work done this afternoon?' she asked when Sally had settled down on one of the sumptuous sofas in the airy living room.

'I certainly did,' Sally replied, 'tons, in fact. I surprised myself. I wrote about five thousand words. The sentences positively flowed, practically wrote themselves. I'm really pleased.'

'And so am I. I knew you could do it,' said her friend encouragingly. 'Food's ready. We're just waiting for Jo; she should be here any moment. She lives in Brighton. She finishes work at 7.30 and she's driving straight here.'

'What does she do?' asked Sally.

'She's working at her family's restaurant at the moment. Just for the summer. She goes to the University of Sussex in October; she's reading Philosophy. I'm very proud of her; she's probably the brightest student I've ever taught.'

'How did you get together?' Sally queried. 'It isn't like you to mix business and pleasure. I know I'm being nosy, but I prefer to think of it as healthy curiosity.'

'Not at all,' Katie said. 'It isn't like me. We always got on very well. I gave her special tutoring for her French A Level – not that she needed it, she's so quick. I liked her, but never thought of it as anything other than a professional relationship. On Helen's birthday, we went for a meal in Jo's family's restaurant – the food's great. We must go while you're here. Jo was our waitress and I introduced her to Helen. When we got home, Helen said she was sure that Jo fancied me. I told her she was hallucinating and thought no more about it. About a week later, I popped into a club in Brighton and Jo was there. We got chatting. Jo had had a few drinks, by this time, and eventually she told me that she had feelings for me but hadn't thought it was proper to mention it while she was still at school.'

'Not one of your leather and bondage clubs?' Sally teased. Although she knew that Katie was as interested as she was in the kinkier side of sex – the more so, in fact, because Sally knew that Katie had gone to clubs and done things, whereas Sally was still only at the fantasising stage – they'd always stuck to straightforward sex. Katie was so close to her that she was the obvious person for Sally to share her fantasies with: and yet something had always held Sally back. She wasn't sure what it was – fear, perhaps, of losing a good friendship if it didn't work out? Or altering the balance of their friendship? – so she stuck to teasing Katie rather than admitting just how interested she was, and refused Katie's invitations to the club.

'No, just a straightforward lesbian club.' Katie laughed. 'I'm not a complete perv, you know. I don't spend every second of my spare time dressed up in leather and latex. So, anyway, I brought Jo home with me and we had a long chat. I had all sorts of concerns, as you can imagine; the age gap, the fact that I've been her headmistress. Her parents didn't even know she's a lesbian. I encouraged her to come out and we decided to see each other. That's where you came in.'

'Not quite,' Sally said. 'You've left out the interesting bit. Or am I just being filthy-minded? I can't believe you passed up the opportunity to get horizontal. I want to hear all the details.'

'Actually,' said Katie, 'we haven't.' Her friend looked sheepish, almost embarrassed.

'If I didn't know you better, I'd swear you were blushing, Katie,' Sally said, smiling. 'It's not like you to play hard to get.'

'I know,' answered her friend. 'I've never felt like this before and I want to be sure we're both doing the right thing.'

The bell rang and Katie went over to the entryphone to answer it. 'It's Jo,' she told Sally. 'She's on her way up. I do hope you like her,' she added nervously.

'Of course I will,' Sally reassured her.

Katie went to welcome Jo and Sally helped herself to another glass of the Australian Cabernet.

'I've brought a bottle of wine,' she heard Jo saying on her way upstairs. 'A customer ordered it in the restaurant and then sent it back. There's nothing wrong with it: it's a very good Bordeaux. He was just trying to impress the girl he had with him. Young enough to be his daughter and dressed in a handkerchief.'

'Thanks. I'm sure we'll find room for it,' said Katie as her guest reached the top of the stairs.

Sally heard the two women kiss briefly and then Katie's voice said, 'Come and meet Sally.'

Sally stood up as they entered the room. Jo was tall. Far taller than Sally's own five foot eight; close to six foot, Sally thought. Jo's eyes were a sparkling clear blue; her wheat-blonde hair was short and cut into an elegant short bob. It should have been severe, but it wasn't. Her hair was fine and shiny and full of movement. She was tanned an even coffee colour and her complexion was clear and healthy looking, free of the skin problems that afflicted many teenagers. Her full pink lips formed into a friendly smile as she was introduced to Sally.

'This is Sally Avery,' Katie explained. 'My best friend. She's come to Sussex to get some work done. She needs a break from the lonely garret she normally writes and starves in.'

'I hardly starve,' responded Sally, shaking Jo's hand. 'Pleased to meet you.'

'And this is Jo Carey, my newest friend,' Katie continued.

'Hello,' said Jo. 'Being a writer – is it glamorous?'

'Not at all,' replied Sally. 'It's hard work, mostly, although obviously I enjoy it, when it's going well.'

'I loved *Secrets of the Sea*,' Jo said. 'I didn't even know you were Katie's friend when I read it. I went through a phase of being fascinated by paranormal psychology. I thought you did a great job of straddling both camps; being open-minded yet not gullible, realistic yet not sceptical. And I thought that your ending was wonderful and very brave.'

'Well, I've always been a romantic at heart,' Sally responded, flattered by the younger woman's compliments.

'But not everyone would have opted for your conclusion that the fisherman were protected from harm by the love of their womenfolk. I thought it was radical and courageous,' Jo enthused.

'Fortunately the public agreed with you,' said Katie. 'Let's hope that they go for your new book in the same numbers.'

'I'll drink to that,' responded Sally, raising her glass.

The three women had a relaxed and companionable evening. They ate *spaghetti alla vongole* with green salad and a raspberry pavlova, all of it cooked by Katie. Sally and Katie drank their way through two bottles of wine, although Jo stuck to mineral water as she was driving herself home. They found they had the same sense of humour, similar taste in music and were all fans of Val McDermid's detective, Lindsay Gordon.

Sally couldn't help noticing the rapport between the two women. They were obviously very attracted to each other, but also seemed to be totally on the same wavelength. Katie buzzed attentively around her new lover, filling her glass, fetching her a napkin. Her flushed cheeks betrayed her fondness for the younger woman. And Jo couldn't take her eyes off Katie. She hung on every word, admiration shining in her eyes. They were made for each other, Sally thought. Jo's lively enthusiasm was the perfect foil for Katie's calm wisdom. She was happy for them.

Just after midnight, they said goodbye to Jo. Standing on the doorstep, they watched until the rear lights of her Fiesta disappeared into the distance. They headed upstairs to bed. Neither of them had discussed Sally staying the night. It was just taken for granted between them: an old habit. Silently, they went through the bedroom ritual of removing make-up, applying moisturiser, cleaning teeth in Katie's en suite bathroom. Relaxed after an excellent day, Sally nestled down in the king-size pine bed, waiting for her friend to join her.

'Are you feeling adventurous?' asked Katie as she entered the room. 'Are you in the mood to stretch a few boundaries?' She sat down beside Sally, smiling, her brown eyes twinkling wickedly.

'Why not?' Sally responded. 'I've had a wonderfully productive day and I'm feeling really relaxed. Things can only get better.'

'Good,' whispered her friend, 'let's have some fun.' She ran one slender finger along the length of Sally's torso, between her breasts and down on to her flat belly. 'Close your eyes,' she said.

Sally felt excited and only slightly apprehensive. She knew that her dearest friend would never hurt her but, at the same time, she was nervous about what might happen. What if she didn't enjoy submitting to Katie – if she felt threatened or vulnerable? The thought evaporated almost instantly as she realised that she could simply tell her friend to stop. There was no real risk and no need for fear. It was an opportunity to have some fun and try something new. She smiled trustingly up at her old friend and closed her eyes.

'Should I call you mistress?' she asked jokingly.

'I think you're taking this a bit too seriously,' Katie said, laughing.

With her eyes closed, Sally discovered that all her other senses were heightened. She could hear the quiet hiss of air as she inhaled and, if she strained her ears, she could also hear Katie's breathing. Her skin felt hyper-sensitive. The breeze from the open window caused her nipples to pucker and erect. She shivered as something light and feathery brushed against the skin of her thighs, then her belly and finally her breasts. It felt delicious and she stuck out her chest to try to prolong the contact.

'What is that?' she asked, unable to contain her curiosity.

'It's a silk scarf,' Katie replied. 'Be quiet and just enjoy what's happening.'

She felt the scarf trail along the sensitive flesh of her inner arm. Then Katie took her wrist and lifted her arm above her head. She held her breath, listening hard to the sounds in the room. She could hear Katie moving around the bed, and a rustling, sliding noise that she realised was the silk scarf. But she couldn't work out what her friend was doing with the scarf. She gasped as she felt the silk being wrapped tightly around her wrist and tied in a knot. Katie was tying her to the bed, and she was enjoying it.

'Oh, my God,' she murmured, as she realised what was happening to her. It felt delicious, exciting. 'You're tying me up!'

'Is that OK?' Katie asked, concerned. 'You know you can ask me to stop at any time.'

'I don't want you to stop.'

'That's good,' said her friend. 'I'm going to blindfold you, just in case you're tempted to peek.' Deftly, Katie took another silk scarf from her bedside drawer and wound it round her friend's head, covering her eyes.

'I thought this would be scary,' Sally said, her voice wobbling, 'but it's amazing.' She felt Katie tie her other hand and then her feet to the tall wooden bedposts. Soon she was spread-eagled on the duvet, blindfolded and at her friend's mercy. Her breathing quickened, moisture began to form between her legs. She couldn't remember ever being in such an erotic situation.

The mattress creaked under her as she felt Katie climb on to the bed beside her. She felt her friend climbing over one of her restrained ankles and positioning herself between her legs. The heat from Katie's body warmed her skin, even though they were not quite touching. Something brushed her inner thigh, skimming over her flesh, barely making contact: fingernails, she thought. Then they were gliding over her belly, along her sides. Teasing her, arousing her.

She sucked in her breath as she felt Katie's fingernails gently graze her nipples. Behind her blindfold, she was conscious only of the sensations in her body. She was lost in the pleasure of the moment, her responses heightened and magnified by her inability to see. Katie's nails began to trace small circles around her nipples. They stiffened and extended as Katie teased them. Sally groaned as she felt her lover grip her nipples with the tips of her nails and pull on them gently. Juice flowed between her legs, dripping down the crack of her arse and pooling on the duvet.

Katie was working hard on her nipples now, squeezing and pulling them firmly. Pinpoints of delight radiated out from the hardened buds and spread through Sally's chest. For a moment, Katie's fingers withdrew. Sally felt her friend rest her hands either side of her body and sensed her leaning forward. Hot breath teased her chest and then she felt a warm, wet tongue against her nipple. Katie sucked the nipple into her mouth, drawing hard on it, nibbling it. Sally arched her back in ecstatic response. The delicious sensations she was experiencing intensified as Katie began to nip harder. She felt sharp teeth against the swollen teat, stretching it, biting it. Her lover's fingers worked a similar magic on her other nipple, squeezing, pulling, pinching.

Sally had never felt such intense feelings before. Tingling waves of pleasure engulfed her, overwhelmed her. Her breathing was harsh and rapid. Her bound arms and legs thrashed against the duvet. She realised with surprise that the sensation in her nipples was almost painful, yet it was divinely erotic. This must be what Katie meant about pushing boundaries, she thought. The feelings she was experiencing were so intense that they seemed to take her to the edge of pain. Yet Katie wasn't actually hurting her. On the contrary, it felt unbelievable: the most profound pleasure she had ever experienced. Blindfold, and bound, all she could do was give herself up to the incredible sensations.

She gasped as she felt something brush her inner thigh. With the lightest of touches, she felt a finger stroking her. Teasing the cleft of her buttocks, her labia, tracing the crease between pussy and thigh. She felt an aching between her legs, a tension which needed release. Yet she knew that Katie was in control and would not let her climax until she decided it was time. And she knew that when release did come, it would be an incredible experience. She shivered and wriggled her hips as a finger stroked along her slit and dabbled in the moisture pooled at her opening.

'Please let me come,' she begged. 'I'm going to die if you don't let me come.'

'No, you won't, sweetheart,' Katie reassured her. 'Trust me. Let me take control and I promise you it will be incredible. You can't come yet; you're not ready.'

'Oh, yes, I am!' Sally said vehemently.

'You just think you are, but I know better,' said her friend. 'Now lie back, shut up and let me do the hard work. Or I'll have to think about gagging you.'

Sally lay back, as ordered, and gave herself up to the delightful feelings that were overwhelming her. Still working on her engorged nipples, Katie was now stroking her pussy. Sally seemed to be on fire with pleasure. Spirals of rapture spread out from her breasts and pussy and coursed through her body. Sweaty tendrils of hair adhered to her flushed cheeks. Her hips moved frantically. Katie's fingers brushed her labia, teased her hole, stroked between her buttocks. They explored every inch of her aching pussy but never touched her clit. Sally wriggled, thrusting her groin against Katie's hand, trying to establish a rhythm.

'Patience,' said her friend, sitting up. Sally felt bereft as the mouth withdrew from her nipple. Katie sat between her legs for a long moment, not touching her at all. The room was silent, except for the rasp of Sally's excited breathing. She lay there, tense with desire and longing for release. Then she felt a finger touching her thigh, just beside her knee. A moment later, she felt its twin on her other leg. Fingernails brushed along the skin of her thighs, towards her cunt. They teased the plump flesh of her outer lips, her arse. Then she felt Katie's thumbs on either side of her moist hole. They massaged in small circles, exerting firm pressure.

Her legs began to tremble as the tension in her belly increased. Surges of joy spread out from her loins. Her pussy throbbed. She wrapped her hands around the scarves which bound her to the bed and pulled hard on them, tensing her body and arching her back. She was on the edge, now. Even though Katie had deliberately avoided touching her clit, Sally knew she was about to come. Her partner's massaging thumbs brought her closer and closer towards fulfilment. Her fanny was dripping now, squelching and slurping as Katie's thumbs moved over the slick flesh. Sally started to moan; a concerto burst from her. She sobbed, she gasped, she laughed. The rise and fall of her ecstatic song filled the room. Her cunt began to pulsate, with wave after wave of contractions spreading through her pelvis. Every muscle in her body tensed; she raised her bottom off the bed as the most powerful orgasm she had ever experienced overtook her body. At the peak, she gave an animal cry. Tears formed in her eyes and she began to weep noisily, uncontrollably.

Katie carefully climbed over Sally's bound limbs and lay down beside her. She took her best friend in her arms and held her tightly, rocking her, soothing her. Finally, the tears stopped and Sally's frenzied breathing returned to normal.

'That was . . . incredible,' she murmured. She smiled lovingly up at her friend. 'You are amazing.'

'No, you are,' said Katie, shaking her head. 'How do you feel now?'

'Wonderful,' Sally announced.

'Ready for some more, then?' her friend asked wickedly. Without waiting for an answer, Katie began repositioning herself on the bed. Sally's heartbeat quickened in anticipation. What did Katie have in mind? Still blindfolded, she strained her ears, listening for any clues. The mattress wobbled as her lover moved around. She felt Katie moving up the bed. Then she felt first one, then the other of her hands being untied. She stretched out her arms, which were aching slightly.

'Lie still,' said Katie. 'Let me get into position.' Sally waited patiently, her chest tight with anticipation. Whatever her friend was planning, she was sure it would be as exciting and enjoyable as the incredible experience she had just had. Her heart was pounding. Katie was kneeling near her shoulder now. She could hear the springs squeaking and the soft cotton of the duvet made a sort of swishing noise where Katie brushed against it. Something moved in front of her face and before she had time to wonder what it was, she smelt the familiar perfume of Katie's sweet pussy.

'I want you to lick that, while I'm busy at this end,' her friend explained in mock authoritative tone.

'Yes, please,' Sally responded enthusiastically. 'I'm glad you untied me.' She used both hands to part the fleshy lips of her lover's fragrant cunt. Katie lowered herself until she was sitting on Sally's face. Trapped under her friend's crotch, she didn't have much room for movement. All she could do was lap and suck at the slippery flesh. Katie's cunt was so wet that drops of moisture were trickling down over Sally's face. She smiled inwardly; it was obvious that her friend had really got off on tying her up. That makes two of us, she thought. She pulled Katie's lips further apart, spreading her wide, and sucked on her engorged clit.

She'd been so absorbed that she'd hardly noticed Katie stretching out on top of her. But when she felt her friend's hot mouth claim her pussy, she couldn't ignore it. She bucked her hips and shivered. It felt delicious and Sally was so sensitive from her previous orgasm that she knew it wouldn't take long for her to come again. She spread her still bound legs as wide as she was able and gave herself up to the sensations.

She worked hard on Katie's quim, sucking and licking. Her lips, nose and chin were drenched in juice, making her face slide easily over her partner's slick flesh. She moved her head in big circles, rubbing her lubricated face over Katie's firm clit. She used the hard point of her chin to massage the swollen bud, then the tip of her nose. Between her own legs, Katie was working magic. A hot ball of pleasure gathered in her belly. Her pussy throbbed with excitement. Her lover's hot, wet mouth seemed to suck in her whole cunt, making it ache with ecstasy. She tilted her hips, pressing her crotch against Katie's face.

She was conscious only of the tingle between her legs and the sensation of her friend's wet pussy in her mouth. She licked hard, moving her tongue in quick circles as she sucked on the delicious flesh. The sweet, woman scent of Katie's hot slit filled her nostrils, intoxicating her. Frenziedly, she mouthed the sweet cunt as the heat in her own pussy intensified. She rocked her hips, grinding her spread fanny against her playmate's face. Katie's pussy was moving against her face, its rhythm an echo of her own excitement. She sucked hard on her friend's clit, drawing it into her mouth. Katie was so wet that Sally's fingers kept losing their grip.

The tension in her groin was at breaking point now. She was on the brink. Her hips moved quicker and quicker as she neared orgasm. She sucked hard on Katie's clit as the rush of delight began to spread out from her belly. A deluge of ecstasy coursed through her taut body. Her fanny throbbed and pulsated; her thighs and buttocks quivered. A volcano of pleasure seemed to be erupting between her legs. She mouthed her lover's clit as waves of pleasure continued to unfurl from her womb.

As Sally's orgasm subsided, Katie's movements became more frenzied. Her distended clit was twitching and dancing in Sally's mouth. Sally felt Katie lift her head. She leant against Sally's right thigh and wrapped her arms round it, gripping it tightly. Her torso stiffened. She moved her hips convulsively, rubbing her cunt in quick, short strokes against her lover's eager mouth. Juices drenched Sally's face as she sucked hard on her friend's spread pussy. Katie was panting, groaning, sobbing. Sweat dripped off her body. She ground her crotch against Sally's mouth in shorter and shorter strokes. A low, animal rumble began in her throat and escaped between clenched teeth. Her fanny contracted as she rode her lover's face.

'God,' she shouted as she came. 'Oh! God!' Arching her back, she pressed down on Sally's mouth one last time. Gradually, she relaxed. She released her grip on Sally's thigh, shifted her weight and lay down on the bed beside her friend.

'So, what did you think of Jo?' Katie asked a few minutes later, when they had both recovered and climbed under the duvet.

'I think she's lovely,' said Sally. 'And I think she obviously adores you. I'm happy for you both.'

'I must admit to being somewhat frightened by it all.'

'Relationships are scary; they frighten everyone,' Sally said.

'Do you think that's all it is? I'm not so sure. I think it's more serious.' Sally had never heard her friend sound so uncertain. Katie was usually so confident, so sure of everything.

'I don't think anybody finds falling in love easy. It's meant to be disturbing, unsettling. It's part of what makes it exciting.' She patted Katie's arm fondly. 'Don't worry about it so much.'

'You're right,' said Katie, smiling. 'I know you are. I just don't have any experience of falling in love. I have nothing to compare it with. I expect it's normal to feel as if the entire world is standing on its head.'

'I think it is,' her friend agreed, smiling.

'After Mum and Dad died, I put all my energy into bringing up Helen. Then there was the school. I'd just been appointed and there were all sorts of changes that needed to be introduced. I scarcely had time for romance and, if I'm honest, I didn't even miss it. I had you, of course, and I met plenty of women at the clubs if I felt horny. I suppose I thought you could divide your life into separate compartments and keep it all organised. I never bargained on falling in love and I never realised how vulnerable falling in love would make me feel,' Katie explained.

'You know your trouble?' Sally asked. 'You think too much. You think you can keep everything under control if you can just work it all out in your head and explain it all rationally. Some things need to be experienced and not analysed. Just as you can't have sex unless you take off your clothes, you can't fall in love unless you're prepared to put up with feeling vulnerable for a while. Go with the flow and don't spend so much time thinking about it.'

'Do I hear the pot calling the kettle black?' Katie asked, laughing. 'Perhaps Doctor Sally ought to take a dose of her own medicine.'

'OK, OK,' said Sally. 'Guilty as charged. But, really, I think Jo is lovely – just right for you. I am really happy for you both.'

The two women settled down to sleep. Sally snuggled in against Katie's back, relaxed and happy. She felt safe and loved beside her best friend. She gripped Katie tighter as she thought about how lucky she was to have her. This might be the last time they slept together, she thought. It would be hard to justify continuing their physical relationship, once Katie and Jo became established as a couple. She'd miss it a lot, she realised.

As her mind drifted, she thought about her day. Quite profitable, on the whole. Now she'd finally managed to make a start on *House of Spirits*, she couldn't imagine how she had managed to build it up in her own mind until it had seemed an impossible task. If she continued at this rate, she'd easily be able to finish the chapters by the end of August and make a good start on the rest of the book. She sighed in relief, wrapping the duvet tighter.

Her pussy was still tingling, experiencing pleasant little aftershocks that made her shiver. The sex had been an eye-opener, too. She wished she'd talked about it to Katie earlier. She'd experienced things she'd only ever dreamt about before. Her anxieties about bondage had proved groundless. She had known she was perfectly safe with Katie, so allowing her friend to take control hadn't frightened her. Far from making her feel helpless and vulnerable, being tied up had made her feel sexy and powerful. And she'd never before experienced an orgasm without touching her clitoris. She snuggled down in the big bed, sleepily fantasising about all the kinky games she wanted to try out. And then write about, remembering the pleasure as she worked.

FOUR

Katie sat in her study, working out staff duty rosters for the forthcoming term. The large picture window looked out over the downs; the afternoon sun warmed her. She took a long gulp from the cool drink by her side and smiled to herself as she admired the manicured lawns and formal flowerbeds of the school grounds.

As she wrote down the staff assignments for psychology and sociology classes, Katie thought about all the changes she'd instigated. Seven years ago, Cuckmere had offered only the most traditional A Level courses. Katie had had to work tirelessly but, under her guidance, Cuckmere Manor had increased its scholastic reputation and improved its results. The Board of Governors knew that their school's enviable reputation was due in large part to Katie's skilled yet discreet management. They gave her a free hand. She had modernised the curriculum, introducing subjects such as A Level Psychology, Sociology and History of Art. She had also instituted an information technology policy which ensured that her students had access to the latest computer equipment and the Internet.

Katie was also popular with her students. She had the knack

of relating to all of the girls in her care, from the youngest eleven-year-old with homesickness to the oldest eighteen-year-old with romantic problems. All of them found their headmistress approachable and sympathetic. She loved teaching and was saddened that her responsibilities as head of school didn't give her as much opportunity to spend time in the classroom as she would have liked.

She went over to the open window and proudly surveyed the grounds below. A little way off, a gardener was trimming one of the box hedges. Shafts of sunlight shone on the stone slabs of the walkways. In the distance, she could hear the drone of a lawnmower. Mistress of all she surveyed, she thought to herself, smiling.

The school had been her life for the last seven years. That and her sister. Their mother's death from cancer when Helen was a toddler had created a bond between the two of them. After their father died from a heart attack, ten years ago, Katie had virtually become a parent to Helen. She was fiercely protective of her sister. She glanced down at the framed photo of Helen and her husband Stuart which sat in pride of place on the broad windowsill.

And now there was Jo. Just thinking about Jo frightened and excited her at the same time. And Katie thought about her constantly. Jo's image kept creeping into her mind at the most inopportune moments. Organising the duty rosters had taken her twice as long as it should, because her mind had kept returning to Jo. It was almost as though the younger woman had cast a spell over her. I've got it bad, she thought.

She sat down at her desk and closed her eyes. She took a few deep breaths to calm herself. For the first time in her life, she was out of her depth. At thirty-six, she'd never been in love. She was as overwhelmed and obsessed as one of her students experiencing her first crush. Only she was a grown woman and ought to know better. She did love Sally, of course, but that was different. Sure, there was passion, and fondness. But, most of all, it was a sense of deep familiarity and closeness. There was no spark, no fire like there was with Jo. The younger woman had captivated her somehow. Had pierced the armour she had worn so long and found her heart.

Katie smiled fondly as she thought of her new girlfriend. She was so bright and warm and full of life – it was hard not to like her. But it was Jo's openness which she found most appealing. Jo seemed so willing to share her feelings and her thoughts and her heart that Katie just had no defence against it. If only I could be like that, she thought.

She was getting even more confused. She shook her head, as if to clear the swirling thoughts away. What would she advise a friend in these circumstances? What would she tell Sally, if it were her problem? Katie smiled again. It was easy if you looked at it from someone else's perspective. She knew at once what she would say to her friend, if this were her problem. It was obvious. She'd tell her to ignore her fears and go for it. To seize the opportunity with both hands.

And that's what she would do. When Jo came over, that evening, she'd tell her how she felt. Then she'd take her to bed. It wasn't like Katie to be shy in that department, but fear and doubt had held her back from sleeping with Jo. But tonight she would face her fears and open her heart to Jo.

She felt better now she had a plan. Making a decision seemed to calm her. The knot in her belly softened and her mind stopped racing. She turned back to her papers and was quickly absorbed in her work.

Katie glanced at the clock – it was ten to eight. Jo would be here, soon. Katie's cheeks were flushed with excitement. She checked the table again. The salad was ready; a bottle of Frascati was chilling in an ice bucket. The chicken would come out of the oven in a few minutes and the home-made chocolate mousse was ready in the fridge. She'd even put clean sheets on the bed. Everything had to be perfect. She wanted everything to be perfect for Jo. She could hardly believe how excited she was. Now she had made her decision, her earlier fears had dissolved. The knot of anxiety in her abdomen had given way to a tingle of anticipation. She could hardly wait for Jo to arrive. She took a sip of wine and looked at the clock again. She smoothed the linen tablecloth and rearranged the cutlery.

The doorbell rang and Katie hurried over to answer the entryphone.

'It's me,' Jo informed her.

'Come up.' Katie pressed the button to open the door and hurried to the top of the stairs. 'Hi,' she said, feeling suddenly nervous. Jo was so pretty. Even the simple cotton skirt and sleeveless white T-shirt looked wonderful on her, showing off her long legs and golden tan. Her short blonde hair bounced as she climbed the stairs. The two women hugged.

'You look lovely,' Jo said, appreciatively. 'Is it silk?' She grasped the hem of Katie's scarlet dress and stroked the fabric appreciatively.

'Yes. I'm glad you like it,' Katie said, blushing. 'Come and have a drink. Dinner's ready; I just need to take the chicken out. Help yourself to a glass,' she said, indicating the table. Katie busied herself in the kitchen, suddenly nervous. She took the chicken out of the oven and arranged it on a serving dish, then rinsed the roasting pan and put it in the dishwasher. She carried the chicken into the main room and set it down on the table. Jo was still standing. She sipped her wine slowly, watching the older woman move around. Her blue eyes shone with pride.

'That smells good,' she said as Katie put down the meat.

'Lemon and pepper chicken,' said Katie. 'It's nothing special,'

'You are far too modest, you know.' Jo shook her head. 'It seems to me there isn't anything you can't do. I came here one day and you were mending your own car! You cook like a dream and, when nobody's looking, you play the cello – and you run this place. Yet whenever I pay you a compliment, you tell me "it's nothing".'

'You make me sound like Wonder Woman,' said Katie, blushing.

'You seem pretty wonderful to me,' said Jo honestly.

'Stop it! Or my face will go as red as my dress.' Katie grabbed Jo's wrist and pulled her close. They kissed.

'Let's eat,' said Katie.

Katie hardly tasted her meal. She couldn't take her eyes off Jo. She watched the younger woman's hands as she cut her food. Her fingers were long and slender. Katie watched Jo lift each forkful to her mouth and slip it between her lips. She was fascinated by Jo's mouth: she'd never seen such an expressive mouth. Jo's full lips smiled as she talked, or curled downwards to express sadness or sympathy. Katie couldn't resist those lips; she longed to taste them, to possess them. She refilled Jo's glass with wine and watched, rapt, as the younger woman took a sip.

Jo's hair fell forward as she ate, partially covering her face. Katie reached over and brushed it back.

'I couldn't see your face,' she said quietly.

Jo looked up and smiled, then frowned. 'You're not eating. Anything wrong?'

'Not at all,' Katie answered, shaking her head. 'I'm just feeling a little distracted.'

'I noticed,' the younger woman said. 'At first, I thought I had a blob of mayonnaise on the end of my nose, but then I decided you just like looking at me.'

'Sorry.' Katie blushed. 'I didn't realise it was so obvious. But it's your fault. You're so beautiful, I just can't tear my eyes away.'

'Be careful. You'll turn to stone in a minute,' Jo said, playfully.

'I wouldn't be at all surprised if you had cast a spell on me. I've never felt this way before.' She smiled at the younger woman, slightly embarrassed by her admission.

Jo put down her knife and fork carefully. 'Neither have I,' she agreed. 'What are we going to do about it?'

'I assume that's a rhetorical question,' Katie joked. Jo's blue eyes gazed at her, captivated her. The younger woman didn't speak, but her eyes were more eloquent than any words could have been. 'I did put clean sheets on the bed, just in case,' Katie continued.

'Then let's go and make them dirty,' Jo replied. She stood up and extended her hand. Katie struggled out of her chair, desire making her limbs numb. She took the younger woman's hand and allowed herself to be led. Her mind was racing. She could hardly believe what she was about to do. She'd been looking forward to this moment for so long. She was about to make love to this beautiful woman and she couldn't believe how nervous she was. She'd slept with plenty of women – more than she liked to admit. Yet she'd never felt like this – so what was the difference? This time I am in love, she thought. The significance of it hit her. This was more than just a friendly tumble between the sheets, more than just a physical need. She and Jo were about to make love.

In the bedroom, Jo pulled her close, kissing her. Katie wrapped one arm around the other woman's waist and leant into her. With her free hand, she stroked Jo's sleek hair. Jo's lips tasted of wine. Katie opened her mouth, surrendering to the kiss. Her tongue luxuriated in the warm wetness of her lover's mouth. She felt Jo's hands sliding up and down her back, gliding easily over the silky fabric of her dress. She broke away from the kiss and nuzzled her lips behind Jo's ear, drinking in the perfume there. She sucked the soft ear-lobe into her mouth and nibbled it.

'Let's get undressed,' said Jo impatiently, breaking away from her embrace. 'I want to feel you properly.

'Good idea,' Katie replied. 'Only it means I have to let go of you.'

'I want to see your body.' Jo spoke huskily, her voice betraying her excitement. She grasped the hem of Katie's dress and pulled it off and over her head. Underneath, Katie wore matching black lace panties and bra. The younger woman pulled her close and reached behind her, unhooking the bra. She pulled it away from Katie's body, revealing her breasts. She inhaled sharply in surprise.

'You're pierced,' she said, her voice tight with excitement. She bent her head and kissed each nipple in turn, then she took one of the thick silver rings in her mouth and pulled on it. Katie moaned softly. Jo quickly pulled her T-shirt over her head. She was braless.

Katie reached out instinctively for the small, pointed breasts. She stroked the soft skin. 'You're tanned all over,' she said appreciatively. She rolled Jo's nipples between her fingers.

'I eat my lunch on the nudist beach every day.'

'I never knew you were an exhibitionist.'

'There are a lot of things you don't know about me, but you're about to find out.' Jo pushed her skirt down over her hips, taking her knickers with it.

'You're so beautiful,' Katie murmured.

'And so are you,' her lover replied, stroking her cheek.

'I'm nearly old enough to be your mother.'

'But you're not, thank God.' She kissed Katie lightly on the lips. 'You talk too much.' She knelt down and slid Katie's knickers down her legs and over her feet. She leant forward and buried her face in Katie's crotch. She inhaled deeply, filling her nostrils with the musky scent.

'Sit down,' she hissed urgently. Katie sat down on the edge of the bed. Jo, still kneeling, pushed apart the older woman's legs. She kissed the inside of Katie's left knee, then moved to her right leg and did the same there. She kissed along the inside of Katie's parted thighs, nibbling at the creamy flesh. She trailed her wet tongue along the crease between pussy and thigh. She traced her fingertip along her lover's slit, barely touching her.

Katie looked down at her girlfriend. Jo's face was flushed with excitement. Her blonde hair shook as her head moved, making it glow in the late evening light. Katie's heart filled with tenderness, and she reached down and stroked Jo on the back of the neck. Jo wriggled appreciatively, and Katie felt a hot tongue moving slowly up the crack of her arse. She opened her legs a little wider. Jo used her thumbs to pull apart Katie's labia and licked along the length of her moist slit. She sucked on Katie's hard clit, drawing the sensitive nub into her mouth. She drank Katie's sweet moisture, lapping at her hole, then thrust her pointed tongue deep inside her lover's wet pussy.

It felt divine. Katie was panting, leaning back on her elbows for support as her lover licked her pussy. Tension formed in her belly. She moaned softly as Jo's tongue worked on her hot flesh. She didn't think she'd ever been so wet. She pressed her cunt against her partner's face, rotating her hips. Jo used her fingers to spread her lover's lips wide, exposing her clit. She sucked hard on the reddened bud, her mouth hot against the sensitive flesh. Rhythmically, she teased her partner's clit, sucking, licking, moving her mouth in rhythm with Katie's own urgent thrusts.

Katie's pussy tingled. Prickles of excitement spread out from her clit. Sweat filmed her brow. She was breathing in short gasps, her chest heaving. She lay back on the bed, sinking into the softness of the duvet. She drew up her legs and wrapped her arms around her thighs, spreading them further. She rocked herself backwards and forwards, rubbing her swollen fanny against her lover's mouth. She was close now. A warm knot of anticipation furled in her belly. Her thighs started to tremble. She moaned softly. She pulled her legs up against her chest, and her whole body shuddered as the first throb of her orgasm overwhelmed her. She was conscious only of Jo's mouth on her quim. Nothing else mattered except her orgasm and the shared intimacy of this moment. She cried out Jo's name as the second wave engulfed her taut body. Her head thrashed against the pillow, and tears of joy welled in her eyes. It seemed to go on forever, surges of pleasure crashing over her one after the other, as she thrust her aching pussy hard against her lover's mouth.

'Too much,' she said finally, pulling away. 'I can't bear to be touched when I've just come. It's just too much.'

'Me, too,' said Jo. She kissed Katie's pussy once more gently and rested her face against her lover's sweaty thigh. Slowly, Katie relaxed and her breathing returned to normal. She raised herself up on one elbow and looked down at Jo, smiling.

'Come here,' she said, patting the bed.

Jo stood up gingerly. 'I'm all stiff from kneeling there so long.'

'Lie down here and relax, then – let me do all the work.'

Jo stretched herself out on the king-size bed, clearly luxuriating in the softness of the quilt.

'Comfy?' Katie enquired. Jo nodded her assent. 'Then I shall begin.' Katie slid down the bed and positioned herself between Jo's thighs. The blonde girl smiled invitingly and opened her legs wider. Katie buried her nose in the curly golden hairs that decorated her lover's mound and inhaled the tangy scent. She swirled a fingertip around the moist opening, then ran the flat of her tongue up the length of Jo's slit, exerting firm pressure. She licked the tiny pink clit. Jo's cunt felt hot against her mouth.

Katie tongued Jo's delicious pussy. Her mouth slid easily over the slippery flesh. She fingered the tight opening as she licked. Gradually, she slid two fingers into Jo's hot, velvety hole. She sucked hard on the girl's clit, slowly finger-fucking her as she did so. Jo's muscles contracted, pulling the invading fingers further inside. Katie's mouth moved over her girlfriend's moist fanny. Expertly, she worked the swollen nub.

Jo had spread her legs wide. She threw back her head and pressed down against Katie's mouth. She moved her hips rhythmically, eager for release. She was breathing hard, her chest heaving as she gulped in air. She reached down and laced her fingers through Katie's sleek hair, then rubbed her crotch urgently against her lover's face.

Katie felt Jo's body stiffen. Muscles contracted around her

probing fingers and the sensitive bead of flesh in her mouth twitched. Jo gripped the older woman's hair hard and whimpered; the piercing sound throbbed in Katie's ears. Moisture flooded into her mouth, tasting sweet on her tongue. She pulled away from Jo's clit and licked gently at the deep crevice between the girl's buttocks. Her crack was slippery with juices. She lapped them up hungrily. She parted the creamy globes and buried her face between them.

She found Jo's puckered opening and swirled her tongue there. She sucked at the wrinkled flesh, relishing the sensation of her mouth against the secret entrance.

Jo exhaled softly. 'That's so good,' she murmured.

Katie pressed her tongue into the woman's pussy. The tight opening throbbed as she slid her tongue in and out. She clamped her mouth over Jo's engorged clit, drawing the swollen bud into her mouth. She moved her tongue in small circles, and sucked the clit hard. Jo began to tremble. She pressed down hard on Katie's mouth. Katie slid two fingers into her lover's tight cunt and two into her arsehole. Jo's muscles gripped her like a vice as she started to come. Her pussy throbbed in Katie's mouth. She sobbed.

Katie lay still. She kept her mouth in position, but avoided touching Jo's sensitive clit. She soothed the hot flesh with her tongue. She rotated her fingers inside the girl's fanny, gently, kneading her G-spot. Jo lay back on the bed, her sweat-dampened hair clinging to her forehead. She breathed heavily through parted lips, her eyes closed. Katie's probing fingers circled inside her, coaxing her towards another orgasm, and she felt Jo's muscles begin to tense. She started moving her mouth again, gently licking the hardened clit. She blew softly on her lover's hot flesh, cooling it, then warmed it again with her tongue. She hummed quietly as she sucked, sending shivers of vibration through Jo's loins.

Jo was on the edge now. She thrashed wildly on the bed, grabbing handfuls of duvet in her fists. She ground her crotch against Katie's face. Katie sucked hard, wiggling her fingers inside her lover. Jo's pelvic muscles tensed. She was moaning, sobbing, laughing all at once. Katie held on tight, riding out her partner's orgasm. Finally, Jo's body relaxed and she reached a hand down to Katie.

'Come up here,' she said weakly.

Katie disentangled herself and climbed over Jo's spread legs. She lay down beside the younger woman and took her in her arms. She brushed a damp tendril of hair from Jo's smooth forehead and kissed her. Tenderly, she licked a single tear from the corner of her girlfriend's eye.

'I've never done that before,' Jo said, smiling. 'I didn't know I could.'

'You'd be surprised what you can do,' Katie explained, 'when you have a good teacher.'

Jo burst out laughing. 'Yes, miss,' she agreed. 'And I think you'll find me an attentive pupil.'

'You know what?' Katie asked. 'I'm starving. How do you fancy some chocolate mousse?'

'Have you ever known me to turn down chocolate?'

Katie kissed Jo and got up. Jo sat up and watched her walk across the room. 'Cute arse,' she said.

A few moments later, Katie came back in, carrying a large glass bowl and two spoons.

Katie settled down on the bed beside Jo and handed her a spoon. She balanced the bowl on her stomach and helped herself to a mouthful of the creamy dessert. Jo dipped a finger into the bowl and scooped up a huge blob of mousse. She sucked it off her finger and licked it clean.

'Delicious,' she declared. 'And you made it yourself? You're so clever.'

'I wish you wouldn't say that,' Katie replied. 'It makes me sound like some perfect being, like Wonder Woman. You've got such an idealised picture of me and my capabilities, that I feel as though I can't live up to myself. I'm very ordinary, really,' she said, more lightly than she felt.

'You are not at all ordinary,' Jo insisted. 'And how do you think it makes me feel? Being involved with someone who's good at everything? I can't think what you see in me. I'm nineteen soon, I've never done anything in my life except go to school and work in my parents' restaurant. How can I compete?'

Katie put her spoon down in the bowl and looked straight at Jo. She took the younger woman's hand and brought it to her lips. 'I can see you and I need a talk,' she said. 'First of all, you don't need to compete with me and I hope you don't feel you have to. I'm not perfect, although I admit that I'm quite capable in practical ways. But you have skills that I am in awe of and I'd swap the ability to make my own chocolate mousse for what you have, any day.'

'What do you mean?' Jo asked. 'How could you possibly envy me?'

'Because you're alive and free. You face life with an enthusiasm, a sort of joy that makes me realise how repressed and cautious I am.'

'You, repressed and cautious?' Jo asked, mystified. 'You're so full of confidence, so passionate about things. Are you sure we're talking about the same woman?'

Katie laughed and hugged the younger woman. 'I suppose what I'm trying to say,' she explained, 'is that I like you very much and I admire you. And meeting you has given me the opportunity to express a part of myself that I'd almost forgotten about. And, if I'm perfectly honest, it terrifies me. But, at the same time, it's wonderful – does that make sense?'

'Yes, it does,' said Jo quickly. 'I feel exactly the same way. In fact, I think I'm falling in love with you and I'm terrified. And, of course, everyone keeps telling me how much older than me you are. But we can never know what's going to happen in the future, so we might as well make the most of the present. And, for now, I am happy to be here with you.'

The two women kissed, holding each other close for a long moment. Then Katie released Jo and took a huge mouthful of mousse.

'Tell me about your nipple rings,' Jo asked curiously. 'Did it hurt? And what about your tattoos? I've always fancied having one done, but I'm a real coward.'

'The rings hurt when I had them done,' Katie admitted, 'but they healed quickly. And I love them.'

'Do they make your nipples more sensitive?' asked Jo tentatively, gently pulling on Katie's nearest nipple ring.

'Oh, yes! It makes them semi-erect all the time and, when you pull on them, it's delicious.'

'As delicious as this chocolate mousse?' Jo asked. She spooned a dollop of dessert on to Katie's nipple and sucked it off slowly, drawing the silver ring into her mouth as she did so.

'The tattoos hurt at the time, but not afterwards. But it's annoying looking after them while they heal. So itchy.' She took a mouthful of mousse and sucked it off her spoon, sensuously.

'What are they?' Jo asked.

Katie moved the glass bowl on to the bed and rolled on to her side away from Jo, displaying her tattoos to the other woman.

'The one on my shoulder is a Celtic knot design.'

'It's lovely,' said Jo. She leant over to kiss it.

'And the one on my hip is a stylised version of the moon, a crescent moon.'

Jo bent to kiss the design on the back of Katie's hip. 'Do you think I should get one?' Jo asked, tracing the outline of Katie's lower tattoo with a finger.

'I'm sure you'd look beautiful,' she said. 'But it's a serious commitment: you have it forever. You have to be sure you want one.'

'Are you into all that other stuff, as well?' Jo asked hesitantly.

'What stuff?' Katie asked. She turned back towards the younger woman and set the bowl down between them.

'You know: whips, chains, rubber, pain.'

'I've been known to dabble,' Katie admitted. 'But it's the psychology of it that appeals to me, not the hardware.'

'What do you mean?' asked Jo, taking a mouthful of mousse.

'It's about exploring your limits. Letting go, trust, intimacy. The chains and leather are only symbols. It's about two people sharing their most intimate desires, not about hurting each other.'

'I think I understand,' said Jo. 'I must admit, the subject fascinates me, although I've only read about it. I'd like to . . . explore, I suppose.'

'I'm sure you'll love it,' Katie assured her. 'I'll take you to a club.'

'But you'll be gentle with me, won't you?' Jo asked, in mock concern.

'You can count on it.' Katie scooped up a dollop of the dessert and smeared it on Jo's nipple. She leant over and sucked it clean, licking Jo's warm skin. She drew the taut nipple into her mouth and nibbled it gently, before sitting up and helping herself to a mouthful of mousse. The younger girl ate several mouthfuls of mousse then spooned a big blob of the dessert on to her nipple; Katie smiled. She cleaned the girl's skin with her tongue. Jo scooped up another spoonful and dropped it on to her other nipple; Katie pulled her close and ate the mousse off her chest. Jo smiled playfully and parted her legs. She ladled several dollops of the dessert on to her pussy, then set her spoon down in the bowl.

Katie set the bowl carefully on the floor and slid between Jo's thighs. She pulled the girl close and buried her face in the blonde pussy. She licked up the mousse, smearing her face in it. She sucked Jo's labia into her mouth, cleaning away the chocolate with her tongue. Jo moaned softly.

Katie slowly licked up all the mousse, sucking the sweet chocolate from the curly hairs. The heat of Jo's skin had melted the dessert slightly. A dribble of liquid mousse had run down between the younger woman's buttocks. Katie squirmed in her tongue and licked it away. She parted Jo's lips and tongued her moist opening, relishing the sweet saltiness of Jo's juices. She used the flat of her tongue and licked the length of her lover's slit, then found Jo's hard clit and sucked it.

She held Jo's lips apart and tongued her sweet pussy. Slippery juices mingled with the mousse, making her skin slick and oily. Katie's mouth glided over the hot flesh. She licked, lapped, and sucked. She snaked her tongue into Jo's hole, squeezing it past the muscular opening. The tight entrance contracted as she slid her tongue inside the hot canal. She slid down and sucked at her partner's pink arsehole, probing with her tongue, teasing the wrinkled flesh.

Jo reached down and stroked Katie's face. She smoothed the shiny hair and smiled at her lover. She leant back on her elbows, watching the dark head bobbing between her legs.

'That's wonderful,' she murmured. Katie was concentrating on Jo's clit now, teasing the sensitive bud with her hot mouth. She licked it with the flat of her tongue, sucked it and rubbed it gently with the tip of her nose. Jo's body was tense, her muscles stiff with excitement. Katie wrapped her arms around the younger woman's thighs and pulled her close. She locked her mouth over Jo's hot cunt, expertly working her tongue on the taut clit.

She circled the hardened nub with her tongue, drew it into her mouth and sucked on it. She moved rhythmically pressing her face hard against Jo's engorged pussy. Jo's hips moved frantically and she pushed her aching crotch into Katie's face. Her breathing was rapid and shallow. Katie felt Jo stiffen and then Jo's thighs clamped down on her face, pulling her inwards. Jo moaned, a rumbling growl which echoed in her throat. She ground her crotch repeatedly against her lover's face. Katie held on, her mouth clamped over the girl's twitching clit.

Jo's body relaxed and softened; she lay back on the bed and closed her eyes.

'I need a cuddle,' she said, beckoning weakly. Katie crawled up the bed and lay down beside the younger woman. She pulled Jo close and nuzzled into her.

'That was wonderful,' Jo murmured, 'but I think you're going to need to change the sheets.'

FIVE

Sally sat in front of her laptop, her work spread out in front of her on the dining room table. Things were going well. She could hardly believe that she'd completed one chapter in draft and was halfway through her second. And in only a week! At this rate, she'd easily write three chapters by the first of September. Although she still experienced the occasional bout of butterflies, the crippling anxiety she had come to associate with working on the book hadn't returned. She didn't understand why but, away from her flat and her office, she somehow just didn't seem to feel under the same pressure.

Her stomach growled, reminding her that she'd been working since eight and eaten nothing since last night. She saved her work and stood up, stretching her legs. I could do with a break, she thought, as she looked out of the window. Sun shone on the lawn, making it shine and a gentle breeze ruffled the shrubs and flowers. She frowned as she realised she hadn't been out of the house in a week, not even into the garden. She hadn't spoken to anyone for days. Sally had been so wrapped up in her work that she hadn't had time to feel lonely. But now she realised she was beginning to yearn for a bit of company. She'd go out for a walk through the village.

Her stomach rumbled fiercely again. She was starving. The pub in the village offered lunch, she remembered. She could combine a bit of exercise with lunch and save herself the trouble of cooking. But she'd need to change. She couldn't go out in public in the tatty old clothes she wore to work in. She shrugged off her old T-shirt and headed upstairs to the bedroom. Quickly she changed out of her working clothes and into a cool summer dress.

It was hot outside. The sun warmed her bare shoulders. The light made her squint. She rummaged in her bag for her sunglasses and put them on. Her neighbour sat in his garden, soaking up the sun. He waved in greeting as Sally walked past, as if they were old friends, although they'd only exchanged pleasantries over the fence. People were so friendly here, she mused.

As she turned the corner of the lane into the village's main street, a group of laughing children collided with her. They offered her a giggling apology and went on. Fruit and vegetables glistened in the sun outside the greengrocers. A Royal Mail van pulled up and the postman climbed out to empty the pillar-box. He stuffed the letters down into his sack and disappeared inside the post office. Its bell rang as the door closed behind him.

It's so peaceful here, Sally thought, so English. She loved this quiet village with its slow pace of life and its old-fashioned values. In London, she scarcely knew her neighbours. Things seemed so much more hectic there. No wonder she found it hard to write at home.

She passed the church with its Norman arches and headed towards the pub. The Moonraker had been an old coaching inn in the days before the railway made travelling easy and comfortable. It still had the massive gateway through which the coaches had rattled their way into the yard. Outside, it was painted white and criss-crossed with the wooden decoration Sally associated with Tudor buildings. A group of cyclists passed her on the road and a couple of ramblers sat outside The Moonraker, eating their packed lunches and drinking cool beer.

She wandered through the heavy oak door of the pub and headed for the bar. It seemed dark inside after the brightness of the day but, once her eyes had adjusted, she realised the interior of the pub was sunny and bright. Pale green slate tiles covered the floor, feeling cool underfoot. The lower half of the walls was clad with blonde wooden panelling. The upper part was colour-washed in warm terracotta shades. Among the traditional pub artefacts of brass rubbings and old farm implements were vintage advertising posters and framed prints, giving the place an eclectic and comfortable feel. And it was very welcoming. The landlady – Sally assumed it was the landlady – stood behind the bar, reading a newspaper. She looked up and smiled as Sally entered.

'What'll you have?' she asked welcomingly.

'Can you do me a St Clement's?' Sally asked.

'Coming up,' said the landlady, busying herself with glasses and ice. 'I haven't seen you in here, before,' she went on. 'Are you on holiday?'

She was tall and dark. In a way, she reminded Sally of Katie: something about the warmth of her smile and the shape of the eyes, although her figure was much curvier than Katie's. It was nice to bump into someone so friendly, Sally thought.

'Not really,' Sally said. 'I'm staying in a friend's cottage, but I'm not on holiday: I'm working. I'm a writer and I needed somewhere quiet away from London. I've got a deadline to meet.'

'Well, it's certainly quiet here. It takes some getting used to, after London. I've been here three years and sometimes I still get a yearning for anonymity and noise. But mostly I don't miss it at all.' She smiled warmly and handed Sally her drink.

'Did you have a pub in London?' Sally asked, handing over a five-pound note.

'No, I was a commodities broker. I inherited this place from my parents. I've sunk most of my money into renovating it.'

'And you've done a good job. It's beautiful,' Sally said.

'Thanks; here's your change. Let's hope the locals agree with you. I've turned the old stable block into a restaurant. We opened last week, and it's doing OK so far. I'm Liz, by the way. Liz Godfrey.' She extended her hand over the bar towards Sally.

'Sally Avery,' she replied, grasping the proffered hand and shaking it. It was soft and warm, yet surprisingly strong. She felt a flutter of excitement in her stomach.

'Sally Avery? Author of *Secrets of the Sea*? Don't tell me you wrote that,' Liz said excitedly.

'I did, actually,' Sally admitted, blushing.

'I loved it. I've never met an author before,' she said, laughing.

'We're pretty much like anyone else,' Sally joked. 'Except we have bad eyesight from staring at the computer screen and an unhealthy pallor from never going outside.'

Liz threw her head back and laughed, revealing her white, even teeth. She's really beautiful, Sally thought. And I don't think I'm imagining it – she likes me.

'Any chance of lunch?' Sally asked. 'I've been writing all morning and I'm starving.'

'Of course. You can go through to the restaurant or I could bring you a bar snack,' Liz explained, reaching behind the bar for a menu.

'If I have a bar snack, does that mean I can go on chatting with you?' Sally asked, blushing at her own boldness. Perhaps the country air had made her reckless, she thought.

'It would be my pleasure. In fact, if you don't mind, I can take my break now and join you for lunch.'

'I'd be delighted,' Sally responded quickly, smiling. Silently, she cursed herself for the formality of her invitation. She probably just thinks you're being polite, Sally thought. You've got to let her know that you fancy her.

'So what can I get you?' Liz smiled warmly.

'Could you do me a ploughman's?'

'Of course,' said Liz. 'Take a seat and I'll prepare it myself. Why don't you sit outside, since you've been cooped up indoors all day?'

Sally thanked her and found herself a seat in the garden behind the pub. She sat in the shade of the umbrella that sheltered the table and sipped at her drink. Liz certainly seemed friendly. And she was attractive. Her short, dark hair gave her an androgynous look but her full, curvy figure was definitely feminine. Sally wondered what the landlady looked like under her clothes.

Before very long, Liz emerged from the pub, carrying a tray. She set down their lunch on the table.

'So what's your new book about?' Liz asked.

'It's called *House of Spirits* and it's about a haunted pub in Arundel.'

'Really? How interesting. The Moonraker is supposed to be haunted, but I've never seen anything. I suspect it's just a story someone cooked up to attract the tourists.' Liz smiled, her brown eyes round and earnest.

God, she's beautiful, Sally thought, admiring Liz's smooth, golden skin. She wondered if Liz was like that all over.

'The Green Man seems to be genuinely haunted. There are documented instances going back centuries and they are too consistent to be coincidence. It's been owned by the same family for generations. The ghost is supposed to be a young woman who killed herself. There was talk about an unhappy love affair. It's a very romantic story and the ghost is said to protect and guide the present generation of the family.' Sally hesitated, suddenly concerned that the other woman might not share her enthusiasm for the book she was writing. She blushed. 'But I'm probably boring you,' she apologised.

'Not at all,' replied Liz. 'I think it's fascinating. I could never write a book; I just wouldn't know where to start. It must seem an impossible task, when you start.'

'It certainly does. And, until very recently, I was so overwhelmed by it, I couldn't even begin. That's why I came here. To get away from London and distractions. And it's worked: I'm really getting involved in my work, now.' Sally looked up from her plate and glanced at Liz. The publican met her gaze and smiled warmly. Sally's heart pounded in her chest and she felt herself blushing. She smiled back.

'So why Hailsham Edge?' Liz asked. 'Do you have family here?'

'Not family,' said Sally, shaking her head. 'I did my degree at Brighton and my best friend is headmistress of Cuckmere Manor school. She owns the cottage I'm staying in. How about you? Are you local?' Her curiosity was piqued. She couldn't take her eyes off the other woman. The little dimple that formed at the corner of Liz's mouth as she spoke fascinated her. Stop staring, Sally, or she'll notice, she'll told herself.

'My parents owned this pub and I grew up here. I went to university in London, and afterwards I stayed there. But three years ago, Mum and Dad died in a plane crash and I decided to settle here. I'd seen plenty of my colleagues burn themselves out after a few years and the commodity broking business is . . . Well, I was getting cynical and ruthless, and I didn't like it. After Mum and Dad died, I put all my energy and anger into the pub. It helped. And slowly I realised I loved it here. It's beautiful and quiet and there's a real sense of community. I belong here.' Her dark eyes glowed with sincerity.

'I know what you mean,' said Sally. 'It is peaceful here – sort of tranquil. I feel as though I couldn't be anxious here if I tried.' She glanced at her watch. 'I really should go. I have to get back to work.'

'Of course. Me, too,' replied the landlady, standing up and gathering dishes. 'Please come again. I get the odd night off and I'd be really pleased to see you.'

Is she offering me a date? Sally wondered. Or is she just being friendly? The woman had certainly seemed interested, but it wouldn't be the first time she had mistaken friendliness for a come-on. And she didn't want to embarrass either of them by asking for clarification.

'I will, thanks,' she replied. 'I'll look forward to it.'

She walked the short distance back to the cottage, distracted. Liz was beautiful. She couldn't remember the last time she had been so attracted to a woman. And the signals she had been giving out seemed to suggest that the feeling was mutual. But Sally was nervous. She didn't want to make a fool of herself or risk offending Liz. She was such a coward. Katie wouldn't be so cautious, she thought. Katie would make her feelings absolutely clear. So what if the other woman turned out not to be interested? At least she'd find out where she stood. And surely, that would be preferable to her present dilemma? She cursed herself silently for being so cautious and let herself back into the cottage.

Back at home, Sally couldn't get Liz Godfrey out of her mind. She sat in front of her computer, but she couldn't concentrate on her work. In the two hours since lunch, she'd scarcely written half a page. Her thoughts kept drifting to the pleasant hour she had spent in The Moonraker at lunch. Liz wasn't just gorgeous, she was intelligent and interesting. Sally definitely wanted to get to know her better. And she was so sexy. Her loose, casual clothes had hinted at the ripe curves underneath. She took a deep breath and imagined peeling Liz's T-shirt over her head and revealing full, soft breasts. In her mind's eye, Liz's breasts were topped by dark, chocolatey nipples. Sally sighed. She wondered if she'd ever get the opportunity to find out how the real Liz lived up to her imaginary one.

Had she been suggesting a date when she had invited Sally back to the pub, or was she just being friendly and drumming up trade? Sally wasn't certain. But Liz had mentioned her days off – surely, that suggested that her interest was personal rather than professional? She'd go back to the pub anyway, she decided. She'd have lunch there a couple of times a week and get to know the attractive landlady better. That would give her ample opportunity to take things further if she was really interested in Sally. She smiled, took a deep breath, and turned back to her computer screen.

Later that evening, Sally dumped pasta into a pan of boiling water. She set the kitchen timer for ten minutes and stirred her pan of marinara sauce. She topped up her wineglass and drank a long gulp of the peppery Cabernet Sauvignon. She was tired. She'd worked long into the evening and had only stopped when her aching back became impossible to ignore.

With two chapters finished in draft, she'd easily be able to meet her deadline, she thought. And to think that she'd been convinced that she'd never write the book. It seemed so straightforward, now. She was really happy here. The tiny cottage was cosy and familiar and the rural surroundings seemed to calm her. And Katie was at hand for advice if she needed it. And company. She had other friends, of course: plenty of them. But none of them were as special to her as Katie.

She took another sip of her wine and stirred the cooking pasta. Part of the reason she felt so close to Katie was the relaxed intimacy they shared. When she didn't have a girlfriend, like now, having Katie as a lover was very important to her. She smiled fondly as she thought about her friend. It's more than just a physical need, she realised. Sharing Katie's bed gave her far more than just sex. It was almost as if she gave Sally an outlet for her feelings of love and fondness. Having Katie as a lover enabled her to express a part of herself which otherwise would have had no outlet.

She was so glad Katie had finally found someone to love. Kate certainly deserved it and Sally was delighted for her: yet, at the same time, she felt an unbearable sadness. She was genuinely pleased that Katie had found Jo, but somehow part of her felt empty. She was lonely, that was it. Now Katie had someone else, she had to face the fact that she was lonely, that she yearned for someone that she could love.

The kitchen timer buzzed and she drained her pasta. She carried her meal and wine into the living room and settled herself down on the sofa, browsing through the TV channels as she ate.

The phone rang and she set her tray down on the floor and got up to answer it. 'Hello,' she said. She carried the phone over to the sofa and settled back down among the cushions.

'It's Katie. How's the writing going?'

Sally smiled, pleased to hear her friend's voice. 'Fine,' she replied. 'I have two chapters done in draft and I'm ready to start on the third. I've missed you,' she said. 'We haven't spoken in a week. I was just thinking about you.'

'And I've missed you, too, sweetheart, but I haven't rung you because I didn't think you needed any distractions. I'm glad you've been working.'

'Me too,' Sally admitted. 'It seems so peaceful here – the writing just seems to flow. I really can't thank you enough.'

'Thank me for what? You're the one doing the writing, not me.'

Sally smiled. Katie's being modest again, she thought. She hated it when Sally tried to give her the credit she was due.

'You know I couldn't have done it without you,' Sally said. 'How have you been? What about Jo?'

'Well,' said Katie, 'we went to bed last night.'

'And how was it? Did the earth move?'

'It still is,' replied her friend.

Sally could hear the excitement in her friend's voice. 'I'm

really pleased. I'm only surprised that you left it so long. It isn't at all like you.'

'Well, I've never been in love before,' Katie admitted shyly. 'It didn't seem right before. She's wonderful. She's so full of life and curiosity, and passion. She makes me feel so alive.'

'I could tell. You couldn't take your eyes off her. And she obviously feels the same about you.'

'She seems to,' confirmed Katie, 'although I can't think why.'

'Because you're beautiful, and talented, and generous, and wise,' Sally said. 'Jo is a very lucky woman.'

'And so am I.'

'I'm happy for you both. You deserve it,' Sally said.

'We're going to Brighton, tomorrow night, to check out my favourite leather club. Jo's curious. We wondered if you'd like to come along.'

Sally was about to decline the invitation, as she had so many times before, but she hesitated. Her recent experience at the London club had whetted her appetite. She wanted to learn more about bondage and submission, to learn more about her own desires. Why not? She'd feel safe with Katie and she had nothing to lose.

'I will come, thank you,' she said finally.

'I am surprised,' Katie said with exaggerated shock. 'I almost didn't bother asking you, because you always say no. Even though I know you're dying to come along, really.'

'I finally plucked up courage and visited a club in London, a couple of weeks ago,' Sally confided.

'And? Tell all. How did you get on? What did you think?'

'It was amazing,' Sally admitted. 'I saw a mistress using a riding crop on her slave's arse. I've never been so turned on in my life. It made me realise that I want to explore that part of my nature. It was incredible.'

'I always knew you'd love it. You're a natural,' Katie said. 'Come over at eight and we'll drive into Brighton in my car.'

'OK,' said Sally. 'I'll see you tomorrow.'

As she put down the phone, Sally was unsettled. She was excited and aroused about the idea of visiting another fetish club. Yet there was that lingering sense of sadness, of loneliness, that just wouldn't go away. She'd come to rely on Katie too much, she realised. And she was envious – she wanted someone she could share her bed and her life with. Someone to explore her fantasies and her impulses with. Someone to love.

She wondered again if the attractive landlady was a lesbian. She'd certainly seemed interested. And they had a lot in common. But could she be mistaking the rapport between them for something more? She wasn't sure. She'd have lunch at the pub tomorrow, she decided. Have a chat with her, take things one step at a time.

She relaxed back on to the sofa, uncoiling her tense muscles. She ached all over. She was exhausted, she realised. She'd better pace herself tomorrow. Apart from her lunch break, she'd spent twelve hours in front of the computer today: far too long. Even her eyes hurt. She closed them and breathed deeply. There was no point making herself ill.

A good night's sleep was what she needed. She sat up and began gathering up her dishes and wineglass. She carried everything through into the kitchen and went upstairs to bed. She stripped off the dressing gown she had put on after her shower earlier and climbed under the covers. The feathery duvet and plump pillows were comforting as she nestled down further in the bed.

She wished Katie were here now, she thought. There was nothing like an orgasm to wash away the cares of the day and get her off to sleep. Or Liz, perhaps. Yes, she'd love to be lying beside the beautiful landlady, her tired head resting on Liz's ample chest. She closed her eyes and pictured herself holding the duvet back for Liz to climb into bed with her. In her imagination, Liz's body was honey-coloured. The same shade as coffee ice-cream, she thought dreamily. Although some might think the landlady fat, Sally had always been attracted to curvy women.

She imagined running her hands all over the other woman's creamy skin. Stroking her round buttocks, cupping the soft belly. Sally raised her knees and parted her legs. She ran her finger lightly along her moist cleft. In her imagination, it was Liz touching her, Liz's warm hands on her body. She shivered and cupped her own breasts, squeezing them. She pinched her nipples hard, imagining Liz's mouth on her, sucking the hardened teats, biting them.

She brought her left hand to her pussy and stroked along the slit. Her fingers dabbled in the slippery moisture. She circled her clit lightly, teasing herself. She dipped her wet fingers into her hot hole and pictured Liz kneeling naked beside her, smiling down at her. She could feel the probing fingers in her fanny, Liz's fingers.

Her right hand was still squeezing and pinching her swollen nipples. In her mind's eye, the other woman leant forward and nibbled them. Fingers between her legs were moving fast rubbing her engorged clit hard. She drew up her knees and opened her thighs a little wider, then pulled and stretched her reddened nipples. It was almost hurting now; it felt divine. She thrust her chest out, offering herself up to the other woman's imaginary mouth. She could almost feel Liz's tongue snaking across her flesh.

She was breathing hard, her chest heaving from the effort. She was hot. She threw back the duvet, uncovering herself. Her right hand slithered down her body and found her cunt. She spread her labia wide, exposing her clit. She rubbed herself with two fingers, smearing slippery juices over the tiny button. Her whole body was tense. Her pussy ached, and she was tingling.

Her hips rocked rhythmically. She imagined Liz lying between her legs, Liz's mouth on her clit. The fingers sliding over her swollen flesh were Liz's tongue, Liz's lips. Her fanny was throbbing and spasms of pleasure spread through her pelvis.

She slid two fingers into her wet hole and rubbed her clit hard. She ground her crotch against her fingers, against Liz's imagined face.

Her thighs began to tremble and she lifted her buttocks up off the bed. Shivers of pleasure coursed through her. Her pussy pulsated around her fingers as surges of orgasm overwhelmed her. She imagined she was coming for Liz, coming into Liz's hot mouth. It went on and on. Her climax gripped her, consumed her. Waves of rapture possessed her. She cried out, 'Liz!'

Gradually her body relaxed and her breathing slowed. She covered herself with the duvet again and turned on her side, relaxed and contented. That had been incredible. She couldn't remember the last time she had had such an intense orgasm on her own. Tomorrow, she was definitely going to have her lunch at The Moonraker again, she thought as she drifted off to sleep.

SIX

At noon the next day, Sally got ready for lunch at The Moonraker. She brushed her hair and put on some subtle eye make-up. She hoped she hadn't overdone it. She was wearing her favourite dress; the bright red cotton clung to her curves. She wasn't bad-looking, she thought, as she applied her eyeliner. Her naturally blonde hair fell across her shoulders. Her blue eyes looked intelligent and she had always had a clear complexion. Her pale skin didn't tan, but it suited her, she thought. If there was one thing she didn't like about her fair colouring, it was the fact that her eyelashes and eyebrows were very blonde. Maybe she should have a go at dyeing them. She gave herself a final check in the mirror and trotted down the stairs.

Liz wasn't behind the bar when she entered the pub. She ordered herself a white wine spritzer to give her a bit of Dutch courage.

'Is Liz in today?' she asked the barmaid, more casually than she felt, as she paid for her drink.

'It's her day off. She won't be in again until tomorrow.'

Sally's heart fell. Of course, Liz hadn't said she'd be in the pub today, but Sally had just assumed she would be. She'd been looking forward to it. She was disappointed.

'Will you be having lunch?' the barmaid asked her.

Her appetite had deserted her. She just wanted to go back to the cottage and hide herself away. But she needed to eat. She'd get tired and ill if she went without food – and she couldn't work if she was unwell. 'I'll have a ploughman's in the garden, please,' she said and walked out into the sun to wait for her food. Liz probably wasn't even gay, she told herself. She was just being friendly, yesterday. She'd enjoyed sharing her lunch with a fellow Londoner, but there had been nothing more to it. Sally had been mistaken.

She was lonely, that was it. And her loneliness had made her mistake friendliness for sexual interest. She couldn't go around imagining that every attractive woman she met was a lesbian. She'd have to get a grip. Her cheeks coloured with shame. What if Liz had been embarrassed by her attentions and had deliberately taken the day off to avoid her?

She was being paranoid, now. Liz's day off probably meant nothing; she simply hadn't thought to mention it to Sally. She'd come back to the pub in a couple of days and see what developed. In the meantime, she knew she'd have a hard time thinking of anything else.

Sally picked up her keys and handbag and left the cottage. She was looking forward to this evening. Her visit to the fetish club in London, over a week ago, had piqued her interest. The experience had touched her deeply. She wouldn't have been able to explain why, yet she knew she wanted to explore her impulses.

She settled herself behind the wheel of her car and started the engine. Going to the club with Katie by her side would make her feel more confident, she thought. Katie would be there to explain things to her, and give her moral support. She wondered if she'd be lucky enough to witness the kind of scene she had watched in London – she hoped so. She was getting horny just thinking about it. She wriggled slightly in her seat.

She turned the car off the road and into the drive leading up to the school. As she entered the car park, she saw Jo's Fiesta parked beside Katie's Jeep.

'It's me. I hope I'm not late,' she said, when Katie responded to the buzzer.

'Not at all. Come up,' her friend replied.

Katie was waiting for her at the top of the stairs, smiling warmly. She was positively glowing, Sally thought. They hugged and Katie led her into the living room.

'You look lovely,' Sally said 'but aren't you a little underdressed?'

'I prefer to save my leather gear for the bedroom,' Katie joked. 'Anyway, I'm not half as kinky as you think I am. I'm just interested in the erotic implications of submission and dominance. I don't have to get dressed up in rubber and studs to get turned on.'

'I know,' said Sally, laughing. 'And I can't talk. I learnt enough from visiting that club last week to know I want to try it for myself.'

'I must admit I'm interested, too,' confided Jo, 'although I'm a complete novice.'

'Then I think we have an interesting evening ahead of us,' said Katie emphatically.

It was dark inside the basement club. It was a long narrow room with a bar at one end and a low stage at the other. There wasn't much in the way of décor. The walls were a sort of rough brick. Sally thought it must have been a cellar, at one time. The rustic walls provided an atmospheric backdrop to the club, bringing it the air of a dungeon. Here and there, chains hung from the ceiling. Sally looked around, wide-eyed, drinking it all in.

'Let's get ourselves a drink,' said Katie, nodding towards the bar at the far side of the room. Sally nodded and followed her friends across the room. She glanced around as Katie ordered their drinks. Most people seemed ordinary, dressed in everyday clothes, like themselves. But there were a couple leaning against the bar dressed in leather miniskirts and tight T-shirts. A knot of women near the door sported more outlandish outfits, featuring rubber and fishnets. Sally felt her nipples peak as she watched them. She was already excited.

She glanced over at Jo and the two women exchanged a nervous smile.

'Let's find ourselves a table,' said Katie. They wove their way between the groups of women until they found a free table at the far side of the room, next to the small stage. They sat down.

'There's a cabaret, later,' explained Katie. Jo leant over and kissed Katie lightly. The two women sat close to each other, holding hands. Jo looked around the room excitedly, taking it all in. Sally took a sip of her drink and sat back. A little way away, a dark, heavy woman wearing a short skirt and a leather jacket snapped her fingers. Another girl, wearing fishnets and high-heels with her black mini dress, leapt forward eagerly. The first woman said something Sally couldn't hear and the fishnet girl took out a cigarette and offered it to her companion. She's her slave, thought Sally. The idea excited her; she crossed her legs.

The slave buzzed attentively round the dark woman, lighting her cigarette, holding her drink. Her mistress paid her little attention, talking to the other people in her group and only acknowledging the slave when she issued an order. Sally held her breath. Part of her longed to be a slave, taking orders from a dominant mistress. Did she dare try it for herself? She wanted it very much, yet part of her was frightened. She longed to give herself to a loving mistress, yet she feared the loss of control that it necessarily entailed. Why did she need to be in control so much? Why couldn't she just let go?

Across the room, a couple were standing at the bar. They

were dressed fairly conservatively, in jeans. Yet Sally noticed that one of the women was wearing a dog collar and her partner was holding the leash that was attached to it. She wondered what it must feel like to be led around by her lover, to have everyone know that she belonged to someone else. She imagined the heaviness of the collar around her neck, felt the pull of the leash.

Jo had noticed the couple and she pointed them out to Katie. 'Imagine what it would be like if that were us. The whole club would know I belonged to you.' Jo smiled at her lover, her eyes glistening with excitement.

'I was just thinking that,' said Sally quietly, half to herself. The couple at the bar had finished buying their drinks and the mistress led her slave over to a table. The mistress sat in a chair but, to Sally's surprise, the girl wearing the collar knelt down at her partner's feet. It was incredible! Sally felt her nipples growing tight. She knew she had to try it for herself, but how? There must have been plenty of women in the club who would have been prepared to teach her. Did she dare pick someone up? She was nervous, yet unbelievably excited. Where should she start? Katie probably knew some of the women here; perhaps she could introduce Sally to someone. She would ask Katie.

She turned towards her friend. 'Katie –' she said.

'There seems to be somebody interested in you at the bar. She's been staring at you for five minutes,' Katie interrupted. Sally glanced over at the bar, trying to spot anyone she recognised. She could hardly believe anyone in the club was interested in her. She couldn't see anyone looking at her.

'Where?' she asked her friend.

'On the right there, at the very end of the bar.'

Sally scanned the bar. 'It's Liz!'

'You know her?'

'She's from Hailsham Edge. She's the landlady of The Moonraker. I was planning to talk to you about her, later. We met yesterday. I fancied her – only I wasn't sure if she liked me or not.'

'Well, she obviously does,' Katie said. 'Why don't you go over and talk to her, before her eyes burn a hole in you?'

Sally gulped down the rest of her drink. She smoothed her skirt and stood up. It took her a while to weave her way across the crowded club between the groups of women. Finally, she was standing beside Liz at the bar.

'Fancy meeting you here,' said Liz, smiling. 'You look as though you could do with a drink.'

'Red wine, please,' said Sally. 'I went to the pub at lunchtime today, hoping to see you, but they told me it was your day off.' She took a deep breath. 'I was quite disappointed, so it's really nice bumping into you.'

Liz handed her a drink and smiled. She grasped Sally's hand and squeezed it. 'It's Sod's law, isn't it? You turning up at the pub on my day off. But this is a lovely surprise. This evening is turning out better than I expected. Yesterday, I couldn't decide whether you were gay or not,' Liz confided. 'At least meeting you in here answers that question for me.'

Sally laughed out loud. 'Me, too, and I was too nervous to ask.'

'Well, now we've got that one out of the way, where do we go from here?' asked Liz.

'How about my friend's cottage?' Sally suggested boldly. 'It has a huge double bed,' she added.

'What are we waiting for?'

'I'd better say goodbye to the people I came with,' Sally said. 'Come and meet them.' She swallowed down her drink and grasped Liz's hand. She led her across the room. 'This is my friend Katie, and Jo,' she said to Liz.

'Pleased to meet you,' said Liz, extending her hand. The three women shook hands and exchanged pleasantries.

'I'm going home with Liz,' she said.

'Don't do anything I wouldn't do,' said Katie. She winked at Sally.

'I parked up the road,' said Liz, outside the club, 'just along here.'

'It's only the second time I've been to a fetish club,' Sally confessed nervously as they walked.

'I've been a couple of times,' Liz admitted, 'but I've only ever looked.'

'I must admit, it does interest me, though. At the club in London, I saw a mistress spanking her slave with a riding crop. And I found it very erotic.' She blushed, unsure of Liz's reaction.

'And which one did you want to be?' Liz asked wickedly, smiling at Sally.

'The slave,' she replied quickly. 'Definitely the slave.'

Liz laughed. 'That's good,' she said, 'because I'd have wanted to be the mistress.'

Sally's heart skipped a beat. Could Liz be the partner she had dreamed about? Her heart raced with excitement, but in the back of her mind she still felt a niggling doubt – was she ready for this?

'This is my car,' said Liz, unlocking the door. They climbed inside.

'Have you ever indulged? In real life I mean?' Sally asked.

'Once. With my last partner. She'd always had submissive fantasies and, when we first met, she shared them with me. We started to dabble – role-play, bondage, nothing heavy. And we both loved it.' She switched on the ignition and drove off.

'Really?' said Sally. 'It's always attracted me, but I'm nervous about it. I'm not sure I'd be able to "let go", if you know what I mean.'

Liz nodded. 'Yes, I understand. In the first place, you can't go into it unless you trust the other person completely. You have a safe word, a sort of code word which means "stop now", and you use it if things get too much for you. And, of course, it's really the submissive partner who sets the rules. As long as you trust each other, it's completely safe. And it's . . .' She looked at Sally and smiled. 'Liberating, empowering, unbelievable.' Her eyes shone.

Sally was captivated. She couldn't believe how attractive she found Liz. And now she'd discovered that they shared an interest in bondage and discipline. Liz seemed like a dream come true. Her heart was beating quickly; she was nervous but unbelievably excited.

'That's what I thought,' Sally said. 'I have a big thing about being in control. Not just sexually: with everything. It makes me sort of anxious – constantly. But I sort of think that if I could be submissive in bed, I'd feel more relaxed. Does that make sense?'

Liz nodded emphatically. 'Yes, yes, it does. I think that's what most people find. It is empowering. My ex said to me that once she'd allowed herself to be submissive, she felt she could face anything. It made her feel more confident.'

'I can't believe we're having this conversation,' Sally said. 'Yesterday, I wasn't even sure you fancied me and now we're actually talking about . . .' Her voice trailed away uncertainly. She was suddenly afraid she had misread the other woman – did she actually mean they might experiment together?

'About putting your fantasies into practice?' Liz said. 'Is that what you meant?'

'Yes, only I suddenly thought you might just be talking theoretically. That you weren't talking about us having a go at it.'

'Would you like to?' Liz asked.

Sally took a deep breath. What had she got to lose? If Liz didn't want to pursue that side of things, they were still headed for Katie's cottage and a night in bed together. Liz was very attractive. Ever since they had met, Sally had been desperate to see her naked. And if her companion was suggesting that they explore their fantasies further, that would be a bonus.

'I would,' she said finally, 'although I must admit I'm nervous. But yes, I'd love to.' She smiled at Liz.

'So am I,' Liz confessed. She stroked Sally's knee. 'But I think it could be fun.' Liz pulled up at a junction and put on the handbrake. She leant over and cupped Sally's head in her hands. They kissed. Liz's lips were soft and warm; she smelled of violets, Sally thought.

'Choose a safe word,' Liz said. 'Something you're not likely to say in the normal course of conversation. If things get too much, you only have to say it and I will stop straight away.'

Sally's heart was hammering in her chest. She couldn't believe she was finally going to fulfil her fantasy. But it was about to happen – and choosing a safe word somehow seemed to make it seem real. She racked her brain for a word which seemed suitable. It was important to her that she could use the word if she needed to: it made her feel safe.

'How about walrus?' she suggested.

Liz laughed out loud. 'That's excellent,' she said. 'There's no chance that I'll think you're talking about walruses in a moment of passion. How do you feel?'

'Excited, nervous but mostly unbelievably turned on,' Sally confessed.

'Me, too.' Liz smiled. 'We're just coming into the village. You'd better tell me the way to your friend's cottage.'

Moments later, they were outside the cottage. Sally rummaged in her bag for the key. Her hands were shaking. She was so excited. She leant towards Liz and wrapped her arms around her, pulling her close. Sally's lips found Liz's and they kissed.

'You'd better let us in, or the neighbours will throw a bucket of water over us,' Liz said. Sally fumbled with the key and dropped it. 'Let me,' said Liz, bending to pick it up. She opened the door and held it open for Sally, then followed her in. She set the key down on the table inside the door. 'Where's the bedroom?' she asked.

'Upstairs,' Sally replied. The other woman looked at her expectantly, smiling slightly. She raised an eyebrow. A frisson of excitement spread through Sally's body. Liz has already started, she realised. She wants me to take her to the bedroom. Silently she walked up the narrow stairs, Liz following behind her.

'Slaves don't wear clothes,' said Liz as they stepped into the bedroom.

Sally swallowed. Her heart was racing. She felt her nipples tighten.

Liz was standing, hands on hips, looking at Sally expectantly. 'I expect my orders to be obeyed instantly,' she said firmly. 'But, on this occasion, I will let it pass.'

Sally quickly began to undress. She unzipped her dress and stepped out of it. She kicked off her sandals and unclasped her bra, dropping it on the floor and then bending to slide her already wet panties down her legs. Finally, she stood before Liz naked. It felt wonderful. Although she was slightly self-conscious, she knew that her partner was looking at her body: and the thought aroused her.

Liz reached forward and grasped Sally's nipples. She squeezed them hard. Sally took a sharp intake of breath. Liz's hand was between her legs now, her fingers sliding along Sally's moist crack.

'You're very wet,' said Liz. She brought her juice-moistened fingers to Sally's lips. 'Clean them,' she ordered. Sally took the fingers into her mouth and sucked them clean. Tasting her own sweet juices made her feel wicked.

'Kneel,' hissed Liz. Sally quickly knelt in front of the dark woman and looked up at her expectantly. Her mistress undid her belt and slid it out of the loops of her jeans. She fastened both Sally's hands behind her back using the belt.

'Is it too tight?' she asked anxiously.

Sally could only shake her head. Excitement made her dumb.

Liz stood above her and undressed slowly. First she kicked off her shoes and slid her jeans down, stepped out of them, then unbuttoned her shirt and shrugged it off. Underneath, she wore matching black underwear. She quickly took off her bra. She was as beautiful as Sally had imagined; her generous curves were creamy and smooth, her breasts were full and heavy, and her dark nipples stood out prominently. Sally felt moisture flowing between her own legs.

'Take off my panties,' Liz ordered. Sally frowned. She could have spoken, but she sensed that she should only do so if Liz gave her permission. If her mistress gave her permission . . . Just thinking of Liz as her mistress excited her. But how could she undress Liz without the use of her hands? Would she be untied?

'Use your teeth.'

It was one of the sexiest things Sally had heard. She shuffled forward and leant towards her mistress. It wasn't easy to grasp the panties in her teeth; she panted from the effort. She had to nuzzle in close to Liz and the contact excited her. Finally, she managed to catch the silky material in her teeth. She pulled the flimsy garment down over her mistress's downy thighs. Her face was only inches away from Liz's sweet pussy. She smells divine, Sally thought, drinking in the scent. Liz's mound was topped by a mass of silky dark curls.

When Liz was naked, Sally sat up, waiting for her next order. She was breathless and hot. Every pore of her body felt tingly and alive. Liz walked across the room and sat on the edge of the bed. With difficulty, Sally shuffled round on her knees, never taking her eyes off her new mistress. Liz leant forward, pressing her breasts into her slave's face. Sally sought out a dark nipple and sucked on it hungrily as the warm flesh engulfed her. The teat grew in her mouth, and she could hear Liz's heart beating. She pleasured the nipple, drawing it between her lips, sucking it hard, nibbling it.

Liz pulled away and Sally felt bereft.

'Lie on the bed.' Liz's voice was urgent and thick with arousal. She helped Sally to stand and led her over to the bed. Quickly, she freed Sally's hands, then retied them in front of her. Sally stretched out on the bed. She was excited. She had no idea what was about to happen to her, yet she knew she wanted it. She had never felt so excited in her life. Never felt so focused, or so fulfilled. She shuddered.

Liz climbed on to the bed beside Sally. She kissed each of Sally's breasts in turn, then planted a deep wet kiss on her slave's hot pussy before moving up the bed and brushing Sally's mouth with her lips. Then she knelt beside Sally's head.

She's going to sit on my face, thought Sally, as her mistress straddled her head.

Liz was facing the headboard; when Sally looked up she could see Liz's full breasts and her ripe belly. She opened her mouth and sucked on the hot, wet pussy that was pressing down on her face; her chin was wet with Liz's juices. Her mistress's pussy engulfed her, its scent filling her nostrils.

She found Liz's clit, circled it with her tongue and sucked it. She closed her eyes. She was conscious only of the fanny pressed against her face: the salty, sweet taste of it. The musky perfume intoxicated her. Her mouth moved constantly, sliding against the slick flesh. The duvet underneath her was wet with her own juices. She licked her mistress's clit, worshipping her, loving her.

Liz rocked her hips. She gripped the headboard and ground her cunt hard against Sally's face. She was panting, sweat pouring down her body as she rode her slave's face. Sally drew the hardened nub into her mouth and sucked on it hard. Liz moaned, and Sally sucked rhythmically, matching her lover's movements. She pressed her mouth into Liz's moist pussy as hard as she could. It was divine. Her face was drenched. She relished the sensation of being pinned down, forced to pleasure her mistress. She had no choice but to lick and suck Liz's delicious fanny, no choice but to serve her.

Above her, Liz moaned. Her entire body stiffened. She rocked frantically, pressing her crotch against Sally's face. Sally sucked hard, teasing the sensitive clit with her tongue. She could hardly move; Liz's thighs gripped her. Her head sank into the pillow as her mistress's pussy pressed down on her. Liz groaned; her thighs trembled and she rubbed against Sally's mouth. Sally was in heaven.

Gradually, Liz's movements slowed. She braced herself against the headboard and swung her leg over Sally's head. She slid down the bed and snuggled in beside Sally.

'Did you enjoy that?' she asked.

'It was fantastic.'

Liz smiled and leant forward. She kissed Sally deeply, clearly relishing the taste of her own juices.

'Want more?' she asked. Sally nodded. 'Good,' she went on. 'So far, your mistress is pleased. But a slave needs to be taught obedience. Are you ready?' She pushed a tendril of Sally's hair off her face.

'I am ready,' Sally whispered.

'Mistress,' Liz reminded.

'I am ready, mistress,' Sally repeated, hoarse with excitement.

Liz rose and helped Sally to sit up. Sally swung her legs on to the floor and sat on the edge of the bed expectantly. Liz ran her hands up Sally's sides, barely touching her skin. Her long red nails brushed against Sally's sensitive flesh – teasing her, arousing her until she gasped. Liz massaged Sally's breasts firmly. Her fingers found the nipples and she grasped them. She squeezed them, rolling them between thumb and forefinger, coaxing them to erection.

Sally leant her head back and closed her eyes.

'You like that?' the mistress asked.

'Yes,' Sally replied, her voice deep and throaty with arousal. 'I like it a lot. When I am on my own, I squeeze them hard, almost until it hurts.'

Liz smiled and nodded. 'There's a fine line between pleasure and pain,' she said, squeezing Sally's nipples firmly. 'Sometimes, crossing it can lead to extraordinary pleasure.'

'Yes!' Sally hissed.

Liz worked her slave's taut nipples. She pulled on them, stretched them. Sally's chest heaved. She breathed short gasps. It felt amazing. It should have been painful, but somehow she felt only pleasure. Her nipples were tingling and sensitive. Liz leant forward and took Sally's left nipple between her lips; her mouth felt hot and wet. She sucked, she nibbled, she nipped. She was biting harder now, all the while working Sally's other nipple with her fingers.

Sally was panting hard, her body tense. She moaned softly as Liz bit her nipple; she could hardly bear it. Pleasure and pain were blurred and all she felt was an intense sensation she couldn't have described if she tried. All she knew was that it was exactly what she wanted.

'I'm going to come if you don't stop it,' she yelled.

Liz sat up. 'A slave isn't allowed to come without permission,' she said severely. 'It's definitely time to teach you some obedience. Bend over the edge of the bed.'

Sally's heart seemed to flip over in her chest. She's going to punish me, she thought. Things were happening so fast, she could barely take them in, yet she knew that she wanted it. Wanted it more than anything. She was practically holding her breath as she stood up.

Liz helped her to kneel and bend over the edge of the bed. Her naked buttocks jutted into the air. She felt exposed and felt excited as she waited expectantly.

She felt Liz's hand on her behind, stroking gently. Her mistress cupped the soft flesh, kneaded it. She's teasing me, Sally thought. She's making me wait. She could hardly bear it. Liz stroked her other buttock, slid her warm hand down Sally's thigh. Briefly, she ran a finger along Sally's moist slit, making her tremble. Then Sally felt it: a sharp slap against the fullest part of her right cheek, followed by a warm, stinging glow. Liz slapped her again, on the other cheek. Sally loved the sound it made, and the burning rush of blood that followed the sound. She could hardly believe it; she was being spanked and she loved it. Her pussy throbbed.

She felt another slap, and another. Her cheeks were tingling now. Every slap of Liz's hand excited her more. Her mistress spanked her again and again. Sally imagined how her reddened arse must look to Liz; she pictured her cheeks glowing scarlet as her partner spanked her. A hot knot of tension formed in her belly and her body trembled. She cried out each time Liz slapped her. Her arse was stinging now. Each loud slap felt more delicious than the last and her cunt ached for release. She thrust her naked buttocks upwards, eager for more punishment.

Liz slid one finger between Sally's swollen labia and rubbed the hardened clit. With her other hand, she spanked her slave's upturned arse rhythmically, each slap a little harder than the last. Sally moaned and circled her hips, rubbing her clit against Liz's hand. She was on the edge now. Her whole body was on fire; blood rushed in her ears. Her pussy contracted, as Liz spanked her hard. The burning in her buttocks somehow intensified every sensation. Every nerve-ending in her body was alive with pleasure. She was coming and it was incredible. She cried out, sobbing and moaning as her orgasm erupted within her. She was shaking; tears welled in her eyes. Waves of rapture crashed over her again and again. Finally, she collapsed forward on the bed, weak and trembling.

Liz was beside her now, helping her on to the bed, untying her wrists. She cradled Sally in her arms, soothing her, rocking her.

'Are you all right?' she asked finally.

'Never better,' replied Sally weakly. 'It was extraordinary.'

'But you enjoyed it?' Liz asked, concerned.

'Couldn't you tell? I loved it. It was amazing.'

'I'm glad.' Liz kissed her tenderly.

SEVEN

Sally woke early the next morning. Sun shone in through the window, warming her face. She felt Liz's soft body against her back, her arm wrapped around Sally's waist. She snuggled against the other woman and smiled to herself. Last night had been the most exciting experience of her life. She'd finally found the courage to test her boundaries and she had loved it. She felt wonderful, energised, alive. And to think she hadn't even been certain if Liz was gay!

She felt hot lips on her neck. She shivered.

'What time is it?' Liz asked sleepily

'Quarter to seven,' Sally answered, rolling over to face her lover. They kissed.

'I ought to get going,' Liz said, stroking Sally's face. 'I have to let the cleaner in at seven. Then I have to do the bottling-up and check to see if any barrels need changing. And we have a delivery this morning.' She sat up and swung her legs over the edge of the bed.

Sally felt miserable. She had pictured a leisurely breakfast, some more sex, perhaps a shared shower. She raised herself up on her elbows and looked at Liz's smooth back.

'My clothes are all over the place,' said Liz, bending to retrieve her underwear. 'We weren't exactly concerned about folding them neatly, last night.' She smiled and glanced back at Sally, then started gathering her clothes.

'Can't you stay to breakfast?' Sally asked, trying to hide her disappointment.

Liz shook her head and carried on dressing. 'Can't,' she said. 'I've got tons to do. Sorry. Have you seen my other shoe? Oh, there it is.' She sat on the edge of the bed and put on her shoes. 'Right, I'm ready,' she said. She leant over and kissed Sally lightly. 'Thanks for last night. I had fun. I'll call you. I'll see myself out.' Before Sally could reply, she was off downstairs. Sally heard her feet on the stairs and the slam of the door as she let herself out.

She threw herself back on the bed and covered her head with the covers. Only I could do it, she thought. I find someone wonderful, have the greatest sex of my life and, the next morning, she doesn't want to know.

It's my fault, she told herself. If you pick someone up in a fetish club, they have every right to think it's only a one-night stand. She had just assumed that Liz wanted the same thing as she did, wanted a relationship where they could both explore their sexuality. She had assumed Liz knew how much it meant to her, how special the experience had been. But they'd never discussed it. She frowned; all they had actually talked about was indulging in a spot of sub–dom sex, nothing more. She had no reason to think Liz was interested in something more permanent. What a fool she was!

'I'll call you,' she had said – everyone knew what that meant. She'd never call. It was simply politeness, uttered for the sake of form. Both of them knew that she'd never pick up the phone and dial Sally's number. She didn't even know the number, Sally realised. How stupid could she be?

A lump like lead had settled in her abdomen. She felt foolish, ashamed, disappointed. Now she'd have to go into the pub and risk making a fool of herself if she wanted to see Liz again. And she knew she wouldn't do it – couldn't do it. She had that much dignity at least.

She tried to look on the bright side. The sex had been great. And she'd finally done it. She'd faced her true nature and explored her secret needs. She'd finally allowed herself to be dominated, to be tied up and spanked. And she had loved it. Just thinking about the sensation of the leather belt constricting her wrists made her wet and tingly. Being spanked had been even better; the stinging heat in her bottom somehow magnified her erotic sensations. She had had the best orgasm of her life. The experience had been worth it for that alone. So what if Liz turned out not to be interested in taking things further? Sure, Sally was disappointed, but she'd get over it eventually, she supposed. At least she knew what she wanted now. She knew that she found something intoxicating and liberating about allowing herself to be dominated. And, above all, she knew there was no going back.

When the telephone rang, it took her by surprise. She'd spent the morning buried in her work and was thankful for the escape it provided. She could all too easily have moped about feeling sorry for herself. She was eating her lunch, sitting at the kitchen table with the morning's newspaper propped up against the coffee-pot. She wiped her fingers on her jeans and went into the living room to answer the phone. It could only be Katie, she thought. No one else knew she was here – at least, not anyone who knew the number.

'Good afternoon,' she said in her warmest voice, assuming she was speaking to her friend.

'Now that's a cheerful voice – good afternoon to you.' For a second, she was confused. It certainly wasn't Katie, but nobody else had her number and there was something familiar about the voice. It was Liz, she realised. Her heart thumped.

'Is that you, Liz? I didn't think I'd given you the number,' she replied, hoping that her voice did not betray the state of her nerves.

'You didn't,' admitted Liz, somewhat sheepishly. 'You told me Katie was headmistress of Cuckmere Manor. I rang her there and asked for the number. I hope you don't mind. She sends her love, by the way.'

'Not at all. It's lovely to hear from you.' She took a deep breath to calm herself.

'I rang to apologise for dashing off so quickly this morning,' Liz went on. 'I hope you didn't think me rude. There's nothing I'd have liked more than spending the morning in bed with you, but it's a full-time job running this place.'

'It's OK,' said Sally. 'I didn't take it personally.' She had, but she wasn't going to say so. She felt better now Liz had apologised, but she still wasn't sure what ground she was on. At least, an apology was a good beginning, she reflected.

'I wondered if you'd like to visit the club again tonight – see what we can get into,' Liz suggested.

'I'd love to,' Sally replied, more enthusiastically than she felt.

'Great,' said Liz. 'I don't normally have two nights off in a row. It was hell to arrange, but I managed it. I'll pick you up at nine – how does that sound?'

'Fine. I'll be ready.'

'OK. Got to go – no rest for the wicked. See you later.'

'Bye,' said Sally. Now she was even more confused. She was slightly comforted by the apology but she still couldn't work out where Liz was coming from. An invitation to a leather bar 'to see what they could get into' didn't suggest that Liz was interested in a relationship. It sounded pretty casual, to Sally's ears. She was just interested in the sex, that was it, Sally decided. Liz had probably been delighted to bump into someone local who shared her kinky tastes. That was all there was to it. She'd been naïve to think anything else.

And yet when they'd chatted in the pub, over lunch, neither woman had known that the other was interested in bondage.

Sally ran her fingers through her hair. She felt more confused than ever, and she was probably reading too much into Liz's actions. Well, it wouldn't be the first time, she reflected. She had a tendency to analyse every word that was said until it was meaningless. She worried far too much. She knew that; yet it was hard to break herself of the habit. And who was to say that Liz wasn't just as confused and uncertain about it all as she was? She'd go to the club with Liz this evening and just see what happened.

If she was honest with herself, she was very excited by the thought of exploring her fantasies with Liz. And the prospect of involving a third party, as Liz's invitation had implied, did turn her on. Having had a glimpse of the possible, she was hungry to experience more. She felt safe with Liz and safety was important to her. She'd just relax and enjoy whatever happened, as much as she could. She'd try not to think about how things might end up between Liz and herself. Why spoil things by worrying about the future and analysing every word? She'd try to live for the moment and have fun.

'I've been looking forward to this all day,' said Liz as Sally climbed into the car.

'Me, too,' agreed Sally. 'Last night was a real eye-opener for me.'

'I'm glad. I liked it, too.'

Liz's response was pretty noncommittal, Sally thought. But she had at least admitted to enjoying it. That was a start. Of course, she'd tried it before, so perhaps it wasn't as mind-blowing for her as it had been for Sally.

'It was fantastic,' Sally said. 'I never knew I could feel like that. I never realised it would be so intense. I'd fantasised about it a thousand times but the real thing was just incredible.' She smiled at Liz, slightly embarrassed by her own intensity. 'Do you know what I mean?'

'Yes, I do. Believe me, I do.' Liz spoke emphatically. 'I felt the same. It's really powerful, frighteningly so. At least, it would be frightening if it didn't feel so natural, so right.' She laughed. 'I guess we're pretty kinky, eh?'

Sally smiled. 'If the cap fits,' she said.

'Here we are,' said Liz as they turned into the road outside the club. 'Now, if I can only find somewhere to park. There's a space there, I think.'

Sally was unbelievably excited as she got out of the car. She wondered what the next few hours held in store for her. She could hardly believe it was happening. Only a week ago, she would never have dreamed of bringing her fantasies to life like this. But a lot had happened in a week. She had nearly finished her three chapters, and that was a miracle in itself. She had felt so different since she'd come to Sussex – freer, more relaxed somehow. Perhaps it was the country air, she mused.

She took a deep breath as they entered the club and followed Liz to the bar. Liz brought them drinks and they sat down at a small table near the stage. Sally looked around the room, trying to spot anyone she recognised. The mistress who led her slave round on a leash was there, near the bar. She pointed them out to Liz. 'That really turned me on when I saw it last night,' she said.

'I can imagine,' Liz replied. 'There's something so blatant about it. Would you like me to lead you around like that?' Her eyes were sparkling wickedly.

Sally's pulse quickened. 'I think I would,' she admitted. 'Perhaps I'll buy myself a collar and lead,' she mused, half to herself.

'A slave doesn't buy her own restraints,' Liz chided playfully. 'It's up to her mistress to decide how and when she should be bound.'

'Stop it, you're turning me on!'

'Look at that,' hissed Liz, gripping Sally's wrist.

Sally looked up just in time to see a couple walk up to the bar. She could see why they had grabbed Liz's attention. The slave was breathtakingly beautiful. It was obvious she was the slave: everything about her demeanour indicated she was the submissive partner. Her dark curly hair tumbled over her shoulders and her creamy complexion was highlighted by her scarlet lips. She was wearing a simple red shift dress and high heels. Sally was surprised she could walk in them, they were so high. And the slave's shoes had a delicate strap encircling the ankle. It was closed with a tiny padlock – she was padlocked into her shoes!

The mistress was tall and slim and dressed from head to toe in black. Tight leather trousers clung to her lithe frame. She wore a complicated leather top with lots of straps and buckles. How delightfully kinky, Sally thought. Her dyed blonde hair was cropped very short. She had a tattoo on her upper arm, another on her shoulder and her left ear was decorated with a cluster of silver rings. Sally wished she had the nerve to dress like that in public, perhaps even wearing her mistress's collar. God, she was wet. She shifted in her seat.

'Now they look like a fun couple,' said Liz.

'They certainly do,' agreed Sally. 'I'd love to be brave enough to walk about in public like that.'

'One step at a time, dear.' Liz laughed.

To her surprise, the two women separated once they had bought their drinks. The mistress wandered off and joined a group of leather-clad women at the other side of the room. The slave loitered dejectedly near the bar.

'Do you think they've quarrelled?' Sally asked. 'I was sure they were together.'

'They definitely were,' said Liz. 'It was obvious. Perhaps the mistress wants to have some fun on her own.

'The slave's beautiful,' Sally said, and she looks so sad on her own.

'She's gorgeous,' Liz agreed. 'Why don't you go and talk to her, cheer her up? Invite her over, if you like.'

'I couldn't.'

'Why not? She's hardly likely to bite your head off. What are you frightened of?' Liz's smile was half mocking.

'I've never been very good at chatting people up,' explained Sally.

'I order you to invite her over,' said Liz.

Was she serious? Sally looked at Liz; her beautiful mouth was curled into a smile and her eyes twinkled wickedly.

'You can't ignore an order from your mistress, can you?' Liz glared at her, challengingly.

Sally's heart pounded. She knew Liz wasn't really serious. There would be no adverse consequences for not obeying, but she had to admit she was aroused by the idea. Approaching the woman because Liz had instructed her to do so somehow made her feel less vulnerable. It also excited her more than she would have believed possible.

She stood up and smoothed her dress. She took a deep breath and walked straight over to the woman at the bar.

'Hi,' she said. Well, she had to say something and it seemed as good as anything. Even if she wouldn't get any marks for originality. The girl looked up and smiled.

'My name's Sally. My friend and I wondered if you might like to come and join us.' Sally smiled encouragingly.

'I'd love to. I'm Ros, by the way,' she said and followed Sally back to the table.

'Ros, this is Liz,' Sally explained.

'Nice to meet you,' said Liz, smiling. 'Sit down.'

At close quarters, Ros was even more beautiful than Sally had thought. Her skin was pale and creamy and her eyes were a piercing blue. Her shapely figure was emphasised by the cut of her dress and her legs were long and lean. Sally was captivated.

'I haven't seen you here before, have I?' Ros asked.

'No,' confirmed Liz, shaking her head. 'We're both comparatively new at this. This is only our second time here.'

'And what do you think of the place?' Ros asked, smiling conspiratorially. 'It's an eye opener, isn't it?'

'You can say that again,' said Sally. 'Yesterday, when I saw that woman leading her slave about with a dog's leash, I nearly wet my knickers.'

Ros laughed out loud. 'That's pretty much how I felt, my first time,' she agreed. 'My eyes must have been out on stalks. Everywhere I looked, I saw people doing things I'd only dreamed about.'

'If it's not a rude question,' said Liz, 'why aren't you with your mistress? I mean, that woman is your mistress, isn't she? The tall one with the bleached hair?'

Ros blushed and nodded. 'Yes, she is my mistress. Well, she's my girlfriend: but when we're here, she's my mistress. We like to experiment with role-play.'

'So why aren't you with her now?' Sally asked curiously.

Ros blushed again, lowering her eyes. 'She's turned on by the notion of me having sex with other people. So she ordered me to get myself picked up,' she said.

Liz raised an eyebrow quizzically at Sally. Sally swallowed hard. She knew that Liz's signal was an invitation. She knew that her lover was suggesting that they have a threesome with this gorgeous woman. And she wanted to. Ros was one of the most attractive women she had ever met and the whole situation made her feel horny. She was tempted.

Yet there was something about it that just didn't seem right to her. In her heart, she only wanted to be with Liz. She wanted to make love to Liz, to explore their feelings and their desires together. Somehow introducing a third person into the equation didn't seem compatible with that. OK, she thought, Liz's interest in me is obviously only sexual – I can live with that. Although she knew that she wanted more than that, she wasn't going to miss this opportunity. She nodded at Liz and smiled, in mute acceptance of the suggestion.

'As it happens, Ros,' Liz said, 'Sally and I are here looking for someone to take home with us –'

'Really?' asked Ros, smiling nervously.

'How about it?' Liz asked.

'Yes, I'd like to,' Ros agreed. 'I'm so glad you invited me over.'

'Thank Liz,' said Sally, laughing. 'She ordered me to.' Ros's eyes widened in disbelief and admiration.

'Liz is your mistress?' she asked.

Sally didn't really know how to answer. It wasn't precisely true, but it was close to the truth, wasn't it? If she was honest, she wanted Liz to be her mistress, but that didn't precisely describe their relationship at the moment.

Liz came to her aid. 'Not exactly,' she said. 'We haven't got that far, yet; we're just experimenting. But, to answer your question, Sally is the submissive one.'

Sally blushed. She liked that description; it made her feel wicked. 'Yes, I'm submissive,' she confirmed, relishing the words as she spoke them. Only a week ago, she would never have dared to be so bold.

Sally could hardly breathe as she let herself and the two women into the cottage. She couldn't remember ever being so excited. Her panties were already drenched with her own juices, her nipples taut and prominent. She trotted up the stairs to the bedroom, Liz and Ros behind her. Her heart was pounding.

'I hardly know where to start,' said Liz, making them all laugh. 'I feel like a kid at Christmas, trying to decide which present to unwrap first.'

'Let's take Ros's clothes off,' said Sally, her voice urgent with desire.

'Good idea,' agreed Liz. She ran her hands up and down Ros's curvy body, then kissed her gently on the lips. Sally stood behind Ros and unzipped her dress. She slid the fastener down and pulled the dress off the girl's shoulders, dropping it to the floor. A sweet, feminine scent rose from her skin; Sally inhaled deeply.

'Mm, lovely,' said Liz appreciatively. She stroked Ros's nipples through her bra. 'Take it off,' she hissed.

Sally unclasped it and peeled it away from the girl's skin. Ros's breasts swung free. They were firm and large, with big rosy nipples. Sally hooked her thumbs into the waistband of Ros's knickers and slid them down. She was beautiful, Sally thought. She stroked the girl's smooth back and plump buttocks. A small butterfly tattoo adorned the top of her right cheek, and Sally bent to kiss it.

Liz drew Ros close and kissed her. She wrapped her arms around the girl's naked body and held her tight. Sally quickly stripped off her own clothes as she watched the two women kiss. She felt hypnotised; she could not tear her eyes away. This was the first time she had been a witness to such an intimate moment and it excited her.

Liz broke away from the kiss. 'Why don't you two get to know each other, while I get undressed?' she suggested huskily.

Sally took Ros into her arms and held her close. The girl's skin felt silky and warm against her own body. She stroked Ros's unruly hair, licked her neck. They kissed; Ros's soft lips yielded to her probing tongue.

'Let's get comfortable on the bed,' said Liz, lying down.

Sally released the girl and lay down beside Liz. Sally noticed for the first time that Ros's pubic hair had been completely shaved. Her mound was naked and smooth. Sally's pussy throbbed with excitement. Of course, she realised – slaves are often shaved.

'I am afraid my shoes don't come off,' said Ros, slightly embarrassed. 'Simone, my mistress, locks me into them.'

'No problem,' said Liz. 'It makes things more interesting. Come and lie down here.' She patted the bed. 'Now, if I sit on Sally's face, do you think you can keep her amused while she licks me?' Ros nodded excitedly and positioned herself between

Sally's parted thighs. Sally gasped as she felt Ros delicately part the folds of her wet pussy. The girl buried her face in Sally's quim; it felt divine. Liz was sitting on her face, her woman-scent filling Sally's nostrils.

Hungrily, Sally licked her lover's fanny. She loved the salty-sweet taste of it. Pussy juice soaked her face. She caught some juice-moistened pubic hairs in her teeth and tugged on them playfully, so Liz moaned. Much as she loved pleasuring her lover, Sally was finding it difficult to ignore what Ros was doing to her. She arched her back as a shiver of delight shot up her spine.

Ros held Sally's lips apart and sucked hard on her exposed clit. She used her thumbs to massage around the hole, and Sally opened her legs further so she could press her wet fanny into the beautiful slave's face while she sucked hard on Liz's clit. Above her, Liz was panting, sucking in short gasps of air. She ground her crotch into Sally's mouth, rocking her hips rhythmically.

Sally's thighs were tensed, her buttocks raised up off the bed. A sheen of sweat filmed her body and fire grew in her belly. Her pussy throbbed. She tongued Liz's hot cunt; her mouth slid easily over the slippery flesh. She sucked her lover's clit, drawing the taut bead between her lips. Ros's mouth was never still. It felt warm and soothing. Sally was conscious only of her cunt and mouth; nothing else mattered. She worshipped Liz's clit as Ros licked her. The air was heady with the scent of sex.

Liz shuddered. She moaned softly and began rocking her hips wildly. Her clit twitched in Sally's mouth. Sally wrapped her arms around her lover's thighs and held tight. She sucked hard as Liz came into her mouth. Liz bucked against her face, rubbing her swollen fanny against Sally's eager mouth, so that juice trickled down her chin. Finally, Liz let out a long, sibilant breath and relaxed. She swung her leg over Sally's head and lay down beside her.

Sally's own orgasm was approaching now. She spread her

legs wide, and Ros's tongue snaked over her hot pussy. She was on the edge. She rocked her hips rhythmically, rubbing her clitoris against Ros's mouth. Her pulse raced and her breathing was rapid and shallow. She moaned softly. She was coming, now, her whole body tingling with pleasure. She was deaf, she was blind, and all that existed for her was the pleasure she was feeling.

Liz wrapped her arms around Sally and held her, pulling her close. A deep, soft roar rumbled in Sally's throat. Tears welled in her eyes. Her buttocks were raised off the bed and her thighs trembled. She rammed her aching pussy into Ros's mouth as the final spasms of climax possessed her.

'You look as though you enjoyed that,' said Liz when Sally had calmed down.

Sally nodded, too exhausted to speak.

'I certainly enjoyed it,' said Ros, looking up from between Sally's legs.

'And you did most of the work, too,' laughed Liz. 'I really think it's your turn now.' She crawled towards Ros.

'Lie down here,' she said, 'and I'll see if all that pussy-licking has made you wet.'

'It has,' said the slave girl. 'Please let me lick you, too.'

Liz lay back on the bed. 'Climb aboard,' she said patting her chest.

Ros straddled Liz eagerly. She positioned her crotch above Liz's waiting mouth and hungrily dipped her tongue into Liz's pussy. Sally, still exhausted from her recent orgasm, raised herself on one elbow and watched the women sixty-nine each other.

Liz looked ecstatic as she licked the slave's shaved pussy. Sally could imagine how smooth and soft it must feel, how easily her lips would slide over the skin. Liz licked Ros's clit, her mouth never still. Ros's rear end looked divine, thought Sally. From where she lay, she could see the plump pussy lips slightly parted, revealing the pinker flesh within. And the furled rosebud of her arsehole was just visible; peeping out between the buttocks.

Sally could hardly wait to explore Ros's naked slit for herself. Watching Liz lavish attention on Ros's fanny was unbelievably exciting. Sally slid a hand between her legs and stroked her clit slowly.

Sally knew how much Liz would love having her fanny licked by the gorgeous slave. Ros was obviously an expert. Sally imagined Ros pleasuring her mistress for hours on end, not being allowed to stop until Simone commanded it. How she longed to serve a mistress in that way. To serve Liz.

Ros's head bobbed between Liz's legs. She wriggled her arse, giving Sally a clear view of Liz's tongue in her juicy cleft. She could see that Liz was concentrating on the girl's clit now. Teasing it, licking it, sucking it. Sally stroked her own hot bud, her fingers flying over the slippery flesh. Ros was riding her partner's face now, rubbing her cunt against the questing tongue. Liz's lips were shiny with moisture; juice trickled onto her face. She sucked hard.

Ros bucked her hips frantically. She was gasping, grunting. Sweat glowed on her back, her thighs. She ground her cunt against Liz's mouth and trembled, then cried out. Sally watched the slave come and frigged herself excitedly. She had both hands between her legs, now, with two fingers thrust inside her tight hole as she rubbed her clit.

Her orgasm over, Ros buried her face between Liz's spread legs. Her mouth sought out the tiny hard clit, teased it, and nibbled it. Liz lay back on the bed, gazing up at Ros's gorgeous pussy, and bit her lip. She was close, Sally could see that. Sally rubbed her own clit hard, finger-fucking herself as she did do.

Liz wrapped her arms around Ros. Her head thrashed from side to side and sweat filmed her upper lip. She was breathing hard and fast. She sighed as Sally's fingers moved between her legs. Her cunt throbbed. Her body shook. Liz's eyes were closed; her lips curled into a smile.

'Oh, my God,' she hissed as she came.

Sally stroked her clit and thrust her two fingers deep inside herself. Her orgasm surged through her, making her gasp. Her fanny pulsed around her invading fingers and she moaned.

'And we've got the whole night ahead of us . . .' said Liz wickedly.

EIGHT

Early next morning, Sally sat at the kitchen table reading the morning paper, surrounded by the remnants of her breakfast. Liz had left early again, closely followed by Ros, who needed to drive into Brighton and change her clothes before work. Her first experience of making love with more than one person had certainly been enjoyable. Sally smiled to herself. Ros had been beautiful, she mused.

Sharing her bed with two gorgeous, horny women had been delightful. It offered so many more exciting possibilities than conventional sex did. She would definitely try it again, she thought. She folded the newspaper and swallowed the last mouthful of coffee. She had certainly had her eyes opened since she'd met Liz.

Last night's experience could not compete with the night she had spent alone with Liz, though. What she had discovered about herself then was mind-blowing. The sex itself had been incredible: almost as if there were some mystical, spiritual connection between the two of them. But it had been much more than just another sexual experience.

Giving herself to Liz so totally, allowing herself to be

dominated and punished, had touched her on a much deeper level. She'd never felt so alive, so powerful. She had never felt so certain of who and what she was. Never felt so complete.

Did that make sense? Volunteering to be another woman's slave ought to make you feel vulnerable and afraid, shouldn't it? Having your hands tied and your arse spanked ought to be humiliating, shouldn't it? But it wasn't, it was exciting – liberating, somehow. She did not feel diminished by the experience; she felt enriched. But why?

There was no fear, she realised. Sex for her had always been incomplete. She had always held part of herself back. There had always been a part of herself that she found terrifying. Its intensity frightened her so she suppressed it, stamped it down and tried to ignore it. But it had refused to die and, the night before last, she had decided to face the demon. And it had been incredible.

The chaos she had feared did not ensue. The locked attic door had not been concealing a monster, but a woman, inquisitive and innocent and blinking in the unaccustomed light. She smiled at the image. All these years she thought she had been hiding her wickedness, her shame. But it wasn't true. She had been hiding her creativity, her spontaneity, her trust.

It was so obvious to her now. She did not need to be in control any more. Control was her enemy, not her friend. It didn't protect her: it stifled her and blinded her to the truth. Without it, anything was possible, she realised. Anything at all. And she was hungry for more.

It was a pity Liz had to work tonight, she thought. There was a lot more she wanted to explore. How she envied Ros, having a mistress of her own. She longed to serve another woman, to explore her submissive nature and her limits as Ros did. But she could, couldn't she? It was so obvious, she realised. She could go to the club on her own.

What an exciting thought! She tingled. She had found the courage to chat Ros up last night; she could do it again. Perhaps

Ros would introduce Sally to her mistress. And if Ros wasn't there, she could find someone else. She smiled to herself. She was becoming so brave, she hardly recognised herself.

At the club that night, Sally surveyed her make up in the cracked mirror. She could do with a bit more lipstick, she thought. She touched up her lips, then tidied her hair. A tall woman in a leather basque and mini skirt came out of one of the cubicles, teetering on the highest stilettos Sally had ever seen. She smiled at the exotic creature and received an enigmatic grin in return. It was getting late; nearly eleven, and she still hadn't spotted anyone in the club she liked the look of. Perhaps it wasn't her night, after all. She took a final look in the mirror and went back into the club.

It was pretty crowded now. The place had really filled up while she had been in the toilet. Probably because the pubs closed at eleven and the club had a late licence. She headed towards the bar, weaving between the groups of women. She squeezed herself between the sweaty bodies, bought herself another drink and leant on the bar. A fug of cigarette smoke hung in the air. The juke box pounded out loud rock music – Iron Maiden, she thought. She'd had to shout to make herself heard when she'd bought her drink.

She looked around the room, taking in details she hadn't noticed on her previous visits. A huge wrought-iron chandelier hung from the ceiling, the kind of thing you might expect to see in a medieval hall. Here and there, metal rings were set into the wall. A bullwhip and a flat leather flogger hung above the bar. She was right when she thought it reminded her of a dungeon. The resemblance was clearly intentional. All it needed was some half-naked slaves suspended from the chains and it would look like a proper torture chamber.

And she'd never seen so many tattooed and pierced people in one place. At least, not since Katie had talked her into visiting a body modification convention. Here, people proudly displayed their adornments. Pierced noses and eyebrows were commonplace. As were bellybuttons and tongues. She felt quite boring, with only her ears bearing evidence of the piercer's talents. She'd even seen a few pierced nipples. And a girl at the bar had rings through her cheeks, the bridge of her nose and her lips. She had a lot to learn, she mused.

Two women squeezed in beside her, holding hands. They were not just holding hands, Sally realised – they were handcuffed together. Who had the key, she wondered? And who had shackled them together? Were they a sub/dom couple or were both of them slaves to a third party? Their joined hands rested on the bar, advertising their enforced union. Sally could not take her eyes off the shiny chrome cuffs. Where did you buy such things? She would ask Katie.

'A penny for them.' The familiar voice broke into her reverie.

She looked up. It was Ros. Sally had been so engrossed in the couple with the handcuffs that she had not noticed Ros and Simone enter the bar.

'Hi,' she said, smiling.

'Where's Liz?' Ros asked, leaning over to kiss Sally.

'She has to work tonight. I thought I'd come and see if I could find some fun on my own.'

Ros nodded. 'This is Simone, my mistress,' she said, indicating the tall woman on her left.

Simone was striking. Sally had thought so yesterday and, close up, she was even more breathtaking. She wore a clinging leopard-print catsuit under her leather jacket and thigh-length boots with the highest heels Sally had ever seen. She towered above Sally. Her slenderness gave her an androgynous look and her bleached, cropped hair and high cheekbones reminded Sally of David Bowie.

She smiled at Sally. 'Hi,' she said. 'My little slave told me all about the fun she had with you and your girlfriend last night.'

Sally blushed, unused to having her sexual conquests discussed in public. But she was being silly and she knew it. Simone wasn't jealous. She had positively encouraged Ros to go home with her and Liz. She had wanted it to happen and she was pleased that Sally had enjoyed it.

'Yes,' she said. 'It was great.'

'I couldn't help overhearing you telling Ros that you were here to have some fun,' Simone said suggestively. 'Since you were kind enough to entertain my slave last night, perhaps you'd allow me to return the compliment.' She leant forward and ran one long finger down Sally's neck. Sally shivered.

'I'd love to,' said Sally. 'Thank you.' She hesitated. She did not just want sex with Simone; she wanted to be her slave. She wanted to find out what it felt like to serve a mistress, as Ros did. 'I want . . . I'd like . . .' She took a deep breath. 'But I don't just want sex,' she said. 'I want to be your slave. Is that OK?'

Simone smiled. 'Of course,' she said. 'That's what I had in mind. I think you will find I am a benevolent mistress. As long as my slaves are obedient,' she joked.

Sally laughed out loud.

'We'll go home straight after my set. In about half an hour – is that OK?'

'Your set?' asked Sally.

'Simone is part of the cabaret,' Ros explained. 'She sings with her band.' She nodded towards the small stage in the corner, where a group of musicians were tuning their instruments.

'And I'd better go. We're on in a few minutes,' Simone said. She swallowed the remains of her drink and headed off across the bar.

'I'm glad you're coming home with us,' said Ros, squeezing her hand. 'You're going to love it, I know.'

'I hope so. I'm really excited,' she said.

'I can see you are,' Ros nodded. 'Your eyes are glistening and you're hyperventilating. I bet you're wet, too.' She leant forward and slid her hand under Sally's mini-skirt. She slipped her fingers between Sally's thighs and stroked her slit.

'You're not wearing knickers!' Ros sounded surprised.

'I thought it would get me in the mood,' Sally confided. Anyone who looked over would have been able to see Ros's hand up her skirt. But, somehow, she didn't care. Knowing they could excited her.

'Simone will punish you for having no knickers on,' said Ros. 'She'll call you a slut, I'm sure.' She slid her fingertips across Sally's clit and pushed her fingers deep into Sally's cunt, then leant in closer and bit Sally hard on the neck.

'I can't wait to see her punish you,' she whispered urgently.

Sally felt the slave girl's breath against her neck. She knew they were being watched. She could feel hot eyes burning into her soul. Let them watch, she thought. She turned her head and kissed Ros on the mouth. Ros broke away from the kiss, sliding her fingers out of Sally's pussy as she did so. Sally felt incomplete without them. Ros brought her juice-moistened fingers to Sally's lips, and Sally sucked them clean.

She heard a woman near her at the bar gasp. She looked up. The stranger stared at her, her blue eyes glowing with a look of unconcealed envy. Sally smiled. She felt wicked; she felt sexy.

'Simone's going to sing now,' said Ros as the band began to play. Ros grabbed Sally's hand and pulled her nearer to the front of the small crowd that had formed in front of the stage. Simone slid off her leather jacket and stood in the spotlight. The club was hushed. Simone stepped up to the microphone, her pale face serious and serene. Then she started singing. It was a song Sally knew well; she played it often at home. David Bowie's 'Life on Mars'. So, her resemblance to The Thin White Duke hadn't been coincidence, Sally thought. It was eerie. Simone *was* Bowie. She might have been possessed. This was no mere imitation; Ziggy Stardust was strutting around the stage in front of her.

The audience clapped appreciatively and Simone launched

into her next number, 'All the Madmen'. Sally glanced over at Ros. Her playmate was gazing at the stage. Her eyes glistened with pride as she watched her mistress perform. Ros and Sally were in love, Sally realised. Theirs was no abusive relationship, based on threat and fear. They loved each other. Although they chose to explore power and submission together, there was no hint of exploitation about it. They shared themselves totally and their union was closer, more intimate as a result.

How she envied Ros and Simone. She longed for that intimacy. For a relationship where she withheld nothing and gave herself totally.

The song ended and Simone took a bow.

'Isn't she incredible?' Ros asked, shouting to be heard above the applause.

'Yes, she is. The likeness is uncanny,' Sally replied.

'She doesn't imitate him on purpose,' Ros explained. 'It's just the way she sings. She loves Bowie, so she started performing his stuff. She's very popular.'

'You're very proud of her, aren't you?' Sally asked.

Ros blushed. 'I suppose I am, but I love her, so I can't help it,' she said.

Sally opened her mouth to speak but the band started playing again, cutting her off. She turned her eyes back to the stage.

'Ground control to Major Tom . . .' sang Simone and the audience erupted in delight. Sally watched, rapt, as Simone finished her set.

'This is our house,' said Ros. The Victorian terrace was a short walk from the club and, like many similar buildings, had been converted into flats.

'We live on the top floor,' said Simone as she unlocked the door.

Sally followed the two women upstairs. Her palms were sweaty and her heart was pounding. She could only guess at the events that would unfold in the upstairs flat and her pussy was wet with anticipation. Simone unlocked the flat door and ushered Sally and Ros inside. A long narrow hall led into the living room. High Victorian ceilings and plaster moulding gave the small, sparsely furnished room a classical air. There was a long Habitat sofa with a wrought iron side table at each end, and a couple of floor lamps. The wall opposite the sofa was floor to ceiling shelves, containing books, videos, CDs and records. A TV and stereo system were set into the shelves. Very minimalist, Sally thought.

On one wall there was a life-size print of Marilyn Monroe from *The Seven Year Itch*, her skirt billowing up around her legs as she stood on a subway grating. A classic image of the twentieth century and one of Sally's favourites. Seeing it here made her feel as though she was in familiar territory.

'Let's go into the bedroom,' said Simone. She led the way into a large bedroom which was dominated by an enormous bed, covered in plain white bedding.

At first, Sally thought there was no other furniture in the room, but she realised that there was a big built-in wardrobe along one wall. Ros started to undress, shedding her clothes quickly until she was standing beside Sally, gloriously naked except for her padlocked shoes.

'Undress our guest, please,' said Simone. 'Since it is her first time, I will not punish her for keeping her clothes on.' She stroked Sally's cheek.

'Slaves do not wear clothes in this room,' she said.

Sally shivered, goose pimples rising on her chest. She was unbelievably aroused. Ros moved behind her and pulled Sally's top over her head, quickly unclasped her bra and slid it off. Sally's nipples peaked as they came into contact with the air. It was so exciting, Sally thought, being undressed like this in front of Simone. Ros unzipped Sally's skirt and pulled it down over Sally's hips. She wasn't wearing knickers, she remembered as her skirt was removed. And Ros had said she would be punished for it. She held her breath.

'The slut isn't wearing knickers,' Simone observed. She ran her nails along Sally's sides. 'That has earnt you a punishment,' she said, twisting Sally's nipples. Sally's cunt throbbed, as she wondered what her punishment would be. Whatever it turned out to be, she knew she would enjoy it. Could hardly wait, in fact.

'But first,' said Simone, 'she must be properly prepared. See to it please, Ros.'

'Follow me,' said Ros.

Sally was confused. How did Simone want her to be prepared? Could she ask? She did not think it would be a good idea. She sensed that she wasn't expected to speak unless she was spoken to. Not knowing what would happen to her was somehow exciting. Ros led her into a big white bathroom and instructed her to sit on a wicker chair in the corner.

She's going to shave me! Sally thought. Ros was shaved – it made sense that Simone would want her to be shaved, too.

Ros knelt between Sally's legs and began clipping her pubic hair with a small pair of scissors, working deftly. Sally wondered if she had done this before. Shaving a fellow slave for her mistress seemed delightfully wicked to Sally. Soon, all the hair on her mound was clipped short and Ros moved further down. Expertly, she trimmed the hair on Sally's labia. Sally was very wet and she knew that Ros would be able to see the evidence of her arousal. She wondered if Ros was turned on, too, if the dark haired slave's naked pussy was as slippery as her own. She hoped she'd have the opportunity to find out.

Ros set down the scissors and picked up a can of shaving foam. She shook the can vigorously and squirted a big blob on to her fingers. She spread the sweet-smelling cream over Sally's pussy. It felt cold and silky. Ros put a fresh blade into the razor and rinsed it under the tap. Sally shivered in anticipation, knowing that she was going to be shaved, like a good slave should be. Shaved because her mistress wished it. And she wanted it; oh, how she wanted it.

Ros began shaving her, gliding the razor through the silky white foam. Sally hoped her fellow slave would be very careful. Even a small nick would be painful on her sensitive flesh, she thought. But Ros was obviously skilled at the job. She shaved Sally smoothly and efficiently, so each sweep of the blade felt like a caress.

Ros took a wet flannel and cleaned Sally's pussy. Gently, she wiped away the shaving foam. The rough fabric felt strange against Sally's newly bare skin. Ros rinsed the flannel and wiped along Sally's slit, washing away the foam. Sally trembled as the coarse material slid over her swollen clit. Ros looked up at her and smiled in recognition as she patted Sally's shaven pussy dry with a fluffy towel. Gently, she smeared some soothing cream over Sally's naked flesh; her warm fingers on her secret flesh felt heavenly, Sally thought.

'Come,' said Ros finally and led Sally back into the bedroom. The dark-haired slave stood obediently at the end of the bed, waiting for instructions. Simone was naked now, Sally noticed. Her slender body was muscular and taut. Her breasts were small and firm, her nipples thick and prominent. A spectacular red and green dragon tattoo encircled her small waist.

'Sit on the edge of the bed, and let me look at you,' she said.

Sally's body was alive with desire. Slippery juices oozed between her legs. Her nipples were erect and red. Her newly shaved pussy felt super-sensitive. Every touch, every sensation seemed magnified and intense. A light breeze blew in through the open window, caressing her naked flesh as she sat down on the bed, spreading her legs wide for Simone's inspection.

Simone knelt at Sally's feet and pressed Sally's thighs apart, exposing her crotch. She stroked the naked mound, then ran a finger between the shaved lips. 'Beautiful,' Simone murmured. 'Now you look like a slave.'

Sally's heart was pounding in her chest. She really felt like a slave, too. Her naked pussy was a symbol of her submission to

Simone, and she loved it. She wondered what else her mistress would require of her slave, tonight: what other gestures of obedience she would be asked to make.

Simone smiled. She leant forward and licked Sally's slit; her extended tongue barely brushing the slippery flesh. Sally trembled and Simone dabbled her tongue into the moisture pooled at her slave's opening. It felt divine. Sally leant back and closed her eyes, knowing that Ros watched, wide-eyed, as Simone's pointed tongue probed and licked at Sally's hole.

Suddenly, Sally felt her mistress's hot, wet mouth against her cunt, licking and sucking. It was incredible. Simone's mouth slid easily against her hairless flesh and the newly shaved skin was highly sensitive. Simone sucked each labia into her mouth in turn, sucked on the swollen flesh, nibbled it. Sally moaned. A thin sheen of sweat filmed her taut body and a scarlet flush spread over her chest and throat.

Simone sucked Sally's swollen clit into her mouth. She swirled her hot, wet tongue round the sensitive bead, teasing it. Sally fought for breath; tension grew in her belly. It was unbelievable. She would never have imagined that having her pussy shaved could add so much to the experience, but it did. It was deeper, more intimate, more intense. Her pussy tingled.

'That's enough for now,' said Simone, standing up. Sally's heart fell; her cunt felt aching and empty. She wanted an orgasm; she wanted Simone to clamp her warm mouth over her clit and make her come. But she knew that her mistress was in charge: that it was Simone who would decide when, and if, she would be allowed to come. She was sure that when it eventually happened, it would be incredible. But what did Simone have in mind now?

'Fetch the crop, Ros,' she said.

Simone was going to punish her with a riding crop? Sally was nervous, but unbelievably excited. Liz had only spanked Sally with her hand. What would a riding crop feel like? The slave at the club in London had certainly seemed to enjoy it.

Ros handed the black leather riding crop to her mistress. Simone flexed it slowly, and Sally couldn't take her eyes off it. Simone swished the crop through the air dramatically and brought it down on the bed a couple of times. Crack! Crack! The sound excited Sally more than she would have believed possible. She wanted it.

'Have you ever had a crop used on you before?' Simone asked her.

Sally could only shake her head; she didn't trust her tongue to speak.

'Then I will use it on Ros, first,' said the mistress, 'show you what to expect. And Ros is always happy to take a beating.' She held the handle of the crop to her slave's lips and Ros kissed it reverently. She bent over the bed and braced herself against it, resting her hands on its surface. Her rounded buttocks looked delightful, Sally thought. She longed to cover them with kisses. Yet she also longed to see them striped by the crop. Was it wrong to want another person to be punished? she wondered. Not if they wanted it, she decided. And she knew that she was as eager to feel the crop on her own naked cheeks as Ros was to receive her punishment. She held her breath.

Simone raised her arm, then swished the crop through the air and brought it down across the fattest part of Ros's arse. She smacked the slave again a few inches higher; and again, and again. Sally was rooted to the spot and the hairs on the back of her neck stood on end. She watched red stripes forming against Ros's creamy skin, and she knew that she was next. She could hardly wait. She was counting the strokes – six, seven, eight, nine, ten, until a criss-cross of scarlet lines marked Ros's round cheeks.

Simone dropped the crop on to the bed and knelt behind her bending slave. She gently stroked the glowing marks, kissed them tenderly. Finally, she helped Ros to her feet and embraced her. The two women kissed deeply. Ros wrapped her arms tightly around her mistress. Simone cupped the back of her lover's head with one strong hand.

Sally was enthralled. Moisture flowed between her legs as she watched the two women kiss. She was seconds away from receiving her punishment and her knees were weak with excitement. Simone had been right – watching Ros being whipped first had certainly heightened her anticipation. She didn't think she'd ever felt so horny.

Simone broke the kiss and turned to Sally. 'And now it's our new friend's turn to take her punishment,' she said. 'Do you still want to go ahead?'

'Yes, I'm sure,' Sally replied.

'Do you have a safe word?' she asked gently.

Sally nodded. 'Walrus,' she said.

'OK,' said Simone. 'Say it if you want me to stop. Bend over like Ros did.' Her voice had regained its authoritative tone.

Sally bent over the edge of the bed and supported her weight with her hands. She could hear her own heart beating, smell her own sweat. The crop hissed through the air. She tensed her muscles, expecting to be hit, and held her breath. But the anticipated blow never happened. She exhaled. Simone was playing with her, she realised – teasing her. She felt the crop against her skin; Simone was stroking her with it, lightly brushing its leather tip against her buttocks, then she tapped her with it gently, giving her half a dozen light strokes across one cheek.

Swish! Simone had hit her! There was a sharp, stinging pain but it was quickly replaced by a warm glow. Swish! Her mistress delivered a second slap, then a third.

Sally was in heaven. She leant her weight on her hands and gripped the duvet tightly. Her legs were weak and trembling. Her pussy throbbed. Her mind raced, trying to make sense of the sensations that were overwhelming her body. It hurt, but it was more than just pain. The shock of impact was quickly succeeded by a fiery glow of pleasure. It was like when she pinched her own nipples, she thought. Somehow her arousal and the situation took her to a place where pain itself became pleasurable; or at least the two became indistinguishable. She didn't understand it, but it didn't matter. She knew she wanted it.

Simone slapped her again. She arched her back, unconsciously raising her buttocks to meet the crop. Her eyes were closed, and sweat dripped off her body. She moaned softly as the crop came down again and again. Her behind felt on fire, each nerve-ending alive with pleasure. She imagined the bright red stripes standing out against her white skin, and groaned.

She felt something hard against her fanny. It stroked along the length of her moist slit, teased her clit, and then it was inside her. It was the handle of the crop, she realised; Simone was fucking her with the riding crop. The hard leather handle circled inside her and Sally pressed down against it. She was panting, her cunt ached and her whole body quivered as her orgasm erupted in her belly. Simone reached between Sally's legs and grasped one nipple, squeezing it hard. Sally sobbed, her pussy pulsing around the invading leather handle. Wave after wave of ecstasy radiated through her. Then she collapsed on to the bed.

Sally woke early. Light shone in through the window. She could hear seagulls calling and Ros's warm body was pressed against her back. She looked at her watch; it was just after seven. She eased herself out of bed, trying not to disturb the two women. She'd take a quick shower, then head for home, she decided. She knew that Ros and Simone would be getting up for work soon, and she did not want to be in the way.

She washed and dressed quietly, not wanting to wake her hosts. She eased open the bedroom door and looked back at the bed. Simone was wrapped around Ros's back, holding her close, and Ros seemed to be smiling. She looked blissful, Sally thought: at peace in the arms of the woman she loved. She envied the beautiful slave, she realised. She longed for a mistress of her own; someone she could give herself to totally. She smiled at the sleeping women and let herself out of the bedroom.

It was extraordinary, Sally thought as she walked back to where she had parked her car. Last night had been amazing. She'd been shaved and beaten and she had enjoyed it – loved it, in fact. It had felt so right, so natural. She felt . . . stronger, freer somehow. Liz had been right when she said it was empowering, although Sally hadn't really understood it at the time. She felt complete at last, as if a weight had been lifted from her shoulders. It was a huge relief, now that she didn't feel the need to hold part of herself back.

She unlocked her car and climbed inside. She felt a tingle of pain as she sat down. Of course, her arse was still sore from last night's beating. But it felt good; she relished the physical reminder of the pleasure of submission. An echo of the lash.

The fresh tang of the sea filled her nostrils as she turned out of the side road where she had parked. She'd take the coast road home, she decided. It was a nicer drive than the A27 and she wanted to make the most of the beautiful morning. She turned on her radio, cycling through the stations until she found some music that matched her positive mood. She wound her windows all the way down, letting in the sea's ozone perfume, and breathed deeply, drinking it in.

She sang along to the radio as she drove. Her mind was overflowing with images of leather and whips and naked flesh: Ros's upturned buttocks as Simone whipped them, the tattooed dragon that snaked its way round Simone's narrow waist, her own shaved pussy. It was incredible. Only a week ago, such things had been unknown to her. They might have been part of her fantasy life, the things she'd written about in stories, but she'd never have dreamt that in a few short days she would become so intimately acquainted with them. Katie was right: Sally was a subbie at heart. If it had been so obvious to Katie, why hadn't she recognised it in herself? What had taken her so long to acknowledge her desires and act on them? Why had she waited so long? After last night's experience, she was eager for another taste of submission. She had a lot of catching up to do.

It seemed so obvious now, and so natural to her that it was hard to understand why she had suppressed her needs for so long. Something that Katie often said came back to her then. 'When the student is ready, the teacher appears.' She hadn't understood it before, but now it made sense. She was ready to learn; she had finally acknowledged her fantasies and was ready to explore them, so an opportunity had presented itself for her to do so. Liz had come along, then Simone, and taught her what she needed to know. Katie would be so pleased that she'd finally taken the plunge, Sally thought. She could hardly wait to tell her.

It was not quite eight, so Katie would be up. She would already have taken her morning dip in the school's indoor pool and would probably be sitting down to an early breakfast. Sally could pop in on the way home. She was driving through Polegate – the school was only minutes away. She pulled into a layby and rummaged in her handbag for her mobile phone. She punched in Katie's number and turned down the radio.

'It's Sally,' she said, when her friend answered.

'You're up early.'

'I know. I'm on my way home from Brighton. I'm in Polegate. I wondered if I could pop in for a chat. I've got a lot to tell you.'

'Of course. I'll put some croissants in the oven, they'll be ready by the time you get here. And, since you stayed in Brighton last night, may I assume that you got your leg over?' she asked wickedly.

'I did,' Sally said, giggling excitedly.

'I want to hear all the sordid details,' replied Katie, 'so drive fast.'

Sally was at the school five minutes later. She parked beside

Katie's jeep and rang the bell. The door buzzed open and she rushed up the stairs and into Katie's waiting arms.

'Come into the kitchen,' Katie said. 'I made a fresh pot of coffee.' They sat down at the kitchen table and Katie busied herself pouring coffee and passing croissants and butter. 'So tell me what you've been up to.'

'I hardly know where to start,' Sally said, 'so much has happened.'

'Why don't you start with what happened the other night, after you went home with Liz? I've been dying from curiosity, ever since,' Katie said.

'We talked about our fantasies – well, bumping into each other in a fetish club is a bit of a give-away isn't it? And it turns out that she is dom, but not very experienced. She'd tried it with one partner but not since. So we decided to explore things a bit together.'

Katie's eyes widened with interest.

'Close your mouth!' Sally said, laughing. 'There's no need to look so amazed; you haven't got a monopoly on kinky sex, you know.'

'Sorry. I didn't mean to look so stunned; it's just that I never thought you'd really do it. I thought you needed to be in control too much. So how was it?' Katie's eyes twinkled wickedly.

'Amazing. She tied my hands and sat on my face. Then she spanked me! And I loved it; it was unbelievable. It felt so right, so . . . Liberating is the only word that comes close. I feel so much freer, somehow. Does that make sense?'

Katie nodded excitedly. 'Yes, it does. It was the same for me. I couldn't understand why I was obsessed with kinky sex, why I was attracted to chains and handcuffs and spanking. It seemed wrong, shameful and I was terrified of it. I felt as though the world would end if I let it out, as if everything would tumble into anarchy – do you know what I mean?'

Sally nodded.

'I tried to ignore it,' Katie went on, 'to suppress it, but it wouldn't go away. Finally, I met a woman who persuaded me to try it for myself. And it was like an epiphany, like Saul on the road to Damascus. It was almost mystical. The world didn't end, far from it – it began for me, somehow. I didn't feel out of control at all: I felt more confident, certain. It was as if I had been wearing blinkers before and I'd taken them off and seen the world properly for the first time.'

'That's exactly how it was for me,' agreed Sally. 'Somehow, I'd always thought that the part of myself that I stamped down and hid from was the bad part and that letting it out would lead to disaster. But it turns out that I'd been squashing down my spontaneity, my joy. I feel like a kid who's been let loose in a toyshop.'

Katie laughed. 'So have you been with Liz ever since?'

'No,' Sally explained, shaking her head. 'She left early the next morning. I was a bit upset at the time, but later she rang to explain that she'd had to get back to the pub and to suggest that we go back to the club that night to see what we could get into.'

Katie's eyes widened. 'My, my. You have been busy.'

'I know,' said Sally, 'and you don't know the half of it, yet. We went back to the club and, to cut a long story short, we ended up taking a girl called Ros home with us. She's submissive. Her mistress, Simone, padlocks her into her shoes! We had a threesome, but nothing kinky. It was lovely: twice as much woman to enjoy. I didn't know what to do with myself.'

'But I am sure you managed,' said Katie, laughing.

'You bet. Liz had to work, that night, but I was hungry for more. I went back to the club yesterday and went home with Ros and her mistress,' Sally explained.

'You've certainly made up for lost time, haven't you?'

'Simone ordered Ros to shave me,' Sally said excitedly. 'I'll show you, later. And she spanked me with a riding crop because

I wasn't wearing knickers. I loved it! I want more!' she said earnestly.

'I'm really pleased for you,' Katie said. 'When my mistress first handcuffed and spanked me, I nearly died of pleasure.'

Sally's mouth fell open; she started to speak, then thought better of it. She stared at her friend in disbelief.

'Don't tell me you thought I was a dom,' said Katie, laughing.

'I suppose I just always assumed that you were,' Sally confessed. 'You're so confident and assertive, I just took it for granted.'

'Well that just goes to show that you shouldn't make assumptions about people,' Katie told her. 'So, are you seeing Liz again?'

Sally shook her head; her smile dissolved into a frown. 'I don't know,' she said. 'I hope so. I like her, but I'm not sure how she feels about me. She seems to blow hot and cold. After all, suggesting that we both go to a fetish club to pick someone up doesn't exactly suggest that she wants a meaningful relationship, does it? I like her a lot, but I can't make her out. I wasn't even sure she was gay, in the first place, and I've never had that problem before. There's just something about her. I could go to the pub and invite her over, but I don't want to make a fool of myself, or make her feel awkward. If she's only interested in sex, she'll think I'm stalking her if I keep hanging around The Moonraker. I don't know what to do.'

'I thought she liked you,' said Katie helpfully. 'When we met her in the club she couldn't take her eyes off you. Give it time. A lot's happened for you both. I understand the temptation to want to know where you stand, but sometimes you just have to let things unfold naturally. Apart from anything else, worrying about the future stops you from enjoying the time you do spend together.'

'You're right,' said Sally. 'After all, we've only been out

twice. I'll try to relax and just have fun. But what about you and Jo? How are things between you two?'

Katie's eyes lit up. 'She is wonderful. When we went to bed, it was everything I imagined. Her body is gorgeous and she's so sexy. She makes even more noise than you do! I ate chocolate mousse off her pussy – we had to change the sheets.'

Sally smiled at her friend. She reached over and squeezed Katie's hand. 'I'm so glad that you're happy. Nobody deserves it more than you do. Actually, seeing you with Jo the other night made me realise how lonely I am and how much I rely on my friendship with you. Having occasional sex with you has stopped me from acknowledging just how much I need someone of my own. Don't get me wrong, I'm not jealous,' Sally continued. 'I couldn't be happier for you both, but I suppose I do feel just a bit sorry for myself. That's partly why I am so concerned about things working out between me and Liz, I think – I can't bear the thought of us not being close any more.'

'We'll always be close, Sally. Nothing can change that,' Katie said. 'And you will find someone special, even if it isn't Liz. And actually, I feel rather guilty because our friendship, and us sleeping together occasionally, has stopped you from finding someone else. I knew that, but I was selfish and I'm sorry.'

'Don't be silly,' said Sally. 'You have nothing to be sorry for. I owe you so much. And I will always love you.'

Katie smiled at her. Was it her imagination, or was there a tear in the corner of her friend's eye?

'I love you, too,' said Katie, squeezing her friend's hand. 'Why don't you come into my boudoir and show me your hairless pussy?'

'Are you sure?' said Sally.

'I've never been more certain of anything in my life.'

NINE

Katie pulled Sally's top over her head, quickly unhooked her bra and dropped it to the floor. She unzipped Sally's skirt and slid it down.

'Oh, my God!' Katie said. 'It's lovely. I'll have to take a closer look at that.' She pushed her friend back on to the bed and began tearing off her own clothes. Sally lay back against the duvet, watching Katie undress, then Katie clambered on to the bed beside her and positioned herself between Sally's parted legs. She stroked the naked flesh experimentally. 'It's so soft!' she said. 'You'll have to keep shaving, or it will get all stubbly and itchy.'

'I do like it,' Sally admitted. 'I might keep it for a while.'

Katie kissed Sally's bare mound gently. She moved lower and kissed each shaved labia, enjoying the sensation of the soft skin against her lips. She opened her mouth and bathed Sally's tender flesh with her tongue. Sally shivered and Katie parted Sally's lips and lapped at her clit. She sucked the taut bud into her mouth, circling it with her tongue; her thumbs massaged Sally's opening as she licked.

Sally stretched her legs wider and propped herself up on her elbows. She looked down at Katie, seeing the way her friend's dark head bobbed as she worked on Sally's wet sex. Katie's eyes were closed as if in prayer. She looked beautiful, Sally thought as Katie's tongue squirmed against her clit. It felt wonderful. She was tingling all over; a warm glow of pleasure formed in her belly.

She rocked her hips and pressed her crotch into her lover's face. In response, Katie slid her thumb inside her partner's tight hole, then lapped and sucked Sally's clit, matching her rhythm with her partner's urgent thrusts. The air was heavy with the scent of sex as Katie licked, probed and sucked at her friend's tender flesh. She nipped and nibbled each naked labia; she pushed her tongue into Sally's hole.

Sally reached down and stroked her friend's soft cheek. Katie's eyes opened briefly; she winked, then her lids snapped shut again. Sally knew that Katie was lost in the sensations of mouth against cunt, that her nostrils were filled with womanscent, and her closed eyes helped her to shut out everything else. Sally didn't think she had ever felt so close to Katie as she did at this moment. She closed her own eyes and lay back on the bed, giving herself up to the sensations that were overwhelming her.

Her breathing quickened. Katie teased Sally's rigid clit with the tip of her tongue and Sally ground her pussy rhythmically against her partner's face, until Katie wrapped her free arm around her lover's thigh and pulled her closer. She sucked firmly on Sally's reddened bud, clearly relishing its slippery hardness against her mouth. Sally moaned softly as a knot of tension throbbed in her lower belly, and she gripped the duvet tightly. Her thighs began to tremble; her cunt throbbed around Katie's thumb. Her skin felt electrified, with tiny shocks of pleasure racing up her spine and spreading through her torso, making her tingle all over. She pressed her feet down into the mattress, lifting her buttocks off the bed. Sally's cunt quivered, and waves of pleasure surged through her body. She sobbed, muttering and moaning incoherent phrases as she came.

Katie held tight, riding out the storm. She crushed her mouth against Sally's clit. Finally, Sally relaxed, her breathing slowing, and she patted the mattress by her side. Katie crawled up the bed and took her in her arms, and they kissed.

'That was lovely,' Sally said lazily.

'It certainly was,' Katie confirmed. 'I might get Jo to shave me.'

'I can recommend it.' Sally wrapped her arms around Katie and kissed her gently. Her mouth found Katie's ear-lobe and sucked it, then her lips trailed down Katie's neck, along her shoulder. She kissed Katie at the base of the throat, bathed the soft skin with her tongue, gently at first then harder. Katie moaned softly and pulled Sally closer.

Sally nipped her lover at the junction of her neck and shoulder, knowing this was a particularly sensitive spot. Katie's creamy skin formed into goose pimples. She shivered as Sally glided one hand down her smooth body, stroking her friend's strong back and then cupping her muscular buttock. Lightly, Sally traced a finger along the cleft of Katie's bottom. Her hand slid between Katie's legs, finding her warm slit.

'You're very wet,' Sally murmured. She lowered her head, seeking one of Katie's pierced nipples. She drew the swollen nub into her mouth and nibbled it. Her fingers moved across her lover's clit; she stroked it lightly, pinched it until she heard Katie gasp. Katie spread her legs apart, giving Sally greater access to her pussy.

Sally teased Katie's clit. She stroked round it in a circular motion. At the same time, she sucked on her friend's nipple; she caught the silver ring in her teeth and sucked it into her mouth, pulling and stretching the nipple. She slid two fingers deep inside Katie's hot pussy and rotated them, all the while stroking her partner's clit with her thumb. Katie wriggled appreciatively and she let out a hissing breath through her teeth. Her eyes were closed; her dark hair was wet with sweat.

Sally's fingers moved between Katie's legs. She rubbed her lover's clit hard, now, circling the reddened nub with quick fingers. Katie's body was tense. Her legs were wide apart, her feet braced against the mattress. She thrust her breasts out towards Sally's eager mouth, breathing fast. Her hips rocked rhythmically and Sally knew she was nearing the edge. She sucked harder on Katie's nipple and stroked her lover's clit, her fingers mimicking the rhythm dictated by Katie's urgent thrusts.

She caught Katie's nipple between her teeth and nipped hard; meanwhile, she massaged her partner's clit, her fingers sliding easily over the slippery flesh. Katie ground her crotch against Sally's hand. Her hips bucked wildly, then her body stiffened and her buttocks lifted slightly off the bed. Katie cried out, giving voice to the exquisite sensations that were obviously overwhelming her. Gradually, Katie's breathing slowed and her taut muscles softened. Sally released the nipple she had been sucking and wrapped both arms around Katie, pulling her close. They kissed, and Sally brushed a tendril of damp hair away from Katie's face.

Sally frowned. Lovely as the experience had been, she was beginning to feel guilty. After all, Katie was involved with Jo. How would Jo react to the news that she and Katie had spent the morning in bed together? she wondered. If she were Jo, she wouldn't be too pleased.

'Katie, that was lovely,' she said, 'but what's Jo going to think? Will you tell her?'

'Of course I'll tell her,' Katie replied. 'She already knows about us. She'll understand.'

'I hope so,' said Sally. 'I'd hate to think I'd caused a problem between the two of you. It's just that we've been friends and lovers for so long, it isn't easy to just stop after all this time.'

'I feel the same,' Katie assured her, 'and it seemed important to go to bed one last time. I don't regret it. Don't worry, she'll understand.'

★

Katie waved goodbye as Sally drove off. She shut the front door and hurried back up the stairs. In the kitchen, she busied herself clearing up the breakfast things. She was not looking forward to telling Jo about her indiscretion with Sally. At the time, going to bed had seemed the most natural thing in the world. Both of them knew it would never happen again and somehow they had needed to share an intimate moment one last time. It was no threat to her relationship with Jo. Surely Jo would understand that?

Only moments earlier, she had assured Sally that it would not be a problem, but now she had her doubts. She had been looking at it from her own perspective, she realised – hers and Sally's. Both of them knew that the incident would never be repeated, that Katie was committed to Jo. But things did not seem so cut-and-dried when you looked at it from Jo's point of view. In fact, things looked alarmingly like adultery.

Jo was a sensible and mature young woman, Katie thought as she dried up the breakfast dishes. Surely she would understand that Katie and Sally had felt the need to make love for old time's sake? Surely she knew how fond Katie had become of her? Katie bit her lip uncertainly. She did not regret what she had done, but she was beginning to think things would have been better if she had resisted the temptation. Perhaps she wouldn't tell Jo at all. After all, why did Jo ever need to know about it? It would never happen again and things would certainly be less complicated if Katie kept it to herself.

She dried her hands, folded the tea cloth and hung it to dry over its rail. She shook her head. It was no good. She did not want to lie to Jo. It did not seem right to begin a relationship on a dishonest note. If their relationship was to work, she owed it to both of them to be honest. She would confess and rely on Jo's good sense and generosity. Surely Jo would understand the situation and accept that the incident was no threat to their relationship? All she could do was hope.

★

That evening, Katie buzzed about the flat nervously. She checked the casserole again and tossed the salad she had prepared earlier. She paced the living room floor. Get a grip, she told herself. She was really looking forward to seeing Jo; she had thought of little else. But she had not been able to shake off the doubts that had plagued her all day. Would Jo be as forgiving and understanding as Katie had assured Sally that she would be?

And how should she break it to Jo? When would be the appropriate moment to introduce it into the conversation? As soon as she came through the door? During dinner? In bed? The longer she left it, the more difficult it would be, she thought. Yet she couldn't just launch into it when Jo arrived. She gazed at herself in the large mirror that hung over her mantel piece. She smoothed her hair and wiped away a thin film of sweat from her upper lip.

The doorbell rang and she rushed over to the entryphone.

'It's me,' said Jo.

Katie's heart leapt at the sound of her lover's voice. 'Come up,' she said, pressing the button to open the door. Jo rushed up the stairs and into her arms. They kissed.

'I've been thinking about you all day,' said Jo. 'My knickers got so wet, I had to change them.' She pulled Katie close and buried her face in her lover's hair. 'You smell so good. I can't wait any longer. Take me to bed,' she said.

'I . . .' Katie hesitated. Her hunger was as fierce as Jo's, yet she felt burdened by the weight of her confession. It did not seem right.

'Don't tell me you've gone off me,' Jo teased, biting Katie's neck.

'Of course I haven't,' she said, as Jo's hands found the hem of her dress and snaked underneath.

'Then I've got to have you now,' Jo said urgently, stroking Katie's buttocks. She pulled away and ran towards the bedroom, pulling her dress off as she did so. Katie could only follow. Jo was in her underwear by the time she reached the bedroom. The younger woman unclipped her bra and slipped out of it. She slid her panties over her hips and down her legs, then beckoned to Katie.

'I think you're a bit overdressed,' she said as Katie approached. She went behind Katie, unzipped her summer dress, and slipped it off. She unhooked the bra and dropped it to the floor. Jo reached round and massaged her lover's breasts. She grasped the silver hoops between her fingers and pulled on them gently, making Katie moan. Her hands travelled down the slopes of the older woman's sides, over her hips, so she could hook her thumbs into the waistband of Katie's panties and pull them down.

'Come here,' she said urgently, pulling Katie towards the bed. She lay back on the mattress, pulling her lover down on top of her, then she wrapped her arms and legs around Katie, pulling her close. Their tits pressed together. Jo ran her fingers through Katie's sleek hair, then cupped the back of her neck and kissed her. Katie felt teeth gently nibbling her lower lip. Their tongues explored each other's mouths.

Katie kissed Jo's neck, gently nibbling and licking the creamy flesh. She was lost in the moment, all thoughts of confronting her lover forgotten. Jo leant back against the pillow and arched her neck. Katie's mouth found her ear-lobe and she sucked it into her hot mouth, and nibbled it.

Jo sighed softly. 'I want to lick your pussy,' Jo said.

'Ditto,' murmured Katie.

'Why don't you turn round and sit on my face, then? You can lick mine at the same time,' Jo suggested.

'Mm,' Katie agreed, 'sounds like heaven.' She kissed Jo passionately, holding her tight. Then she clambered round on the bed, repositioning herself on top of her lover. With her pussy poised above Jo's mouth, she buried her face between her partner's open legs. She nibbled on the blonde hairs, enjoying their musky flavour, and lowered her hips, bringing her crotch into contact with Jo's eager mouth. Jo wrapped her arms around Katie's broad hips, pulling her closer.

Katie used her thumbs to part Jo's lips. She was wet, moisture dripping down the crack of her arse, wetting the duvet. Katie inhaled the sharp, musky scent. She stuck out her tongue and ran it along the length of her lover's slit. Jo trembled as the tongue passed over her clit. Katie blew gently on the nub of flesh, cooling it with her breath, before sucking it into her hot mouth.

Jo lay back against the pillow, no doubt to enjoy the vision of her lover's sex above her face, Katie thought. She knew that her pussy was glinting with juices. The dark red gash would point the way to her puckered rear opening and the twin orbs of her buttocks topped off the image: and Jo was clearly excited by the sight, because she clamped her mouth over Katie's tiny purple clit and sucked hard.

Katie was bathing Jo's fanny with her tongue. She sucked each swollen labia into her mouth in turn. She dipped into the moist hole, relishing the sweet flavour of the juices forming there. She slid one finger from each hand just inside the tight entrance, holding it open, and tongued Jo's clit. Jo stiffened under her and thrust her crotch into Katie's face but, pinned underneath Katie, her movements were restricted. Katie hoped that the younger woman relished the immobility. She wanted to feel captured by her – controlled by her, with no choice but to pleasure her lover.

As she lavished Katie's hot pussy with her tongue, Katie's tongue flicked Jo's clit, poising two fingers just inside her hole to provide an exquisite pressure.

The scent of sex filled Katie's nostrils. They were slick with sweat; bodies sliding against each other. She could feel her heart pounding, and Jo's pussy ground against her face, while she pressed her own cunt down on to Jo's face. Her lover's squirming tongue never lost contact with her clit. It felt wonderful.

Jo's body stiffened. She rocked her hips rhythmically, crushing her pussy against Katie's face and gripping her lover more tightly. As her cunt started to quiver in Katie's mouth. Katie circled her fingers inside Jo and sucked hard on her clit. The younger woman's thrusting hips moved more quickly as she started to come. She wriggled under Katie, writhing against the duvet as her orgasm ripped through her.

As her climax subsided, Jo returned her attention to her lover's clit. She sucked hard, and Katie used her hands to push herself upright, shoving her cunt right down on Jo's face. She shifted her weight, swaying her body back and forth; her clit rubbed delightfully against Jo's mouth as she rocked. Katie arched her back, and her taut thigh muscles strained as she moved. Jo wrapped her arms around her lover's thighs and clung on tightly, sucking on Katie's clit so hard that Katie uttered a deep, throaty moan. Her body tensed. She circled her hips, grinding her cunt against Jo's face. Her pussy throbbed. She cried out – half sob, half moan – as wave after wave of pleasure crashed over her, beginning in her belly and spreading through her body.

At last, Katie fell forward and rolled off Jo. She lay back on the bed, sweaty and breathless. She pushed her hair out of her eyes and took some deep breaths.

'I don't want to spoil the moment,' said Jo, 'but can I smell something burning?'

'Oh, shit,' said Katie, getting up. 'The casserole. I'd forgotten all about it.' She dashed into the kitchen and opened the oven. Jo followed at her heels. She found her oven gloves and removed the casserole. She set it down on a trivet and opened it. 'It's fine,' she said. 'We just caught it in time. Let's get dressed and eat.'

'Sounds good to me,' said Jo. 'I'm starving.' She ran off in the direction of the bedroom. By the time Katie had caught up with her, she was already dressed. She threw Katie's clothes at her playfully. Katie discarded the underwear and slipped into her dress.

'No underwear? Ms Elliott, I am shocked.' Jo teased, 'If my parents had known you went around like that, they would have taken me away from the school. And if they'd known about your tattoos and nipple rings, they'd probably have rung the *News of the World*.'

'Tattooed lesbian headmistress in kinky sex scandal,' said Katie. 'It's a good job I've always kept my professional and private lives totally separate.'

Jo pulled her close. They kissed. 'But I am glad I managed to penetrate your professional façade,' Jo said.

'Me, too,' agreed Katie. 'Now, let's eat that casserole before it's ruined.'

'This coq au vin is marvellous,' enthused Jo. 'It's better than the one we have on our menu at the restaurant. I'll have to get chef to ask you for the recipe.'

'It never tasted this good, before,' said Katie. 'It must be because it's been in the oven so long.'

'I'll tell him to try burning it then.'

Katie smiled weakly. She knew she had to tell Jo that she had spent the morning in bed with Sally, but how could she start? She looked at Jo's beautiful trusting face and couldn't bear the thought of hurting her. And she was pretty sure by now that Jo would be hurt. How could she have convinced herself that her lover would understand? How could she have been that selfish?

'Is there something wrong?' Jo sounded concerned. 'You've been sort of distracted, ever since we got out of bed.'

'It's nothing,' said Katie. 'I've just got something on my mind. I wanted to tell you something, but I don't know how.' Her voice faltered; she could not meet Jo's eyes.

'I'm not that unapproachable, am I?' said Jo brightly. 'What is it?'

Katie shook her head. She opened her mouth to speak, but somehow the words just would not come.

Jo's face blanched. She took a mouthful of wine. 'Is it bad news? Please tell me, Katie. I'm getting worried,' she stammered.

This was terrible, thought Katie. Jo obviously thought there had been bad news; she was concerned for her. But what she really had to tell her would break Jo's heart – she didn't know where to begin. She swallowed. 'It isn't bad news,' she began. 'At least, not the kind of bad news that you mean. But it certainly isn't good news. I don't know how to tell you, but if we're to make a go of things, we have to be honest with each other.' She looked at Jo. Her blue eyes were wide with concern. 'I had sex with Sally this afternoon.' The words rushed out in a jumble. Katie could tell Jo was shocked. 'But it didn't mean anything,' she went on. 'It doesn't change what I feel about you.'

A single tear rolled down Jo's cheek. Her lower lip trembled. 'It didn't mean anything?' Jo screamed. 'Why bother, then?' She was crying hard now, her face red and swollen.

'I didn't mean that. It didn't mean what sex with you means: it was different. I hoped you would understand.' Katie was jabbering and she knew it. Her usual poise and eloquence had deserted her.

'I understand, all right. You've had sex with Sally – someone you've been sleeping with for years – and you tell me that it meant nothing! How can I believe that? I thought you were serious about us, about me. Now I realise you just think I'm a gullible teenager. How could I have been so stupid?' She wiped her eyes with her linen napkin, streaking her mascara.

'I am serious about you: you've got to believe that. And I can't justify sleeping with Sally. It made sense at the time and I told her you'd understand. I'm sorry – I'm so sorry, Jo.' Katie was crying too now; tears poured down her cheeks and landed on her lap.

'It's no good being sorry after the event,' Jo sobbed. 'If you cared about me at all, you wouldn't have done it. I think I'd better go.' She gave her face a final wipe with her napkin and stood up, knocking over her chair.

'Please don't go until we've sorted this out,' Katie begged.

'How can we sort it out? You can't change what you've done and I don't think I can ever forgive you.'

'Please don't let it end like this. Call me, talk to me when you've calmed down,' said Katie, sobbing.

'At this moment, I don't feel as though I'm ever going to calm down, but if I do and I feel as though I want to, I'll be in touch. I wouldn't hold your breath, though. Don't get up. I'll let myself out.'

Katie sat helplessly in her chair as Jo let herself out of the flat. She heard the front door slam and the engine of Jo's car starting. She cried helplessly, her shoulders heaving as she sobbed.

What would she do now? She hadn't explained things very clearly and that had seemed to make matters worse. She had not meant to say that sleeping with Sally had meant nothing, of course she hadn't. But she had hoped that she would be able to make Jo understand why she had done it and forgive her. She wiped her face on her napkin and pushed her unfinished meal out of the way. She had made a mess of the whole thing. Now Jo had gone and Katie didn't know if she would ever come back.

What would she do if Jo didn't come back? She couldn't bear to think about it. In the short time they had known each other, Jo had come to mean a lot to her. The thought of living without her was unbearable. She was sure she would fall apart if that happened. What could she do to make Jo come back? To talk to her, at least? She'd ring Sally – Sally might be able to suggest something helpful. At least she would provide a familiar shoulder to cry on, and Katie needed that, right now.

She went into the bathroom and washed her face. She wet her flannel and wiped away the ruins of her make up – then held the cold cloth against her face, soothing her eyes. The mirror showed her that she looked a wreck. Her eyelids were red and swollen, her face blotchy.

She dried herself and went into the bedroom, then lay down on the rumpled bed and pulled the phone over from the bedside table. She dialled the number of the cottage and took some deep breaths to calm herself down. Please let Sally be at home, she thought. The phone rang and rang. Finally, the answering machine cut in.

'It's Katie,' she said, through her sobs. 'Jo and I have quarrelled. I told her about us and she got upset. She's gone and I don't know how I'm going to cope . . .' She dissolved into tears. 'Please ring me as soon as you get in.' She hung up. Perhaps she could reach Sally on her mobile, if it was switched on. She punched in the number carefully, her vision clouded by tears.

'The phone you have called is switched off, please try later,' the message told her. She crashed the handset down into its cradle and dumped it back on the bedside table.

She'd never felt so alone. She wished she could call Helen. After Sally, her sister would normally be her next choice in a crisis. But Helen and her husband were on holiday in Barbados and she didn't even know the name of their hotel. She hoped Sally got home soon and picked up her message. She had never handled anything so badly in her life. Normally she was so capable: but, where Jo was concerned, she just didn't feel confident. Why hadn't she explained herself properly and made Jo understand? She was so angry with herself.

Katie sat up and reached for a tissue, then blew her nose and wiped her eyes. She took off her dress and threw it towards her laundry bin before crawling under the covers and hugging her pillow. She would try to sleep, if she could stop crying. Perhaps things would look better in the morning – although she had to admit she wasn't very hopeful.

TEN

Back at the cottage, Sally stared at the computer screen. She hadn't written a word for at least half an hour, just sat in her chair gazing at the text that glowed in front of her. She sighed. So much had happened during the past few days, it was hard to concentrate on her work. At least the anxiety she had come to associate with the project had finally deserted her. She now knew she would meet her deadline.

She smiled. She had certainly made a lot of changes over the past week or so; she hardly recognised herself. It was almost like losing her virginity again: as if she had been let into a secret which everybody else already knew. And she liked it.

And it was not just sexual. It could not be coincidence that she'd finally expressed her submissive nature and overcome her writing problem at the same time. Maybe it was getting away from London and the usual distractions – and the countryside helped. Somehow, surrounded by this beautiful landscape with its slower pace of life, she just seemed to feel more relaxed. The consequent and unaccustomed absence of anxiety had made her feel reckless. The old Sally would never have admitted to Liz that she was curious about being dominated. And she would certainly never have been brave enough to go back to the club alone.

She stood up and started pacing the room restlessly. Being in control had been holding her back professionally as well as sexually, she knew. Allowing herself to be dominated in the bedroom had somehow freed her spirit. Did that make sense? Free from anxiety and the need to be in control of every aspect of her life, she was finally able to experience things fully. Sex wasn't just a momentary connection between two separate individuals: it was a meeting of souls with nothing withheld or denied. And writing her book was not an impossible and overwhelming ordeal but an exciting and creative process.

Now everything seemed different and new, richer somehow. And she was hungry for more. Last night's experience had shown her that she needed a mistress of her own. How she envied Ros and Simone. Would she ever find a mistress to serve? She sat down again and began drumming her fingers on the table. It was Liz, of course, who she wanted as her mistress. She knew that now. Especially now that Katie had found Jo. It was as if there were a gap in her life. There was part of herself, which she was not able to express fully except when she was with Liz.

She frowned. She still couldn't work Liz out though. She seemed to be sending mixed messages. Either that or Sally was so blinkered by her own feelings that she wasn't able to pick up on the usual signals. It had been Liz who had suggested that they got together in the first place, hadn't it? And she had been keen enough to go home with Sally when they had bumped into each other in the club. But she had run off at the crack of dawn and then suggested that they got into a threesome. Not the actions of someone who was looking for romance, surely?

Sally ran her fingers through her hair. She rubbed her eyes. She wasn't going to get any work done now, she realised – she was too hyper. She saved the work she had done earlier and switched off her computer. She looked out of the window;

another beautiful day. She didn't belong inside on a day like this. She was in the heart of the British countryside on a glorious summer's day and yet she was cooped up indoors. She would go for a drive, she decided; she would put her laptop in the car, open the sunroof and go off exploring. Perhaps she would find a quiet pub later where she could have a cool drink and a snack. And if she found a nice spot, she could do some work in the fresh air.

Quickly she loaded the car with a few essentials: her laptop and mobile phone, her handbag, a jacket in case it got cold, her favourite CDs and a bottle of mineral water. She rolled down all the windows and opened the sunroof, turned the music up loud and set off.

She decided not to look at the map; she would just drive, see where she ended up. The old Sally wouldn't have embarked on a journey without a proper destination in mind and a thorough route planned. But what a lot she missed that way. She couldn't enjoy the scenery, because she was focused on taking the right turnings and not getting lost. And when she arrived, she was somehow disappointed because there was no surprise, no sense of discovery or spontaneity. It was a metaphor for her life, really. She was so worried about the destination that she never enjoyed the journey. She laughed out loud, chuckling and giggling to herself as she drove. Her shoulders shook, her stomach was beginning to ache, and tears welled in the corner of her eyes. Yes. It was a wonderful day to be alive.

She drove past sun-streaked fields. Crimson black-hearted poppies waved their heads at her from the flower-strewn verges as she passed by. The sun beat down on her through the open roof of the car, warming her skin. It was a good job she had applied sunscreen before she set off; she could easily get burned. A cool breeze blew in through the open windows, ruffling her hair. She passed by grey stone farm buildings where a group of cows were lined up ready for milking. Two teenage boys kept them in order with gentle pats and soothing words. She saw a knot of hikers in heavy boots walking the Cuckoo Trail that wound its way from Blue Beach through the Cuckmere valley. One of the walkers carried a baby in a papoose-style backpack, and a small scruffy dog ran along behind them, darting back and forth and yapping excitedly.

Katie was certainly lucky to live and work in such a beautiful part of the country. No, not lucky – Katie never left anything to chance. If she made her home and her career here, it was because she had chosen to. And Sally could understand why. There was a tranquillity here, and a sense of union with nature that she found captivating. Making love with Katie, that morning, had been special. There had been a finality about it, a completeness that had made it seem poignant. Like they had needed to say goodbye to that part of their shared lives and move on. Her brow wrinkled into a frown. She hoped Jo would understand. She would hate to think of anything she did causing a problem between the two of them. But Katie had seemed sure that her new lover would understand. And she ought to know.

She kept to the country roads, deliberately avoiding towns and motorways. She meandered through farmland and villages. It was the thatched-cottage, cricket-on-the-green, chocolate-box view of England, that tourists loved and natives mocked. Sally drank it all in. It was a landscape that she knew well, but somehow she had never realised how beautiful it was.

She snaked back and forth across the Sussex Downs, through villages and hamlets that sounded as though they had been invented by a team of unimaginative sit-com writers. Upper Dicker sounded like the kind of place where men were men and women were glad of it. Was Muddles Green where Frank Spencer lived? How about Blackboys? Was Plumpton populated by refugees from a McGill postcard? And as for Fulking, her imagination ran riot. Any minute she expected to turn a corner and bump into Captain Mainwaring leading Pike, Godfrey and the rest of the platoon on some secret manoeuvre.

Sally yawned, and then shifted in her seat to ease the stiffness that seemed to have developed in her lower spine. It was already twenty to four and she had left home after lunch – probably at about half past one. A glance at the odometer told her she had driven just over a hundred miles. And last night's activities were catching up on her. She hadn't got much sleep at Simone and Ros's; there had been far more exciting activities on the agenda. Come to think of it, she had not had much rest at all during the past three days. First there had been her night with Liz, then Ros and Liz, and then last night's fun with the slave and her mistress. She had certainly been busy. No wonder she felt tired. She would stop at the next village she came to and hope they had a pub that stayed open all day where she could get a drink and maybe some food.

She had no idea where she was. The last village she could remember driving through was Houghton, but she had no idea where she was geographically. Her limbs were aching now. She had lost her concentration a couple of times, too. She really needed to stop soon. At the approach to a roundabout, she changed gear and decelerated, ready to negotiate the turn. The road sign at the junction told her that Chichester and Bognor Regis were straight ahead and Arundel to her left. She knew where she was, now. She took the first turning and headed for Arundel. According to the sign, she was only a couple of miles away from the town. She would stop there.

Imagine, driving all that way and finding herself in Arundel. She laughed softly. Hailsham Edge was only about fifty miles away from Arundel; probably less. You could easily drive it in an hour. Yet she had been on the road for over two hours and now she was exhausted. Perhaps it was fate. Arundel had always been one of her favourite places. She had got to know it well when she had been researching *House of Spirits*. The Green Man pub, in the town centre, was the subject of her book. She had got to know the family who owned it quite well. Especially Anna, their adult daughter. She was sure Anna had fancied her.

Anna had flirted outrageously at the time, but Sally had never quite had the nerve to take her up on it.

She was approaching the outskirts of the town now, driving past the imposing castle, which looked medieval but was, in fact, mostly nineteenth century. How about spending the night in The Green Man? She liked the idea. She had to admit that she was far too tired to drive the fifty miles back home, this evening. Staying at The Green Man would mean that the place would be fresh in her mind. She would be able to inject the right ambience into her book. And, apart from that, she would quite like to renew her acquaintance with the landlady's lovely daughter. Her nerve would not desert her, this time.

She turned into Tarrant Street. The Green Man was a couple of hundred yards down the road. She drove under the arch where coaches had entered in days gone by and parked in the small cobbled yard that served as the pub's car park. She got her few possessions out of the back seat and locked the car.

The Green Man was divided into two parts. The hotel was located in the main building and the pub was housed in an extension, which had been built during the nineteenth century. The hotel's reception was deserted, so Sally rang the bell.

'Can I help you?' said the landlady as she came into the reception from the pub, behind Sally.

'I'd like a room, if you have one,' said Sally.

'I think we can manage that,' she said, and walked across the tiled lobby and squeezed herself behind the small reception desk, took the register from under the counter and looked up at Sally. She smiled in recognition. 'Sally,' she said, 'how nice to see you.' She put out her hand and Sally shook it warmly.

'I didn't think you'd recognise me,' Sally said.

'Of course I recognise you. It isn't every day we have best-selling authors here, wanting to write about the place. How's the book going, by the way?'

'It's going very well, actually.' Sally was glad she could say that. 'Although it hasn't always been. I had a sort of crisis of anxiety and couldn't start on it. Fortunately, I seem to have got over that now. It's well on the way. I'm staying at my friend's cottage near Eastbourne, at the moment, to work on it. Only I came out for a drive and didn't realise I had driven so far. I'm simply too tired to drive back home tonight.'

'No problem. It's lovely to see you. Would you like to have the same room as last time?'

'That would be nice,' Sally agreed. 'Since I am here, I might as well soak up some atmosphere. Spending the night in your "haunted" room will help to refresh my memory. Thank you, Mrs Lee.'

'Who knows,' said the landlady lightly, 'you might even see our ghost.'

'Well, I didn't last time.' Sally laughed. 'I need a snooze. How late do you serve dinner?'

'Half past nine. Is that OK?'

'Fine,' Sally confirmed. 'If I'm not down by half past eight could you give me a wake-up call?'

'Of course. Here's your key. Do you remember the way?'

Sally nodded her assent and thanked the landlady. She plodded up the broad oak staircase, her legs heavy with exhaustion. She walked along the narrow corridor, up the second, steeper set of stairs, and let herself into her room, then threw off her clothes and crawled into bed.

The cotton sheets were cool and smooth. Her head sank into the fat feather pillow. She gave herself up to the soft cocoon of the bed. She stretched her aching limbs and closed her eyes.

She was drifting; a distant, gentle rumble of traffic reached her ears through the open window. A breeze fluttered the curtains. She listened to the comforting sound of her own breathing. The gently rhythmic rise and fall of her chest and the susurration of her exhalations seemed to hypnotise her. It became a mantra, a lullaby which soothed her to sleep.

She felt Liz's arm snake round her waist. She snuggled against the familiar warmth of her lover's body. Liz rocked her, muttering gentle words of love and stroking her face. It was safe and warm in Liz's arms. Somehow, she belonged there. She relaxed, pressing her back against Liz's strong body. She slept.

Wisps of sensation penetrated her slumber. She stirred. Hands were caressing her back; fairy, feather-light strokes which made her tingle. Fingers brushed against her breasts. Her nipples hardened. She sighed appreciatively, as the familiar, animal odour of arousal filled her nostrils. Strong hands cupped her face; lips found hers. They kissed. A hot wet tongue snaked between her lips. She opened her eyes. Liz's beautiful face smiled at her. She wrapped her arms around Liz and pulled her close. Her body felt soft and warm against Sally.

Fingernails traced the length of her spine; she felt hot breath on her back. A kiss was planted on the tip of her shoulder. Yet Liz was still in her arms, her mouth hungrily sucking on Sally's ear-lobe. There must be somebody else in bed with them. Yet there was no shock, no surprise attached to this realisation. It felt good to have more than two arms holding her, more than two mouths kissing her. How lucky she was. Hands parted her legs, found her slit. Fingers teased her clit, smearing her slippery juices over the taut button. So, there was a third woman in the bed with her now. She sighed.

Soon a hot, wet mouth replaced the probing fingers between her legs. It was divine. Liz was sucking her nipples now, alternately drawing each teat between her lips and nibbling it gently. Behind her, fingernails teased her buttocks; lips planted wet kisses on her shoulders and back. An expert mouth worked her pussy.

She closed her eyes. Without her vision, the distinctions between her three lovers blurred, and it was impossible to distinguish between their caresses. Three mouths kissed her; six arms held her; six hands touched her. She was warm and safe, enveloped by love. There was no beginning and no end: just pleasure. She floated on a wave of ecstasy.

Hands roamed her body, stroking, squeezing. The mouth

between her legs worked her clit. Heat grew in her belly and she groaned. Her hands were above her head now, pinned down somehow. She struggled to move her arms but they felt heavy, stiff. And her feet were restrained too, she realised. A tingle of excitement rose in her chest. Somehow, her lovers had tied her up or shackled her. She was spreadeagled on the bed, helpless. She ground her aching fanny hard against the unknown mouth. Fingers teased her nipples, squeezing them hard, pulling them. She was riding the edge of pain now. And, somehow, every sensation in her nipples seemed to intensify the pleasure she was experiencing in her cunt. She thrashed around on the bed, straining against her invisible bonds, and groaning.

Distant images began to break through her consciousness. She was cold. There was an uncomfortable numbness in one arm, and the eerie wail of a police siren pierced her awareness.

The sexual tension in her pelvis evaporated instantly as she was wrenched out of her dream. She had been so close to coming, as well.

She looked at her watch. It was ten past eight; she had been asleep for hours. She sat up, rubbed her eyes and stretched. Hunger gnawed at her belly. She had not eaten anything since she had shared breakfast with Katie, twelve hours ago. She got up, washed and dressed and went down to dinner.

She seated herself at a small table in the corner of the restaurant, smiling politely at the couple at the next table as she sat down. The pub must be doing OK; most of the tables were taken and the bar next door had seemed pretty full too, when she passed by. She was glad the Lees were doing well. They deserved it. They had done a lot of work on the place, adapting the premises to accommodate the modern requirement for en suite bathroom facilities without sacrificing the character of the old building. They had managed to straddle two camps: catering to the tourist trade but still retaining the loyalty of the locals. It was one of the reasons she had so liked the place on her previous visit. It was comfortable and unpretentious, and it didn't try to be something it wasn't.

A white-aproned waitress backed out of the kitchen door, holding a plate in each hand. She turned round and headed towards the table next to Sally's. It was Anna. Sally smiled, knowing that Anna had not yet seen her as the waitress set the dishes down in front of the couple.

'Enjoy your meal,' she said and turned to face Sally.

'Are you ready to order?' she asked. 'Oh! Sally.' She looked at Sally for the first time. 'Mum didn't tell me you were staying. What a lovely surprise.'

'I could say the same,' said Sally, smiling.

'But where are my manners?' said Anna. 'I'm standing here reminiscing and you're probably starving. Have you had a look at the menu? Have you seen anything you fancy?'

'Yes, I have, actually,' said Sally provocatively, staring straight at Anna, 'only I'm not sure it's on the menu.'

Anna's face creased into a broad smile. She laughed. Sally had forgotten how beautiful Anna was when she smiled. 'I think you'll find that particular item is on the menu, but it isn't available until after we close up, say around midnight. Can you wait that long?'

'As long as I've got some food inside me, I think I'll be able to make it through. Do you still have your calves' liver with prunes on the menu?'

'We do.'

'I'll have that please, with half a bottle of your house red – no, make it a bottle. And will you deliver my dessert to my room personally?' Sally said.

Anna smiled in complicity and trotted off towards the kitchen.

Sally was becoming so bold, she hardly recognised herself. But she liked it. She could ask for what she wanted and that made her feel so much more in control. Before, she would never have been so direct. She would have relied on Anna to take the initiative and then spent hours worrying whether her feelings were reciprocated. She was beginning to realise how positive and empowering honesty was. She needn't wait for things to happen by chance; she could ask for what she wanted and she'd probably get it. It was ironic. She used to be so concerned about being in control – organised her life and her work around it – yet she had not been in control at all. She had been repressed. Yes, that was the word. She had mistaken the repression of her feelings and her impulses for being in charge of her life. But now she finally knew what being in control meant. It meant freedom: the freedom to make her own choices and decisions.

Anna was around twenty, Sally guessed. And she was tall; that was one of the first things Sally had noticed about her. Close to six foot, she'd guess. The second thing she had noticed was Anna's hair; a tumbling cascade of chestnut curls which caressed her shoulders as she walked. Sally longed to bury her face in that abundant hair and inhale its scent. Anna's ivory skin was dusted with golden freckles. Sally guessed that Anna did not like them, because sometimes she wore a heavy make-up to conceal them. But Sally found them very attractive. They gave Anna a girlish, innocent quality and a sort of mischievous look that she rather liked. Although she had only ever seen Anna wearing the restaurant uniform of black skirt, white blouse and white apron, Sally always sensed that there was an alluring body concealed beneath the unflattering clothes. There was something about the way her hips swayed as she walked which suggested womanly thighs and a broad pelvis. And Sally had occasionally caught a glimpse of creamy cleavage when Anna had bent over her table to put down plates, or collect glasses. She smiled to herself. She was looking forward to peeling off those drab clothes . . .

Anna hurried back into the dining room, carrying a tray. She came over to Sally and quickly delivered the wine and a glass, a basket of rolls and some butter and a dish of olives.

'To keep you going,' she said, smiling. 'Food's on its way.' And then she was gone.

Sally buttered some bread and ate it. She quickly devoured the marinated olives and poured herself a glass of wine. The warm, spicy liquid was soft and rich on her tongue. She glanced at the couple at the adjacent table. The woman caught her eye and smiled with slight embarrassment, Sally thought, then looked back down at her plate quickly. Perhaps she had overheard her flirting with the pretty waitress; had heard them arrange their assignation. Sally smiled to herself. She hoped the woman had heard. And she hoped she was jealous. Anna was gorgeous.

When her food came, she ate slowly, relishing each delicious mouthful. Waxy baby new potatoes were the perfect complement to the rich prune sauce. Firm yet tender garden carrots provided a textural contrast to the soft smoothness of the calves' liver. Afterwards, she ate a crème brûlée, crunching her spoon through the crisp sugar layer and into the thick vanilla cream underneath. It was a symphony of a meal; all her five senses were satisfied. Like good sex, she reflected. She enjoyed two cups of strong black coffee, while slowly munching on the chef's home-made chocolate truffles. Nodding politely to her neighbours, she walked across the dining room and headed upstairs.

She had nothing with her except the clothes she stood up in and the few essentials she had packed into the car earlier. She would have liked to change her clothes. But at least she could take a shower. She stripped off her clothes and folded them neatly on to a chair, before going into the bathroom and turning on the shower. There was complimentary shower gel and shampoo provided, so she could wash her hair. But she had no toothbrush. There was chewing gum in her handbag; that would have to do. She climbed under the jet of water and allowed it to beat down on her back. It felt good. When she'd washed her hair, she turned off the water and climbed out of the shower, wrapped herself in one of the hotel's white, fluffy towels and rubbed her hair with another.

She wandered back into the bedroom and rummaged in her handbag for her hairbrush. She found the chewing gum and popped a pellet into her mouth, then brushed her wet hair in front of the full-length mirror. She dropped the towel and looked at her body. It was the first time she had had a proper look at her own shaved pussy. She liked it. She felt exposed: even more naked than usual, somehow. She stroked her mound with an exploratory finger. Stubble; if she wanted to keep it smooth, she would have to shave it again tomorrow. Didn't want it to get prickly.

In the bedroom, she located a socket and plugged in her computer. She climbed naked under the covers and set the laptop on her knee. She leant back against the pillows and read through her first two chapters. They were pretty good. Apart from the odd word here and there and a final bit of tinkering, she was happy with them. Now it was time to start on her third chapter. She knew what she intended to write about; it was just a question of finding the words. She closed her eyes, took some long, deep breaths to clear her mind and, after a few minutes, she opened her eyes and began typing. Her fingers fluttered over the keys; words tumbled out.

She worked with complete concentration. The only sound in the attic room was the gentle, rhythmic clacking of her computer keys. It was getting dark. An hour ago, she had had to turn the bedside lamp on. A sound broke through her consciousness: a sharp rapping at the door. She took off her reading glasses.

'Come in,' she said.

The door creaked open and Anna tiptoed into the room. 'I didn't want to disturb you if you were sleeping,' she said, smiling.

'No, I've been working,' she said. 'Give me a minute and I'll save the file and switch off.'

'I wish I could work in the nude, like that,' said Anna. 'It gets pretty hot in our kitchen, this time of year.'

'I'd certainly eat here more often, if you did.' Sally closed her laptop and set it down on the bedside table. 'But aren't you a bit overdressed at the moment?' she asked, raising an eyebrow wickedly.

Anna smiled. She was still dressed in her working clothes, although Sally noted that she had taken off her apron. She pulled her white shirt out of her skirt and began undoing the buttons. At last, Sally was about to find out what Anna had been concealing under her uniform. On her last visit, she had enjoyed quite a few erotic dreams on the strength of Anna's imagined charms. She watched as Anna fumbled with her shirt buttons. Sally did not think she was going to be disappointed. Finally, the beautiful waitress undid the last button, stripped off the white blouse and threw it across the room. She was wearing a plain white cotton bra. She undid the zip at the side of her skirt and shimmied it down her legs to reveal white knickers which matched her bra. She kicked off her flat black shoes and wriggled her toes.

Her figure was curvaceous and muscular. Sally knew that Anna cycled along the riverbank each morning before the pub opened; the toned columns of her thighs were evidence of this. Full breasts heaved beneath the cotton confines of her bra. Sally's heart was pounding with anticipation as Anna reached behind her and unclasped her bra. Anna peeled it away from her skin slowly, tantalising Sally. Largish breasts and pale pink nipples came into view as Anna dropped her bra on the floor. She bent forward to remove her knickers, forcing her breasts forward and creating a delightfully deep cleavage.

Sally licked her lips.

Her knickers off, Anna quickly stood upright again. A rounded, womanly belly and two creamy, toned thighs seemed to frame her pussy. An abundance of strawberry blonde curls nestled between her legs. She was every bit as beautiful as Sally had imagined all those months ago. More so, if that were possible. She held back the duvet and shifted across the bed, making room for Anna.

'I've been keeping your place warm,' she said, smiling.

Anna climbed under the duvet with her. She wrapped her arms around Sally, pressing her body against her. They kissed. Anna's lips were soft and wet. Sally buried her face in Anna's chestnut mane so that the soft, shiny curls tickled her nose. Coconut shampoo, she thought, and a faint hint of cooking smells from the hotel's kitchens where Anna spent most of her day. Sally rubbed her face in Anna's soft hair, relishing the scent and the texture.

Anna's mouth was on Sally's neck, exploring the flesh with her tongue. She kissed, she nibbled, and at last rolled on top of Sally. She cupped Sally's face in both hands and kissed her gently. She kissed the tip of Sally's nose; she kissed each closed eyelid. She kissed Sally's temples, her cheekbones, the tip of her chin. Her lips found Sally's and they explored each other's mouths, tongues snaking against each other.

Anna's weight felt good on top of Sally. She was pressed down into the mattress, pinned down, almost. Their tits pressed together; she could feel Anna's hard nipples against her skin. Anna wriggled down her body and trailed her tongue across Sally's chest, to find a nipple. Sally closed her eyes and laced her fingers into Anna's unruly hair, stroking her head.

Anna teased Sally's nipples, sucking one while she fingered the other, her hot breath warming Sally's skin. Chestnut curls tumbled everywhere, tickling Sally, and Anna slid lower. She dipped her tongue into Sally's shallow belly-button, tasting the saltiness there. She parted Sally's thighs, pressing the legs apart with her strong hands, then wriggled down the bed until her face was poised above Sally's pussy.

'No hair!' She stroked the naked flesh experimentally.

'Someone thought it might be fun to shave me. Do you like

it?' Sally leant up on her elbows, watching Anna's face between her legs.

'It's smooth; your skin feels so soft. And I can see everything; it's all on display. I like it. I wonder what it will feel like to lick . . .' She dipped her head and rubbed her lips against the bare skin. Sally purred and an expression of rapture formed on Anna's features. She rubbed her lips all over Sally's shaved pussy. 'It's lovely, so soft against my face,' she said.

'Believe me,' Sally assured her, 'it feels pretty good from my end, too.'

Anna wrapped her arms around Sally's parted thighs and pulled her close. She buried her face in Sally's pussy, drinking in the musky scent. Sally lay back against the pillow and closed her eyes. She felt Anna's tongue tracing the contour of her labia, sliding along her slit. The pretty waitress pulled Sally's lips apart gently with her thumbs, exposing the clit, then ran her tongue along the moist cleft, relishing the copious juices welling there.

Sally sighed and brushed a wayward strand of hair out of her eyes. She parted her legs a little wider and circled her hips, increasing the intensity of the sensations building in her cunt. Anna bathed Sally's wet pussy with her tongue. She darted it inside the tight entrance, flattened it to tease the clitoris. Her thumbs held Sally's lips apart, allowing her full access to the juicy slit. She circled the tiny hard bud of Sally's clit, exerting firm pressure with her tongue, and Sally pressed her crotch into Anna's eager face.

Anna drew her partner's clit inside her mouth. She sucked on it gently, lapped at it with her tongue. Sally moistened her dry lips with her tongue. Sweaty strands of hair clung to her forehead and neck. Anna's tongue moved rhythmically between her legs and she circled the swollen nub of Sally's clit with her tongue, sucking on it firmly as she did so. Her wild hair fell everywhere, spread across Sally's lap as if it had an existence of its own. It brushed against her in perfect synchronisation with the rhythm of Anna's mouth, moving against her cunt. Sally's skin was on fire where the soft curls stroked her. Heat welled in her belly, and a tense ball of pleasure formed in her womb.

A soft moan escaped from between Sally's lips. Her eyes fluttered and darted beneath closed lids. She pressed her heels down into the mattress, grasping handfuls of sheet with her hands. Her hips circled frantically as she thrust her cunt against Anna's probing tongue. Anna gripped Sally tight and sucked hard at her clit, matching her rhythm to her lover's urgent lunges.

Sally's thighs stiffened as her cunt began to throb. Sally sobbed loudly, grinding her hot pussy against Anna's face. Electric surges of delight erupted from her womb. They spread through her body, weakening as they did so, bathing her in a warm glow. Pinpricks of pleasure, as they ran up and down her spine, made her nipples tingle. Anna's talented mouth seemed to coax orgasm after orgasm from her. Sally shook uncontrollably, tears pouring from her eyes as she came.

Anna rode out the tempest of Sally's orgasm; her strong arms were wrapped around Sally's thighs. Eventually, Sally's body relaxed and she lay back on the bed, exhausted. Anna released her and scrambled up the bed to lie beside her. Sally pulled her close and kissed her passionately, relishing the taste and aroma of her own juices. She licked and sucked Anna's wet face clean. She smoothed down Anna's wild hair, cupped the freckled face in her hands and traced the girl's enviable cheekbones with a finger.

'You are quite beautiful,' she said quietly. Anna laughed and shook her head.

'Not me,' she said modestly, shaking her head and making her curls bounce. 'You must be thinking of someone else. I'm just a gangly, freckly girl with brillo-pad hair and legs that are too skinny. You're the beautiful one.'

'Thanks,' said Sally. For the first time, she did not feel the need to reject the compliment; if Anna thought she was beautiful, she must mean it. It felt good to be thought beautiful. 'But I assure you, you are gorgeous. Let me see what I can do to help you appreciate just how lovely you are.' She rolled on top of the pretty waitress and kissed her.

ELEVEN

Sally was handcuffed, wearing only her underwear; her hands shackled behind her as she knelt. She did not know where she was. There was cold parquet floor underneath her. She looked up at a high vaulted ceiling. Hundreds of candles glittered down from an iron chandelier dangling from a beam. Their glow seemed to warm the stark room. She coughed. The hoarse sound echoed round the room in ghostly parody. She shivered. The room was huge, she realised, although she could not see into all of its dark corners.

She had no idea where she was, or why she was here: yet she felt no fear. Although there was a chill in the room which left her trembling from the cold, she was strangely calm. Then she heard footsteps: high heels clacking on a tiled floor and coming progressively closer. The footsteps echoed, as her cough had done, and the sound filled her with anticipation. Who was it, and what did they want with her?

The footsteps halted and she heard the sound of bolts being drawn back and latches being turned on the double oak doors she had just noticed were set into one wall of the room. She held her breath, hardly able to contain her curiosity about the identity of her captor. The heavy doors swung open and a figure walked in, shrouded in a long black velvet cloak. It was a woman, Sally sensed that. And she meant Sally no harm. She didn't know how she knew that, but she did. Part of her brain knew that she was dreaming, yet the images and sensations she was experiencing seemed totally real. She allowed herself to let go, to enjoy the dream as it unfolded, safe in the knowledge that it could not harm her.

The cloaked woman lowered her hood, then unclasped her cloak at the neck and dropped it to the floor. It fell around her feet in a fluid heap. She kicked it aside and walked towards Sally. In spite of the obvious antiquity of her surroundings, the woman was dressed in modern clothes; a short black, silky dress clung to her ample curves and matching suede stilettos made her legs seem unnaturally long. And she was masked, wearing the kind of black eye-mask that eighteenth-century ladies hid behind at masquerade balls. The woman was familiar, but Sally could not seem to identify her. She trawled through her memory, trying to dredge up information that would let her recognise the woman, but her mind felt clumsy and slow.

The woman reached Sally and stood in front of her with her hands on her hips. Sally looked up hungrily at the muscular legs and curvaceous body. Whoever she was, she was beautiful. The woman knelt. She placed one strong hand on the nape of Sally's neck and pulled her close. She kissed Sally gently on the mouth, a kiss which seemed to touch her soul.

She knew who it was, then; how could she have been so blind? It was obvious. There was no mistaking that kiss, the taste of those lips, the scent of that skin. It was Liz. Was Liz her captor? Or had she come to release Sally from her confinement in this stark room? Liz stood up again, grasped the hem of her dress and pulled it up to her waist. She was naked underneath and Sally could smell the familiar aroma of her pussy. Liz parted her legs provocatively, revealing a glimpse of her violet quim, peeping out between the dark curls.

'Lick me,' she commanded. Sally leant forward, raising herself up on her knees. It wasn't easy moving around without using her hands, but she struggled to get herself properly positioned. Liz was not helping her. She just stood impassively, legs parted, hands on hips, waiting for Sally to obey her command. Sally shuffled nearer until her mouth was only centimetres away from her mistress's dark curls. She pressed her face into Liz's bush. She inhaled deeply, relishing the complex melange of scents. The musky aroma of arousal, the clean smell of soap, the slightly meaty perfume of fresh sweat, deodorant.

She nuzzled her way down Liz's mound. She found the clitoris, hiding beneath its secret cowl, and she licked it. She shaped her tongue into a hard point and poked it into the crevices and hollows of Liz's pussy. She licked along the length of the lilac slit, smearing her face in the fragrant juices. Liz took a step backwards, out of reach. Sally crawled forward on her knees, eager to re-establish the intimate contact. She panted from the effort. Finally, she was kneeling before Liz again.

She leant forward again, hungrily seeking her lover's cunt. She fastened her mouth over Liz's swollen clit, sucking on it. She circled the hard bud with her tongue, squeezed it between her lips. Sally's knees hurt, and the muscles of her shoulders ached from the strain of holding herself upright. The metal cuffs which bound her wrists chafed the delicate skin. Yet none of it mattered. She was aware of her physical discomfort; the unyielding wooden floor she knelt on would not let her forget it. But it was irrelevant. Nothing mattered to her except her mouth and the woman she was worshipping. It was bliss.

As she licked, she was conscious of the juices flowing between her own legs. Her body felt alive, each nerve-ending sensitive to the slightest sensation: a wisp of breeze caressing her skin, the pressure of her underwear against her clit. She mouthed Liz's clit, lavishing it with love.

Liz stepped backwards again, and again. She was three feet away, beyond Sally's reach. Sally felt empty. Painfully, she shuffled on her bruised knees after her mistress. Inch by painful inch she crossed the floor between them. At last, she was next to her mistress again and she thrust her face forward, burrowing between Liz's parted legs. She worked her mistress's clit, eagerly sucking on it. Sally's nipples were erect and sensitive, and a knot of excitement settled in her pelvis. Her cunt was on fire; as she licked Liz's clit, her own tight bud seemed to respond. She was covered in perspiration. Her hair clung to her head in damp clumps. Here and there, dirt from the floor stuck to her sweat-slicked legs. She was panting.

It had suddenly got darker, no – not dark. The room was filling with mist. Tendrils of milky vapour were seeping into every corner. Her vision clouded; she was floating. And where was Liz? She struggled futilely against her bonds. What was happening?

She opened her eyes, blinked.

'Good morning,' said Anna. She was holding Sally, cradling her shoulders with one strong arm. 'Were you dreaming? You were sort of murmuring.'

'I think I must have been,' Sally admitted. She became aware of her arousal, then. The tension in her belly, which had been part of her dream, was still with her. Anna's hand was pressed between Sally's legs, expertly fingering her clit.

Sally smiled. 'I thought I was dreaming that,' she said. 'It's nice to find out I wasn't.'

'Unfortunately, I don't have much time,' Anna apologised. 'I have to go downstairs and help with breakfast. In fact, I am probably already late. So I only have time for a very quick one.'

'OK by me,' said Sally. She relaxed back against her pillows and opened her legs wide. 'I'm pretty near, anyway.' Anna held her close, dipping her head to kiss Sally's neck and shoulders. Her other hand moved between Sally's legs, teasing her clit. Sally closed her eyes as a familiar tingle mounted in her belly. Anna fingers slid against Sally's juicy slit, circling the sensitive clit and pinching it. Sally sighed softly.

Anna kissed her breasts, gently nibbling on the plump globes. Her mouth found a nipple. She trapped it between her lips and nibbled on it. Sally groaned. Anna mouthed her nipple, sucking it firmly and nipping it with her sharp teeth. Her fingers moved between Sally's legs, stroking her taut clit. Sally writhed in Anna's arms. She was on the edge now, and Anna's mouth on her nipple was taking her closer to fulfilment.

She rocked her hips back and forth, creating a delicious extra friction where Anna fingered her. She pressed her head into the pillow, tensing her jaw. A snake of fire coiled in her belly, and her fanny pulsed. Her body stiffened, and then ripples of pleasure spread out from her clit, overwhelming her. Anna bit down hard on her nipple, and Sally could not distinguish between the pleasure and the pain; all she knew was that it felt wonderful. She pressed her crotch against Anna's hand, milking every last drop of pleasure as she gyrated her hips.

Anna's strong arms encircled Sally's quaking body as she came. Sally felt safe: protected, somehow. She lay in Anna's embrace long after her orgasm had subsided, enjoying the afterglow.

Anna stroked her hair, kissed her forehead, then said, finally, 'I really have to go. There will be guests wanting breakfast and nobody to serve it.'

'Of course,' said Sally, feeling guilty at having detained Anna. 'You go. I'll be down for my breakfast in a little while.'

Anna leapt out of bed and quickly got into her clothes. She bent over the bed and kissed Sally. 'See you later,' she said and was gone.

Sally stretched. What a delightful way to wake up. A delightful way to go to sleep, too. Anna was lovely. Not only beautiful, but generous and modest as well. She was starving, she realised. Sex always seemed to give her an appetite. She threw the duvet back and climbed out of bed.

It was just before eight when she went down for breakfast. She took a seat next to the window. Sun poured in through the leaded windows, making diamond patterns dance on the white linen tablecloths. She could smell the savoury aroma of cooking bacon and sausages, and her stomach growled.

Anna came out of the kitchen with a glass pitcher of orange juice. She spotted Sally, smiled and walked over to the table, and filled her glass. 'Good morning,' she said brightly. 'Full breakfast or continental?'

'Since I started the day by being wicked, I think I'll carry on that way.' Sally laughed. 'I'll have the full breakfast.'

'Coming up,' said Anna. 'Help yourself to cereal.' She pointed to a table near the wall, where cereal, fruit, rolls and milk were set out. 'Would you like coffee or tea? And how about a newspaper.'

'Coffee, please,' said Sally, 'and have you got an *Independent*?'

'I'll bring it straight over.'

'The service here is very efficient,' observed Sally, smiling wickedly.

'I think you will find,' said Anna, lowering her voice conspiratorially, 'that the room service is even better.'

Sally laughed out loud. Two elderly people at a nearby table looked up disapprovingly from their newspapers. It was the couple who had sat next to her last night. No doubt they now thought her loud and ill-mannered in addition to immoral. Let them; she didn't care.

It was peaceful here, just as she had remembered it. And she had got an amazing amount of work done last night. Then there was Anna. She had certainly turned out to be an unexpected bonus; Sally would be sorry to leave. She went over to the buffet table and helped herself to muesli and yoghurt. She spooned a couple of stewed figs into her bowl. But she didn't have to leave, did she? She could work here just as easily as she could at the cottage. What was to stop her staying on for a few days longer? She would have to buy herself a few necessities: some toiletries and a few clothes. But there was no reason for her to rush back to Hailsham Edge, if she was enjoying herself here. Her quiet room up in the eaves of the old building was obviously conducive to working and she had to admit that she'd like to spend more time with Anna. Plus she waited to work that dream into a story.

And, apart from anything else, she did not seem to feel so troubled by thoughts of Liz, here. Of course, she knew that eventually she would have to deal with her own complicated feelings about Liz and resolve things between them, but for now it didn't seem so urgent. If she stayed in Arundel a couple of more days, perhaps she would feel a little more objective about the whole Liz situation. Perhaps the distance – both geographical and emotional – would bring her a new sense of perspective. She certainly hoped so.

She finished her cereal and set the spoon down in the bowl. She swallowed the last of her juice, poured herself a cup of coffee and opened the newspaper, which Anna had brought over while she was getting her cereal. There was a big article about the take-over at Eden's. She spread out the newspaper, smoothing its folds with quick fingers. She was mentioned, or at least *House of Spirits* was, as a forthcoming publication. Only a fortnight ago, reading this news would have sent her into a panic. But not today. She felt excited: excited and slightly proud. She would probably be able to deliver her three completed chapters to Margaret within the next few days and was well on course with the rest. And she was looking forward to it; the joy of creation she had experienced thus far had fired her with enthusiasm. She was inspired. She smiled to herself.

'Your breakfast, madam,' said Anna in mock servility.

Sally had not noticed her standing there. Quickly she folded the newspaper and moved it out of the way.

Anna set her breakfast down. 'Enjoy your meal,' she said.

'Anna,' Sally asked, 'is my room available for a few more days?'

Anna's eyes widened. She smiled. 'I should think so, although

I'll have to speak to Mum. I'll find out for you and let you know.' She leant forward and brought her freckled face close to Sally's. 'I'd like to think I played a small part in your decision to stay.'

'You played a big part, actually. And I hope you will continue to deliver my room service personally, as long as I am here. But really, I just fancied a couple of days away. I can work here as easily as anywhere, and it's nice and restful. I just felt like staying.'

'That's good enough for me,' said Anna. 'I'll talk to Mum now and let you know.' She smiled at Sally and walked off towards the kitchen.

Sally enjoyed her cooked breakfast. She wolfed down the sausage, bacon and eggs and followed it with toast and marmalade. She leafed idly through the newspaper as she ate, languishing in the unaccustomed luxury of a meal someone else had cooked.

Anna's mother came out of the kitchen and headed for Sally's table. 'Anna tells me you'd like to stay a little longer?'

'Is that OK? I don't want to mess up your arrangements if the room is booked,' Sally said anxiously.

'Not at all. We have plenty of bookings, but no one has asked for that particular room. So you can stay as long as you like,' she said, smiling.

'Thank you very much, Mrs Lee. It's very kind of you.'

'Not at all,' said the landlady. 'When your book comes out, we'll be turning customers away. I should be thanking you.'

Sally laughed. 'I hope you're right,' she said. 'There's an article about Eden's in the paper today. It mentions *House of Spirits*. It seems to make it more real, somehow. But, in the meantime, I'd better get upstairs and get back to writing the thing. Thank you again.'

She drank the last of her coffee and went back up the stairs to her room, carrying the newspaper under her arm. She opened the two windows wide and set up her laptop on the small table that rested along one wall. She turned on the radio, flicking through the channels until she found a station she liked. She powered up her computer and called up the chapter she was working on.

Sally worked away quietly. The drone of the radio soothed her. Distant street sounds drifted in through the open window, providing a comfortable backdrop. She was really in her stride now. The two chapters she had already completed had set the scene for the book. Now she was working on the meat of her story, weaving beguiling word-pictures which, she hoped, would enthral her reader. She was totally engrossed in her work. It was almost as if she were inside the story, telling the tale as it unfolded before her eyes.

Her stomach rumbled. A sudden awareness of hunger snaked into her consciousness; pulled at her concentration. She looked at her watch. Half past twelve; time for lunch. She could do with a break, anyway. If she went down to the bar for a snack and then for a walk in the town that would give her the chance to pick up a few necessities and give her some fresh air at the same time. Sally picked up her handbag, locked the door of her room and put the key in her pocket. She trotted down both flights of stairs and walked into the bar. As a resident, she could have eaten her lunch in the hotel's restaurant. But she fancied something lighter, less formal – just a snack. And perhaps a glass of shandy.

She was delighted to see Anna serving behind the bar. 'They keep you busy,' Sally said as Anna approached her.

'Yes, they do. They exploit me shamefully. I have to lick the kitchen floor clean and black-lead the grate before I'm allowed to go to bed at night. Then it's up at four to get water from the well and polish the coal.' Anna's eyes shone mischievously.

Sally laughed. 'What bar snacks are you doing? Could I have a sandwich? I've been working all morning and I'm starving.'

'We offer a huge selection of freshly cut sandwiches and rolls,' Anna said formally, offering Sally a menu. 'In fact, you name it and we slap it between two pieces of bread. Let me get you a drink while you're deciding.'

'Thanks,' said Sally. 'I'll have a pint of lager shandy. And a chicken salad sandwich, if it isn't too much trouble.'

'Anything for you,' said Anna huskily, suddenly serious. 'Shall I come to your room after I've finished work, tonight?'

'There's nothing I'd like more.' Sally smiled.

Anna set her drink down in front of her and briefly rested her hand on top of Sally's. 'One chicken salad sandwich coming up.' Anna disappeared behind the bar into the kitchen.

Sally took a long swallow of her shandy. Bliss. She looked around the bar, its dark wooden beams and panelling decorated by horse-brasses and sepia prints of old Arundel. A huge copper warming-pan was suspended over one window and sheaves of fragrant hops hung in swathes above the bar. A couple of elderly men sat quietly on an old church pew in one corner, enjoying a companionable game of dominoes. A pair of hikers noisily consumed cold beer at the bar, their thirst boosted by exercise.

'There you go,' said Anna, setting Sally's sandwich in front of her.

Sally ate quickly and finished her drink. She nodded her goodbye to Anna and went out into the street. The sun made her squint; she wished she had got her sunglasses from the car. She headed towards the shopping centre. The midday sun beat down, bleaching colour from the town and bathing it with warmth. She found a branch of Boots and wandered round its aisles, stocking up on toiletries. She threw a pack of disposable razors and some shaving foam into her wire basket; she did not want to get stubbly.

She hit M & S and bought a multi-pack of cotton knickers. That ought to keep her going. She picked out a couple of bright T-shirts and a long printed skirt. If she washed out the clothes she had on, that ought to be enough.

She passed a kiosk selling ice-cream. A thread of smiling children queued at the small window, waiting to be served.

Sally joined the queue. She eyed the list of available flavours greedily as she waited, and finally selected a double cornet in chocolate chip and toffee ripple and carried it carefully over to a nearby bench. She sat down beside a mother with two small children in a buggy, both of whom were messily enjoying ice-creams. Pink smears of melted strawberry goo embellished their happy faces. Their mother looked on indulgently, tissues at the ready.

Sally finished her treat and licked her fingers clean. She gathered up her purchases and headed back to The Green Man.

The pub's interior was pleasantly cool after the heat outside. She trotted up the two flights of stairs and let herself into her room. The bed had been made, she noticed. She had forgotten how unobtrusively efficient they were here. She took her carrier bag into the bathroom and arranged her new toiletries on the glass shelf above the wash basin. She really needed to shave her pussy again, she reflected as she unpacked the razors and foam. She'd do it now; have a shower to cool her down and get it out of the way. She stripped off her clothes and dumped them into the bath. She'd give them a rinse later. She turned on the shower, climbed into the cubicle, and stood under the steamy jet. She fiddled with the temperature control until the water was coming out tepid, then stood still, allowing the water to cool her.

Sally turned off the water and stepped out of the shower. She positioned herself in front of the full-length mirror and squirted a big blob of shaving foam onto her hand. It smelt lemony and fresh. Sally smeared the white cream over her pubic mound and lips, then rinsed her fingers under the tap and took a razor out of the pack. Shaving her triangle was easy. The blade slid easily over her skin, removing the stubbly hairs. Very quickly, she was smooth again. But shaving herself underneath proved more difficult. She couldn't see what she was doing in the mirror and she didn't want to nick herself.

She hobbled into the other room, careful not to drop foam

on the carpet. She fetched the chair and placed it in front of the mirror. By putting her foot on the chair, she managed to see her pussy in the mirror. She used her fingers to stretch the skin as she carefully shaved each labia, then wet her new flannel and wiped away the remaining foam. She stroked the naked skin. Smooth. Satisfied that she had done a thorough job, she dried herself and applied some moisturiser to the newly shaved area. She didn't want to get a rash.

Sally carried the chair back into the other room and set it down in front of the table. She rummaged through her carrier bags for a new pair of pants. Deciding to go without a bra, she put on one of the new T-shirts and the skirt. The clothes were comfortable and the soft cotton skirt felt good against her skin. She settled herself in front of her computer, put on her reading glasses and began working.

She must have been writing for hours. It was growing dusk. She had taken off her watch when she had had a shower, so she had no idea of the time. She went into the bathroom, stretching her stiff limbs as she walked, emptied her bladder and flushed the toilet. She retrieved her watch from the side of the sink: ten to seven. Deciding to sleep for an hour then go down for dinner, Sally took off her clothes and folded them on to the chair. She climbed under the duvet and gave herself up to the cool, soft embrace of the bed, closing her eyes.

Her door opened; the sound of the creaking hinges breaking into her slumber. She lifted her head; it felt so heavy. She was still tired. A woman stood in the open doorway, silhouetted against the light that poured in from the hallway. Light shone on the woman's curly hair, making it look like an unruly halo. It was Anna. Sally smiled weakly. She was so tired; her limbs felt like lead. She could hardly keep her eyes open.

The door closed, its hinges protesting noisily as Anna pushed it shut. It was suddenly darker in the room; Sally was momentarily blind. Anna climbed into the bed with her, and they kissed. Sally buried her face in the wild hair. It smelled sweet, of vanilla and spice – like a cake or an old-fashioned rice pudding. She inhaled deeply, half intoxicated by the exotic scent.

Anna enfolded Sally in her arms. She pulled her close, rocking her gently, smoothed Sally's hair and planted a single chaste kiss on her forehead. Sally looked up at Anna's beautiful face, reached up with one hand and pulled Anna down to her for a kiss. She tasted Anna's sweet lips and wiggled her tongue between them to claim her mouth.

Anna sat up. Sally's eyes were becoming accustomed to the darkness now. She watched as Anna began undoing the front of the long white nightgown she was wearing. It seemed to fasten with narrow ribbons, Sally noticed. It must be antique. Anna's chestnut curls tumbled down her back, almost to her waist. She shrugged off the nightgown and sat before Sally, naked, with her breasts chastely concealed behind her plentiful hair. Sally hadn't realised how long Anna's hair was, the previous night. She seemed even more beautiful than yesterday, if that were possible.

Sally pulled the pretty waitress on top of her. Anna's abundant hair fell over them both, covering them like a thick blanket. It tickled Sally's skin as Anna wriggled on top of her. It fell in Sally's face, filling her nostrils with its pungent aroma. She wrapped her arms around the woman above her, realising that there was a fragility, an insubstantial quality about Anna's body that she had not noticed before. Perhaps her excitement the previous night had clouded her perceptions. But that didn't seem right.

She was cold; a biting chill in the air made her tremble. She reached behind Anna and flicked up the duvet, covering them both. She was cold to her marrow. The last time she had felt like this, she had had the flu. She snuggled under the covers and held Anna tight, trying to keep warm.

It was wonderful in Anna's arms. Sally felt calm and safe, all worries gone; she did not think she had ever felt so secure. She felt strong, powerful, and grounded, somehow. Nothing bad could happen to her while she was safe in Anna's arms. She could hear something; she cocked her head to one side, straining her ears. It was coming from outside. The sound drifted in through the open window. She could not identify it, yet it was familiar. And it was getting louder. No, getting closer: it was horses' hooves, the clatter of a team of horses trotting over cobbles. Now it was directly outside, under the window. And there was a commotion in the yard, raised voices and the thump of luggage being unloaded and whinnying horses. It didn't make sense, but it didn't seem to matter. Nothing mattered while she was safe in Anna's arms.

'I want you to remember something,' said Anna, her voice hissing with urgency. 'It's important.'

Sally nodded. She gazed into Anna's broad face; her eyes seemed to burn into Sally's soul.

'You have passion in your soul. You must listen to it. It will guide you. You know what you want and you must pursue it without fear. You already have everything you need; listen to your heart and don't leave things to chance.' Anna's eyes seemed to glow with the passion of her words. Sally stared at her. The hairs on the back of her neck stood on end. Goose pimples formed across her shoulders and chest.

'You're talking about Liz, aren't you?' Sally asked. 'But how do you know? I've never even mentioned her to you.'

'Because I know what is in your heart. Let your heart and soul speak to you and act on it. And don't be afraid; you have nothing to fear now.' How did Anna know about Liz and her dilemma? Had Sally spoken in her sleep? Or was Anna telepathic? Sally couldn't make any sense of it, but somehow it didn't matter. She was safe and relaxed in Anna's arms, and she trusted her. She would do what Anna suggested. It made perfect sense; declaring her feelings to Liz was the only way she would ever find out if the other woman returned them. And she was not afraid now.

'OK, I promise I will,' she said dreamily.

Anna rocked her, cooed softly as she might to an infant she was coaxing to sleep. Sally closed her eyes. Anna's arms soothed her, reassured her. She drifted into sleep.

TWELVE

Sally was woken by a tap on her door. She sat up and rubbed her eyes. Where was she? What time was it? Her confusion passed quickly. Of course, she was in her hotel room in Arundel and she had been having a nap before dinner. But it was dark now; she could see the full moon hanging like a silver pendant in the velvet sky outside her window. Her door creaked open slowly and Anna crept inside, carrying a tray.

'Hi,' she said. 'Did I wake you?'

'Yes,' Sally replied. 'What time is it? I feel as though I've been asleep for hours. I'm all disorientated.'

'It's quarter to eleven. We've just got rid of our last dinner guest. When you didn't come down to eat, I assumed you'd got absorbed in your work. Are you hungry? I've brought you a sandwich.' She set the tray down on the bedside cabinet and sat on the edge of the bed.

'Yes, I am hungry.' Sally looked at Anna. Her head felt thick, her thoughts slow. She wasn't properly awake yet; that was it. She shook her head, chasing away the dreams.

'Weren't you here earlier?' Sally asked. 'I thought you were.

And have you had your hair cut?' She fingered Anna's lustrous curls.

Anna smiled at her. 'No, I haven't had my hair cut,' she said, laughing. She shook her head, making her chestnut mane of curls quiver. 'I've been downstairs all night, working my legs off. We had a party in from the local Rotary Club and they all thought the proper way to attract my attention was to snap their fingers and shout "Miss." One of them even pinched my bottom.'

Sally laughed. 'I must have been dreaming,' she said. 'Only it seemed so real. I thought you were in bed with me.' She looked at Anna and smiled. Somehow, being with Anna seemed to make her feel safe and secure. She couldn't explain it. She knew she was not falling for Anna, so it couldn't be love clouding her judgement. Although she had enjoyed their dalliance, both of them knew it was only a temporary arrangement. So why did she feel so content in the younger woman's company? It was a mystery, but a pleasant one.

'I'm starving,' said Sally. 'I hope you brought me a big sandwich.'

'I made you a hot beef baguette with horseradish. And a slice of pear and almond tart for afters, and a bottle of mineral water. In fact, I brought enough for two. We were so busy tonight, I didn't get around to having my meal. So if you move over, I'll get out of these horrible clothes and join you. And I'll promise not to spill crumbs in the bed.'

Anna unbuttoned her blouse, and stripped it off, then unzipped her skirt and stepped out of it. She unhooked her bra and peeled it away from her ripe breasts; she whirled the garment round her head a couple of times, gyrating her hips like a lap dancer, and draped it over one of the bedposts. She slid her knickers down to her knees then shook her legs until they fell to her ankles.

Sally could not tear her eyes away from this impromptu striptease. She looked on lustfully as Anna undressed. Anna bent down and retrieved her pants. She threw them up in the air and headed them into a corner, like a footballer scoring a goal. Sally laughed and shifted over in the bed, making room for Anna.

Anna slid in beside her. 'Oh it's all warm in here,' she said. 'Let's eat. I'm starving and you must be too.'

They sat up in bed. Anna put the tray on the duvet between them, opened the mineral water and poured them a glass each. She passed Sally her sandwich and a linen napkin from the restaurant.

'Very posh,' observed Sally. 'A paper serviette would have done.'

'Wash your mouth out,' said Anna, laughing. 'This is a very select establishment. I'll have you know, we are in the Egon Ronay guide. Only the best is good enough for our guests.'

'I've noticed. I've never stayed at a hotel with such personal service before,' Sally teased.

'Wait until you get the bill,' said Anna dryly.

Sally laughed out loud; almost spitting out the mouthful of sandwich she was chewing.

They ate in silence for a while. The tender roast beef and creamy, peppery horseradish seemed to melt in Sally's mouth. The crispy, fresh baguette crunched as she bit into it and smelt of yeast. The pear and almond tart was delicate and spicy. Its crisp pastry base was rich with butter.

'I feel better, now,' said Sally, wiping her mouth on her napkin. 'I didn't realise how hungry I was.'

'Me, too,' agreed Anna. 'But now I am all fuelled up, ready for a hard night's work.'

'You do take customer satisfaction seriously, don't you?' Sally observed wickedly.

Anna put the tray back on the bedside table. She snuggled down under the covers, pulling Sally with her, then wrapped her arms around Sally and kissed her. Sally caressed Anna's shoulders and upper back, fingers sliding over smooth skin. The younger woman dipped her head and kissed Sally at the base of her throat. Sally nuzzled against the tousled hair, and the wiry texture tickled her lips. She inhaled deeply: coconut shampoo. Anna rolled on top of her.

'Now I know I was dreaming earlier,' Sally said. 'The other Anna was half your size.'

'She probably didn't eat up all her greens when she was a little girl, like I did.'

'With my mother, it was crusts,' said Sally. 'She told me if I ate my crusts, my hair would curl.'

'Well, it's a bit wavy, I suppose,' said Anna, taking up a strand of Sally's hair and examining it.

'It's got what hairdressers politely refer to as "kink".' Sally laughed. 'Which is probably rather appropriate, in my case. You, on the other hand, must have eaten a lot of crusts.' She stroked Anna's bright hair and wound a long strand around one of her fingers, creating a ringlet.

'Nothing but,' Anna said. 'It was all they could afford and even then I had to compete with the dogs.'

'You're funny,' said Sally. She kissed Anna on the nose. 'And beautiful. You have incredible hair. I suppose you're going to tell me you hate it, aren't you?' she said, as Anna's face creased into a disapproving frown.

'You bet. It's frizzy, it takes hours to dry, and in the summer I almost die of heat exhaustion. It's like wearing a hat all the time. And what with the freckles – believe me, there was a time when I seriously considered walking around with a bag over my head.'

'Listen to me,' said Sally seriously, propping herself up on an elbow. 'You are beautiful. Your hair is glorious, vibrant, unique. And your skin is pale and clear and smooth. The freckles make you look impish. You're like a Pre-Raphaelite princess. I'd kill to look like you, and so would most women I know. Stop putting yourself down. Believe in yourself.' Sally gazed at Anna as she spoke, her face flushed with passion.

Anna's mouth fell open, then snapped shut. 'Nobody has ever called me beautiful before,' she said finally. She spoke quietly, almost embarrassed. 'Thank you.'

'Well, they should have. You are a lovely young woman and you deserve . . .' Sally's voice trailed away. She was suddenly ashamed of herself. Ashamed of using Anna, of sleeping with her when she knew that she'd be leaving soon and would probably never see her again. She had exploited Anna's vulnerability and generosity, she saw that now. She had been selfish.

'I deserve better than this? Better than sharing a bed with anonymous guests who regard me as just one more of the hotel's facilities? Better than a never-ending flow of one-night stands with people who I'll never see again? Is that what you meant?' Anna spoke coldly, dispassionately, no trace of anger or self-pity in her voice.

Sally leant forward and kissed her passionately on the mouth. 'Anna, I owe you an apology. I've just realised that I've taken advantage of your good nature and that's why I was lost for words a few seconds ago. Because I am ashamed of myself, not because I think you've got anything to be ashamed of. I think you are a wonderful, generous and loving young woman and you have a lot to offer. It was selfish of me to think that I could just have sex with you and then just go home. When I said you deserved better, I meant better than what I have to offer you. You deserve happiness and you deserve someone who will be able to return all that love you have inside you. And I hope you find it.'

Anna smiled. She picked up Sally's hand from where it lay on her chest and kissed the palm gently. 'Thank you,' she said, quietly. 'I wasn't offended and you have nothing to apologise for. You've helped me to realise that I do want what you said and that I'm not going to find it this way. I never felt special before, never felt as though I had anything to offer to someone else, except perhaps sex. So thank you for opening my eyes. And I know you'll find what you are looking for, too. Let the passion in your soul guide you and don't be afraid and everything will be all right.'

Sally sat up. It couldn't be true: she must have imagined it. 'What did you say?' she asked.

'I said, let your heart guide you and ignore your fears. What's wrong?'

'I think I'm having déjà-vu,' said Sally. 'The Anna in my dream told me that, too. Almost exactly the same words. It's weird. I'm watching for your head to start spinning around, now.'

'I'm not psychic. I can't read minds or bend forks or anything.' Anna laughed. 'There's a rational explanation.'

'And what is that rational explanation?' Sally's voice was squeaky and strained. This was weird: she felt out of her depth.

'The Anna in your dream was your subconscious speaking to you. You already know what you need to do, but sometimes we need a sort of kick-start. It takes a funny dream, or a memory, or another person to really help you get in touch with what you knew all along. That's all: your subconscious used me in your dream as a way of getting you back in touch with your feelings.'

'I can accept that,' said Sally, nodding her head as she considered Anna's explanation. 'Yes. In fact, that makes perfect sense. But what I can't get my head around is how you happen to say exactly the same words to me. Now that is impossible.'

'No, it isn't,' said Anna reassuringly. 'I'm a pretty good judge of character – at least, I like to think so. And on top of that, I have a sort of knack. Mum says it's a gift that runs in the family, but that all seems a bit too *Twilight Zone* to me. I prefer to think of it as being very empathetic. I sort of know how people feel, almost like I can see inside them. When I am close to someone, I just seem to know what they are feeling. I haven't told you anything you didn't know; you had the answer yourself all along.'

'It still seems a bit spooky to me,' said Sally, 'but I sort of know what you mean. Sometimes I can sense how my friend Katie feels without her needing to tell me. It's like that, isn't it? Only you're a bit better at it than most people,'

'Exactly. At least, that's what I've always thought. But, right now, I think that what you need is a thoroughly good seeing-to.' Anna bent her head and kissed Sally's neck. She licked the hollow of her throat. She left a trail of butterfly kisses across Sally's collarbone, down the centre of her chest. She slithered down the bed until her head was level with Sally's breasts. She licked a finger and carefully wet each nipple. Then she blew on each strawberry bud, making them contract and peak.

Anna mouthed each nipple in turn, sucking and nibbling the swollen flesh. She ran her hands up and down Sally's sides, grazing her nails along the skin. Sally arched her back, thrusting her breasts into Anna's face. Anna teased Sally's engorged nipple, grasping it with her teeth and flicking her tongue over the puckered surface. She grasped its partner between thumb and forefinger, squeezing it, pulling it. She licked down Sally's breastbone, wetting the skin, then slid her tongue down the centre of Sally's abdomen. She circled the navel, dipping into the shallow dimple. Her tongue moved ever downwards towards its fragrant goal.

Anna shuffled lower; positioning herself between Sally's spread legs. She planted kisses all over Sally's rounded belly, her bare mons. She kissed the inside of her partner's thighs, moving progressively downwards. She extended her tongue and licked along the sensitive furrow between pussy and thigh, up the valley between her buttocks. She licked and sucked around the perimeter of Sally's damp cleft, drawing each naked labia into her hot mouth, then ran her fingernails along the length of Sally's sensitive inner thighs.

Sally wriggled. 'That's so good,' she murmured.

Anna dipped her tongue into her lover's sweet honeypot, as delicately as a sparrow drinking from a garden birdbath. She closed her eyes, relishing the taste of Sally's sweet nectar. She parted the plump lips and plundered Sally's sodden slit with her mouth. She pressed her companion's legs wider apart and lapped passionately at her hole, then plunged her tongue into the muscular entrance, spreading the tight sphincter.

The pungent aroma of sex perfumed the air. Sally's heart hammered in her chest. Prickles of pleasure washed over her as Anna's tongue swirled inside her. The younger woman reached up with one hand and grabbed a pillow. She pulled it towards her, all the while continuing to pleasure Sally with her mouth, then grasped Sally's hips and lifted her up until her bottom was a few inches above the bed. She slid the fluffy pillow under Sally's buttocks, tilting her pelvis upwards.

Anna now had total access to Sally. The pillow raised Sally's arse off the bed; a glistening bead of moisture trickled down the cleft between her buttocks. Anna dipped her head and licked it away. She nuzzled her face between the creamy orbs. She licked along the length of Sally's nether crack and circled her pointed tongue against the puckered opening. Her roving tongue moved upwards, poking into Sally's wet hole; then Anna licked along the slippery slit. She brushed her mouth against the hard pink pearl of Sally's clit, teasing it. She slid a finger into her partner's lubricated rear hole, easing it past the tight ring of muscle which gripped it, and pushed two more fingers inside Sally's tight cunt, claiming it.

She fastened her mouth over Sally's engorged clit, sucking the taut pellet into her mouth. Sally moaned softly, unconsciously parting her legs wider. She sank back into the pillow and closed her eyes. Her nipples were erect and prominent. A scarlet rash flushed her throat and chest, standing out against the milky skin. She pressed her heels down into the mattress, tensing her thighs.

Anna's mouth felt hot against her flesh, sliding smoothly over Sally's juice-slicked skin. Anna sucked hard on Sally's clit, flicking across its sensitive surface with her tongue as she did so. Slowly, she finger-fucked Sally, sliding her fingers sensuously in and out. Her hand and mouth moved in perfect synchronisation. She played Sally like a virtuoso, instinctively knowing when to make her caresses soft and fleeting, or strong and deep.

Sally was panting, light-headed. Images of Anna and Liz and her recent dream floated in her mind. In her belly, the insistent beat of imminent orgasm throbbed and grew. Her thighs trembled as she dug her heels into the bed. Her pelvis was thrust forward, pressed into Anna's eager face. She arched her back and rocked her hips, rubbing her ripe clit hard against her lover's mouth.

She threw her arms above her head. Her sweaty hands found the rails of the brass bedstead and grasped them tightly. White-knuckled, she gripped the bedposts, making tendons stand out in her wrists and upper arms. She pressed her soles down into the yielding mattress, lifting her buttocks slightly off the bed, so she could grind her aching cunt hard into Anna's mouth. Pleasure exploded in her belly, bursting at the base of her spine; she drew in a long rush of air. Tingles of ecstasy spread out from her nipples, and a tidal wave of delight spread through her limbs. The hairs on the back of her neck stood up and her upper lip curled, exposing her teeth. Her cunt pulsed around Anna's fingers; gripping them tightly.

Gradually, her strained muscles softened and she caught her breath. She opened her eyes and looked down at Anna, still busy between her parted legs.

'Stop, stop!' she said, as Anna continued to lick her sensitive clit. 'I can't bear it; it's just too much.'

Anna planted a single kiss on Sally's damp pussy and crawled up the bed on her elbows, like a commando on a secret mission. She smiled. 'That's the first time I've ever made a woman beg for mercy!' she said, laughing.

'But not the last, I'm sure,' said Sally, stroking Anna's cheek. 'Now let me see if I can return the compliment.' She rolled on top of Anna, pinning her to the bed. She laced her hands through Anna's bountiful hair, running the glossy ringlets through her fingers. She kissed the girl's smooth forehead, and the freckles dotted across Anna's broad nose, then nuzzled her mouth against the spot where Anna's jaw met her ear. She inhaled deeply, drinking in the scent. The intoxicating aroma which filled her nostrils seemed to embody Anna, to capture her essence somehow. Sally wished she could bottle it.

Their lips met. They enjoyed a long, slow, deep kiss.

'You taste of me,' murmured Sally, as she broke away. She bit the point of Anna's shoulder, gently nibbling at the pale skin. She licked along the curve of the girl's collarbone, wetting her, then moved her attention downwards, peppering Anna's chest with kisses. She licked the upper slopes of Anna's full breasts and circled her tongue around the perimeter of each areola.

Anna's hands rested on Sally's shoulders. She cooed and purred softly as Sally's mouth worked on her body. Her green eyes gazed down fondly at Sally's bobbing face. Sally licked Anna's soft right nipple, circling the tiny flat disk with her tongue and coaxing it into erection. When the pink bud stood out proudly against Anna's white skin, she sucked the raspberry protuberance into her mouth and nibbled it.

Anna arched her back appreciatively and Sally transferred her mouth to the other nipple, lavishing it with the same skilled attention she had given its partner. It quickly became erect, deepening to a rich crimson colour. Sally leant up on her elbows and surveyed her handiwork. She fingered the prominent buds, rolling them between finger and thumb. She pulled on them, gently at first, then more firmly. She twisted them, then squeezed the rosy teats harder, increasing her intensity as Anna's enthusiastic sighs and moans betrayed her enjoyment. She dipped her head and bit each nipple in turn, making Anna squirm with delight.

Sally slithered down the bed until her face was poised above her partner's crotch. She gave both nipples a final squeeze and slid her hands down Anna's toned body. She buried her face in

Anna's pubic triangle, relishing the heady fragrance trapped in the dense curls. She sucked on the damp hair, caught a few tufts between her teeth and pulled on it playfully, before slithering her tongue down the slippery valley between the girl's hairy lips and darting it into the moist depression that was Anna's opening. She devoured Anna's cunt, lavishing attention on the crinkled folds that concealed her tiny clit.

Anna reached down and grasped the back of both thighs. She pulled her knees up towards her chest and held them there so her pelvis rotated forwards, tilting upwards into Sally's face. Sally cupped one of Anna's spread buttocks in each hand and pressed her mouth against the rosy cleft. She worked the girl's clit with her mouth, squeezing it between her lips, sucking on it hard, flicking it with her tongue.

Anna tilted her head back, stretching her neck. Her nipples stood out like ripe strawberries. She thrashed against the pillow, tangling her hair. She pulled her knees closer to her chest and began rocking on her curved spine, setting up a delightful friction between her clit and Sally's mouth. Her heartbeat was a throbbing tattoo of excitement and her swaying hips moved with the rhythm of her urgency, crushing her aching vagina against Sally's face.

A trickle of sweat ran down between Anna's breasts. Her pussy contracted, and the bead in Sally's mouth began to twitch and dance. Anna's body tensed; she let out a strangled sob. Sally sucked hard on the girl's rigid clit, massaging it with her tongue as she did so. Anna ground her spasming cunt into Sally's face, her body trembling. Sally massaged the girl's buttocks, circling her hands as she mouthed Anna's fanny.

Slowly, Anna's muscles uncoiled. She released her grip on her thighs and lowered her legs; pushing her heels into the mattress. She leant up on her elbows and beckoned to Sally. Sally crawled up the bed and lay down beside Anna.

'That was incredible,' said Anna weakly, 'but I'm sorry to be a killjoy. These late nights have been taking their toll on me –

I really must go to sleep now.' She kissed Sally affectionately on the lips, stroked her hair.

'Of course,' Sally agreed, suddenly ashamed for having interfered with Anna's work, 'I'm tired myself. Goodnight.' She closed her eyes and took some deep breaths. Anna's warm body was snuggled against her side. She felt the edges of her awareness dissolving. She was drifting away. Her body felt light; weightless. Her mind softened, relaxed. The room around her seemed to melt. A soothing silence hung in the air.

Anna sat up; her abundant locks falling around her, covering her breasts. Her fragile shoulders seemed to be trembling, and a thin sheen of sweat filmed her brow. Sally thought she saw the flicker of pain passing across her delicate face. Anna gripped Sally's upper arm; her bony fingers digging into the flesh.

'Don't be afraid,' she said. 'Follow your heart with passion and courage and all will be well. Promise me!' she hissed.

'What's wrong, Anna?' Sally said, confused. Her friend looked different, somehow, unwell. Her usually muscular body seemed sort of shrunken and her smiling face was clouded. 'Are you ill?' she asked, concerned.

'Never mind,' Anna said urgently. 'You must seize your dream. Make it happen. Do you understand me?'

'Yes, I will. I promise,' said Sally, and she knew she meant it. Something was different, though she couldn't place it. A moment ago, Anna had been strong, healthy and vibrant. Now she seemed weak, ill. Like in Sally's dream earlier. She was dreaming again: that was it. And it was her subconscious speaking to her; that was what Anna had said. She was dreaming again. That was all. She snuggled in closer to Anna and let her body relax.

Anna was gone when Sally woke up. She scrabbled for her watch on the bedside table; five past nine, already. She'd miss breakfast if she didn't hurry. She leapt out of bed and dashed into the bathroom. She got herself ready hurriedly. The dining room was practically empty when she walked in. Just a couple of stragglers finishing their coffee.

Mrs Lee popped her head round the kitchen door and smiled.

'Am I too late for breakfast?' Sally asked anxiously. She was starving.

'Of course not,' Anna's mother replied reassuringly. 'Have some cereal and I'll get it ready for you. I'll bring you some coffee straight out.' Sally thanked her and helped herself to muesli at the buffet table.

'There you are,' said the landlady, setting down the coffee pot on the table. 'How's the book coming along?'

'Very well, I'm pleased with it.' She smiled proudly.

'It will be nice to see our Anna brought back to life in a book,' Mrs Lee reflected.

'Anna?' Sally gulped. 'I thought the ghost was called Bella – that's what you told me, last time I was here.'

'She was. At least, she was called Annabelle and everybody else called her Bella. In the family, she was always Anna, though. We named our Anna after her. It's quite a coincidence, really, because people who have seen the ghost say that there's a strong resemblance between them. Are you all right?' Mrs Lee asked anxiously. 'You've gone all pale.'

'I'm fine,' Sally replied. 'I think somebody just walked over my grave.' She smiled up at the landlady and poured herself a cup of coffee with shaking hands.

'I'll bring your breakfast in two ticks,' said Mrs Lee, heading for the kitchen.

Sally couldn't take it in. Although she wrote about paranormal phenomena, she was not sure that she believed in ghosts. She could hardly believe that the woman who had come to her last night was the dead spirit of Anna's ancestor. On the other hand, whoever the woman was, she hadn't been Anna, either. Not the modern Anna, anyway; there had been too many differences for that. The girl who had spent the last two nights between her sheets was athletic and strong. Yet the girl in the dream, if that's what it was, was thin and sickly. And her hair was longer and not so healthy looking. But that didn't make her a ghost did it? Sally had convinced herself that she had been dreaming. But had she?

On the other hand, why would the Anna in her dream be so different? If she were dreaming about the landlady's daughter, surely her imagination would recreate her exactly as she was? Bella had consumption, what we'd call tuberculosis. That would make her wasted and pale, wouldn't it? How could her subconscious concoct a detail like that? She could accept that the unconscious part of her mind might make her dream about the ghost. After all, Sally was writing about her, so the subject was fresh in her mind. But she hadn't known there was any link between the two women, apart from the obvious fact that they were related, so why should she give the ghost Anna's face?

It didn't make sense. Yet she still couldn't believe that she had been visited by a spirit from the other side. So how could she explain it? She was certain that the Lees hadn't told her that the ghost was called Anna. All her research notes had the name of Bella; that was what she remembered. And they hadn't described the ghost, either. No one in the family had ever seen her personally. She always appeared to hotel guests, or once to some workmen doing alterations. She had interviewed some of these people, but none of them had said the spirit looked like Anna.

She ran her fingers through her hair. She wasn't ready to believe that she had witnessed an apparition, yet she was unsettled by it all. She'd be much happier if she could find a logical explanation. She drummed her fingers on the table, trying to make sense of it all. The dream had come from her subconscious mind. Sometimes that part of our brain responded to things which our conscious mind had forgotten, or suppressed. Just because she couldn't remember being told that the family called the ghost Anna, that didn't mean that she had never known it. It was quite conceivable that they had told her, had mentioned it in passing, but she hadn't written it down and, over time, she had forgotten it. And something about being back at the hotel and intimately involved with Anna, coupled with her dilemma about Liz, had combined to create the dream. Yes, that made sense.

She felt better now she had a rational explanation for her dream. It was her mind playing tricks, that was all. Mixing up the two Annas with her anxiety about pursuing Liz. And the modern Anna had told her that the girl in the dream had been her heart speaking to her, hadn't she? That was logical too. She knew that she really wanted to be with Liz, only she'd been too nervous to admit it. In the past, fear of rejection had always stopped her from acting. But not now. She was going to listen to what her heart told her. She was going to take control.

How ironic that she had spent all those years frantically trying to keep control of her life, trying to keep so many balls in the air that she didn't know which direction to run in next. She felt so much more relaxed, now that she had stopped trying to be perfect. She could start making informed choices at last. She wanted to be with Liz more than she had ever wanted anything and she knew, finally, what she must do.

She ate her breakfast quickly and dashed upstairs to pack. It didn't take her long to put all her recent purchases into a carrier bag and pack up her laptop. She carried her luggage down the stairs and loaded it into the car. She took her credit card out of her handbag and went back into the hotel. She rang the bell at the reception desk and waited for service.

Anna poked her head round the open office door into the reception area. She grinned at Sally and stationed herself behind the desk. 'Did you sleep well? You looked so peaceful when I got up, I didn't have the heart to wake you,' said Anna. 'I hope you didn't miss breakfast?'

'No, I didn't,' Sally said, smiling. 'Your mother took care of me. I'd like to check out. Can you sort out my bill?'

'No problem.' Anna pressed some buttons on the computer

terminal in front of her and waited for the bill to print. 'I've really enjoyed having you stay. I'll miss you.'

'And I'll miss you,' Sally agreed. 'I hope you find someone, Anna. I really do. You are a very special young woman.'

'Stop, or you'll make me blush!' Anna exclaimed. She fanned her face with a leaflet. 'I start at university in October. I know I'll be a bit older than most people, but I've always been a late starter. After A-levels I just couldn't decide what I wanted to do, so my gap year ended up being two. Who knows – maybe I'll meet someone there.' She handed Sally her finished bill, picked up the credit card from the desk and swiped it through the machine.

'I'm sure you will. They'll probably be queuing up for the privilege.'

Anna tore off the completed credit card slip and handed it over. Sally signed it.

'And you?' asked Anna. 'Are you going home to talk to Liz?'

'I am, actually,' Sally admitted. 'I've finally realised it's what I need to do. She might say no, but at least I'll know where I stand. And she's worth the risk.'

'I've got a hunch that she won't say no,' Anna spoke quietly, mysteriously almost. 'I don't think you've got anything to worry about. If you follow your heart, you'll do OK.'

'Your mother told me you were named after the ghost. I hadn't realised.'

Anna blushed. 'That's right. It's a bit embarrassing. People who've seen her say we look alike, too, only she was scrawny and ill-looking whereas I am built like a brick outhouse. Nothing ethereal about me.'

'I don't know,' said Sally. 'There's a sort of spiritual quality about you, isn't there? The empathetic bit you were telling me about – isn't that ethereal?'

'I guess so,' she admitted. 'I hadn't thought of it that way. She was supposed to have that too, apparently. Perhaps if I'd been born four hundred years ago, I'd have been a witch.'

'You certainly bewitched me,' said Sally seriously, looking into Anna's green eyes.

'I'll walk you to your car,' said Anna. She followed Sally out into the courtyard and stood beside the car while Sally climbed into her seat and started the engine.

Sally wound down the window. 'Thank you. For everything. You've given me more than you can possibly imagine,' said Sally.

Anna smiled and poked her head in through the car window. 'And so have you,' she said simply. 'And I won't forget it.' She cupped one hand round the back of Sally's neck, pulled her face close and kissed her deeply. 'Now go, before I cry.'

Sally turned her car and drove out of the yard.

THIRTEEN

On the outskirts of Arlington, Sally pulled into a layby. She rummaged in her handbag and fished out her mobile phone. She switched it on and punched in Katie's number.

'Hi, it's me,' she said brightly when her friend answered.

'Sally,' wailed her friend and then broke into incoherent sobs.

'What's the matter, sweetheart? Tell me what's wrong,' Sally soothed.

Katie sniffed. She took some deep breaths and blew her nose. 'Jo's not talking to me. She won't even come to the phone. I told her we'd had sex and I thought she'd understand. But I made a mess of it and she got angry. She didn't even give me a chance to explain it properly. She just ran off.' She burst into tears again, strident sobs which hurt Sally's ears.

'Where have you been?' Katie asked tearfully. 'I've been ringing you for days. I've left messages at the cottage and on your mobile. I must have tried fifty times. I even rang you in London. I needed you.'

'I'm really sorry,' said Sally. 'I feel terrible. I had no idea. I've been in Arundel. I spent a couple of days at The Green Man, and I've had my mobile switched off. I haven't been back to the cottage yet'

'I don't know what to do, Sally. I want her back but I don't know what to do. She won't talk to me.' Katie spoke in a small, quavering voice.

Sally had never known her to sound so upset, so uncertain. And it was her fault. She'd wanted to go to bed with Katie so she'd ignored the possible consequences. Of course Jo had been angry: how could they have thought she wouldn't be? It was Sally's fault that she wasn't speaking to Katie, her fault that her best friend was distraught and hurt. She'd have to make it right for Katie. It was the least she could do. Katie had bailed her out so many times, now it was probably time she returned the favour. Especially as she had caused this mess in the first place.

'Don't worry, Katie. Take a couple of aspirin and go to bed. I'm sure things will be OK. She'll calm down and you'll sort things out. I'll come over and see you, later this afternoon. Will you be all right until I get there?'

'Yes,' said Katie quietly. She sniffed. 'I've been in such a state, but I feel a bit better now you're back.'

'I'm really sorry I wasn't here when you needed me, Katie. I shouldn't have let you down. I'll see you in a couple of hours. I just have to do something first.' She rang off and tossed the phone back into her bag. She did a U-turn and drove back towards Brighton at top speed, hoping that she didn't get spotted driving over the limit. Fortunately, police patrol cars were pretty thin on the ground in this part of Sussex.

Twenty minutes later she was driving along Brighton's seafront, keeping her eyes peeled for a vacant parking meter. She spotted one and slid into the space quickly, much to the annoyance of the driver in the car in front of her, who had also had his eye on it. She locked the car and fumbled in her bag for twenty pences, ignoring the hail of abuse and eloquent hand gestures that the motorist was directing at her. She loaded up the meter, smiled sweetly at him and dashed off in the direction of Jo's family restaurant. She knew it was in Marine Parade, although she wasn't sure of the exact address. She had parked a couple of blocks away, so she walked briskly along the seafront.

She looked at her watch. It was just after eleven; the restaurant might not even be open. At least it was before the lunchtime rush, so Jo would not be too busy to speak to her. Assuming that she was prepared to speak to her, in the first place. What a mess! She had not thought twice about going to bed with Katie and now her best friend was at home in tears. How could she have been so selfish? Katie had assured her that Jo would understand, but Sally shouldn't have listened, shouldn't have let her friend put her relationship in danger. She would make Jo listen, make her realise how much Katie loved her and how sorry she was.

She spotted the restaurant a couple of doors away and she quickened her step. Carey's was on the first floor of one of the many Regency-style houses that looked out over Brighton beach. Sally squinted through the window, looking for signs of life. They obviously were not open yet, but the lights were on and gentle jazz music was playing. She tried the door. It was locked. Damn! What should she do now? Knock? Wait until the place opened for lunch? If it did open for lunch – she was not sure.

She saw a figure coming through a door at the very back of the restaurant, carrying a wicker basket of cutlery. It was Jo. She set the basket down on the nearest table and began laying out place settings.

Sally rapped on the door with her knuckles. Jo looked up, and walked slowly towards her. Sally was surprised how nervous she was; she was practically holding her breath. She wanted this to go well. She couldn't afford to mess it up.

Jo slid the bolts back on the inside of the heavy glazed door, opened it a couple of inches and spoke to her through the crack. 'We don't open until 12.00,' she said. Her eyes widened as she recognised Sally. 'Oh, it's you. I suppose Katie sent you.

I've got nothing to say to her and I've got nothing to say to you, either.'

'I don't blame you for being angry with me, Jo,' Sally began. 'Katie didn't send me. In fact, she doesn't even know I am here. She's at home, sobbing her heart out.'

'Is she OK?' Jo asked; her trembling voice betrayed her concern.

'I've never seen her so upset,' Sally answered quietly. 'She loves you and she feels terrible that you won't talk to her. She wants to resolve things.'

'She should have thought of that before she leapt into the sack with you, shouldn't she? But I suppose old habits die hard.' Jo spat out the words.

'As I've said, you've every right to be angry. But why don't you talk to Katie? Sort things out.'

'I told you, I've got nothing to say to either of you.' She stared at Sally through the gap in the partially open door, her blue eyes cold and piercing.

Surely, she didn't mean it, thought Sally. She couldn't really mean that she was prepared to walk away from Katie and the relationship. No, she was angry. Deep down, she was as hurt and upset as Katie. It was all bravado, as much for Sally's benefit as her own. She couldn't bear to let either of them know that she really cared or she would dissolve into tears. She was hanging on to her self-control by her fingernails.

'You've surprised me, Jo, I must say,' said Sally. 'I'm disappointed.'

'Disappointed? What do you mean?'

'I thought you were different. I thought you were courageous. I thought you had intelligence and commitment and flexibility and understanding. I thought you had the qualities you would need to be Katie's lover. Because it's going to take someone really exceptional and special to be worthy of Katie. I don't know anyone more generous than her, or more loving, or more open. I thought you had what it took to make her happy. But I was mistaken. You're a coward, you're selfish, and you're so short-sighted I'm surprised you can see the end of your own nose. Katie hasn't betrayed you. She made a stupid mistake with someone she's been close to since you were in junior school. Of course, it was wrong, we shouldn't have done it and, for myself, I am sorrier about it than you can possibly imagine. But you shouldn't have run away. You shouldn't be hiding yourself here. You should be by Katie's side, trying to do whatever you need to do to sort this out. Because she's worth it. She's worth making the effort for and if you can't see that, then maybe you don't deserve her.'

Jo gripped the edge of the door, her knuckles turning white. She gazed open-mouthed at Sally; tears welled in her eyes. She blinked them away. 'Wait here,' she asked quietly. She shut the door and disappeared back into the restaurant. A moment later, she reappeared and let herself out.

'Let's go for a walk,' she said.

Sally sensed that Jo would talk in her own time. She hoped her outburst had not shocked the girl too much, but she had meant it. If Jo didn't have the sense to resolve this problem, she wasn't worthy of Katie. She strolled along beside the young woman, allowing her to dictate their route. They headed for the beach and walked out over the sand. Jo stooped and slipped her feet out of her sandals, then picked them up and walked on. Sally did the same and fell back in step with her.

The sand was warm. They snaked their way between families sunbathing on towels spread over the sand and children playing with buckets and spades. A dog ran along the water's edge, chasing the tide and barking. After a few more minutes, Jo headed towards a couple of empty deck chairs and sat down. Sally joined her.

'You're right,' she said finally. 'I am a coward. But I'm not frightened of commitment, or intimacy, or the sheer hard work it takes to make a relationship work. I've never met anyone like Katie. She's incredible and I felt . . . blessed, unbelievably lucky, when she showed an interest in me. But what scares me, terrifies me in fact, is having to live up to you. You're a tough act to follow and, quite honestly, I don't think I'm equipped to do it. And I was right, wasn't I? I obviously can't give her what she needs. She was back in your bed quick enough, wasn't she? And it will always be that way. As you said, you were lovers when I was still playing with dollies and wiping my nose on my sleeve. I just can't compete. I shouldn't even have tried.'

'No, you're wrong,' Sally assured her. 'We have been friends a long time, that's true. And we've also been lovers but, in a way, that's just been an extension of our friendship. If we were cut out to be together, don't you think we would be? It would be a damn sight easier, I can tell you. And I wouldn't have wasted the last seven years trying to find someone special if I thought Katie and I could make a proper couple. I don't know anyone who I admire more than her and anyone I meet has to live up to her, but she isn't "the one". She belongs to you. We shouldn't have had sex. It was wrong. It was weak and I was being selfish. I'm sorry and so is Katie. Talk to her.'

'I thought she was serious about me. She told me she loved me. And I believed her. Then, the minute my back's turned, she leaps between the sheets with you . . .' Jo sobbed. 'She can't really care about me if she could do that so easily. I feel so stupid.'

Sally rubbed Jo's arm, patted her shoulder. 'Life isn't as straightforward as we'd like to believe, Jo. She does love you and she is serious about you. We made a stupid and hurtful mistake and I can't justify it. Forgive her, and move on.'

'I wish I could believe you,' said Jo. Tears stained her face. Her lower lip trembled.

'You can. I know Katie better than anyone and she's never even come close to loving anyone like she does you. I'm quite jealous. In fact, seeing you two together has made me realise how much I'm missing, myself. I'm lonely, and having Katie available for a friendly shag whenever I needed one was stopping me from doing anything about it. I want what you two have got and I assure you that, if I were you, I'd go straight over to Katie's and I wouldn't leave until I had sorted things out. And I'm going straight over to see Liz at The Moonraker to tell her how I feel about her: because if there's even a chance that she and I can have what you two have got, I'm not letting the opportunity slip away again.' Sally was surprised by her own passion. But she meant it. She had driven back from Arundel to speak to Liz and, now this had happened, she was more determined than ever. She hoped she hadn't left it too late.

'Have you got your car with you?' Jo asked.

'Yes, it's parked down the road,' Sally confirmed.

'Can you take me to her?'

'Of course, I can. Come on.'

Katie lay on her unmade bed, a cold flannel pressed over her eyes. Her head ached. She had cried herself dry. Her eyes were reddened slits, which peered out from her swollen, blotchy face. Thank goodness Sally had rung her at last. Now at least she had been able to share her distress. She did not feel quite so alone. And Sally had said she would be over later. She was glad; she could do with a hug.

Sally had seemed certain that Jo would come round in the end, but Katie was not so sure. Jo wasn't even speaking to her — just how were they going to sort things out, if they weren't talking? She wasn't sure of anything any more. She had been convinced that she would be able to explain her infidelity in a way that Jo would accept, but she had been wrong. Terribly wrong. And now she didn't know what she would say, even if she could get Jo to listen. How could she have been so stupid?

The flannel over her eyes had become warm. She turned it over and took some deep breaths, to calm herself. She was exhausted, yet she knew she couldn't sleep. The dancing jangle of anxiety that had inhabited her stomach ever since Jo had run away made certain of that. She'd barely got any rest at all during the past few days. She'd cried and tossed restlessly and finally given up all pretence of sleeping and got up. She had prowled around the flat, watching late night TV and scoffing packet after packet of biscuits. She'd tried reading, but she couldn't maintain her attention span long enough to keep up with the plot. Her mind kept wandering and she found herself reading the same sentence over and over again. Finally she had thrown the book across the room, angry at her own self-pity.

And she hadn't been able to work, either. Duty assignments and lesson plans gathered dust on her desk. If she didn't sort herself out soon, she wouldn't be ready for the beginning of term. She was falling apart; she hardly recognised herself any more.

This morning, she had tried to rouse herself and get something done. She had forced herself to get under the shower, letting her tears mingle with the steaming water. She had washed and dried her hair and lavished moisturiser on the ruins of her face. Then she had wrapped herself up in her most comforting dressing gown and sat down at her desk. She gave up the pretence when her tears had run the ink on the exam paper she was marking.

Perhaps she could try ringing Jo again. She had rung several times a day since their argument, although Jo had never come to the phone. Now her parents were getting distinctly tetchy when they answered. She had better not call again, she decided. If word got around about her tearful phone calls, her reputation — as a professional and mature head teacher — would begin to suffer. But if she didn't ring, how would she cope? How could she fill the time until Sally arrived? She felt so alone.

The doorbell buzzed, jolting her out of her reverie. She took the flannel off her face and leant up on her elbows. Who could it be? She wasn't expecting anybody. It was certainly too early for Sally. Afternoon, she had said, and it couldn't be noon yet. She wouldn't answer it. She didn't want to see anybody. And she certainly did not want anyone to see her in this state. If she didn't answer, they'd go away.

The bell buzzed again, twice. They would go away soon; they would think she wasn't in. It rang again, four long peals, which told her the caller was not going to give up. She got out of bed and walked into the living room. She peered out of the window and tried to see her visitors, standing at the doorway below. She couldn't see them; she would have to poke her head out of the window to do that, and she didn't want them to know she was there. As she turned away, she noticed that there was a car parked on the gravel below. It was Sally's car. She dashed over to the entryphone and picked it up.

'Is that you, Sally?' she asked breathlessly.

'Yes, it's me,' the welcome voice replied.

'Sorry I didn't answer before. I'm not fit to be seen and I wasn't expecting you until later. Come up.' She pressed the switch to activate the electronic doorlatch and hung up. She heard feet walking up the stairs. Two sets of feet: Sally was not alone. Katie went out onto the landing. Sally reached the top of the stairs, with Jo a pace or two behind her.

'I've brought someone to see you,' Sally said simply.

Katie looked at Jo; she was as beautiful as ever. She looked tired; dark circles discoloured the skin around her eyes. And she looked as though she had been crying. Katie didn't know what to say. She was so relieved to see Jo. It must be a good sign that she had come, mustn't it? It must mean that she was prepared to talk at least. But her usual eloquence deserted her.

'Sorry,' they both said, at the same moment.

'I'm really sorry. I was stupid and selfish. I shouldn't have slept with Sally. It was wrong of me.' Katie's words came out in a rush.

'And I'm sorry, too,' said Jo. 'I shouldn't have overreacted. I was jealous. I thought Sally meant more to you than I did. I know I was wrong, now.' Jo rushed towards her, her arms spread wide. She practically fell against Katie's chest, resting her head against her lover's heaving bosom.

Katie wrapped her arms around Jo and pulled her close. She dipped her head, burying her face in the girl's blonde hair, drinking in the perfume. 'I've missed you,' she said, her voice husky with emotion.

'Me, too,' agreed Jo. 'I'm so glad Sally persuaded me to see sense.'

'Sally?' said Katie, looking up. In her excitement, she had almost forgotten that her friend was still there. 'You went to see Jo?'

'I figured it was my fault you had argued. I should never have put myself between the two of you, and I am sorry I did. So it was my responsibility to sort things out. It wasn't easy, but I managed to get Jo to accept that I'm not a threat to your relationship.'

'Thank you, Sally,' said Katie. 'I can't thank you enough.'

'All I did was put right the mess I had created. There's no need to thank me. Anyway, I have something else I have to do, now. I'll leave you two alone.'

'Thank you,' said Jo. She released Katie and held her arms open to Sally. The two women hugged. She kissed Sally's cheek, then Katie joined them and wrapped them both in an embrace.

'Thank you for bringing us back together,' she said. 'Now go and see Liz. Tell that woman how you feel about her and put her out of her misery.'

Sally extricated herself from their arms and trotted down the stairs. She let herself out of the flat and closed the door.

'Take me to bed,' whispered Jo into Katie's ear. 'I want to show you how much I love you.'

'But I look terrible,' said Katie, running a hand through her hair. 'I've been crying for days. I look like a Panda with eczema.'

'I've never seen you looking more beautiful,' said Jo, planting a kiss on the tip of her nose. She took her hand and led the way to the bedroom. Katie trailed after her, obedient as a child. Jo loosened the belt of Katie's dressing gown, pushed it back off her shoulders and let it fall to the ground. She ran her fingers down the slopes of Katie's shoulders, barely touching the skin. She skimmed her nails down the front of the chest, over the swell of Katie's breasts, and brushed her nipples. Jo wrapped one arm around her lover's waist and pulled her close, holding her tightly. Her free hand moved up to cup the nape of Katie's head and her fingers laced through Katie's hair.

They kissed. A long, slow, deep kiss that seemed to last for eternity. Jo's lips tasted sweet. A delicate, floral perfume rose from her skin. Katie's hands explored Jo's back. She traced the long line of Jo's spine, cupped her buttocks, and stroked her shoulders. Her tongue explored Jo's mouth, snaking through the parted lips, tasting her.

Jo broke away from her embrace and began undressing frantically. She tore open the buttons on the white blouse she wore for working in the restaurant. She threw the shirt aside and unzipped her black skirt. She wriggled out of it and unclasped her bra. She discarded it, pushed down her knickers, and stepped out of them. She pressed her naked body up against her lover, rubbing her tits against Katie's. Her skin felt warm and soft.

She nuzzled her partner's neck, kissing and nibbling the sensitive area. Katie moaned softly and Jo cupped Katie's rounded buttocks, kneading them. She wormed her hot tongue inside her companion's ear, then used her teeth to tug on the lobe. Finally she pushed Katie back on to the bed and climbed on top.

Katie liked the way Jo's weight pressed down on her. She loved the sensation of Jo's strong body pinning her to the mattress. She wriggled, emphasising the feeling of being trapped underneath her lover.

Jo bent her head and caught one of Katie's nipple rings

between her teeth. She pulled on it, lengthening the dark teat. She sucked the nipple into her mouth and nibbled on it. Slowly, she licked her way across Katie's chest, wetting the tanned skin. Her mouth sought the other ripe nipple. She found it and sucked it inside the warm cave of her mouth. Jo teased the swollen nub. She flicked her hot tongue over the tip. She chewed on it gently. She straddled Katie and sat up. Her fingers ran over Katie's torso, barely touching. She kneaded the ripe breasts, squeezing them, massaging them. She rolled each swollen nipple between a thumb and forefinger.

Katie arched her back, thrusting her proud tits forward. Jo's expert fingers continued to tweak and stretch her pierced nipples. Katie stroked the girl's long thighs, astride her own hips. She ran her hands up and down over the smooth skin. Hot pinpricks of pleasure radiated out from her nipples and warmed her chest. Her cunt ached with arousal. Where Jo's sweet pussy rubbed against her belly, she was slick with her lover's juices. She grasped Jo's hips and pulled her closer.

Jo hooked a finger through each of Katie's nipple rings. She pulled on them hard, making Katie moan. Jo increased her pressure on the rings, elongating the reddened teats, and pulled harder, stretching Katie's aroused nipples. Slowly Jo turned the rings, rotating them through 180 degrees.

Katie was riding the line between pleasure and pain, experiencing a level of excitement she had only dreamt of. Her whole body was quivering and weak. If she hadn't already been lying down, she was sure she would have fallen over. Her breathing was rapid and irregular. Her eyes closed into slits and a sheen of perspiration filmed her skin.

Jo released her grip on Katie's nipple rings. She swung one long leg over her lover's prone body and quickly crawled up the bed. She positioned herself beside Katie's head and turned round then straddled her lover's face and leant forward, supporting herself on her hands. Jo stretched out on top of Katie and lowered her fragrant pussy. She pushed the older woman's legs apart and nuzzled her mouth against the dark-fringed cunt. She quickly located Katie's tense clit and bathed it with her tongue.

Katie wrapped her arms around Jo's hips, pulling her closer. She drank in the heady aroma rising from her lover's hot cunt. She ran her tongue over the moist blonde curls that covered her labia, then slid it along the scarlet slit which bisected them. She sought the hardened bud of Jo's clit, sucking it into her mouth. She lavished attention on her lover's reddened clit, while Jo's mouth moved against her own pussy.

A delicious tingle prickled between her legs and a warm fist of tension grew in her belly. She bent her knees and pressed her heels down into the mattress. She rocked her hips, increasing the friction where Jo's mouth worked her clit. She smothered her face in her lover's quim, smearing the sweet juices over her lips and chin. Her mouth moved frantically against Jo's slippery crotch, finding Jo's clit and teasing the hard bud.

Jo writhed above her. Her sweat-smeared torso slid against Katie's belly and she pressed her pussy into Katie's eager face, establishing a rhythm. The air smelt of sex. Katie's heart pounded in her chest as she ground her aching cunt hard against Jo's face. The first throb of orgasm began to beat between Katie's legs. Her thighs tensed and trembled. She dug her nails hard into the flesh of Jo's buttocks and thrust her cunt against Jo's face. She pulled Jo closer, wildly sucking on the girl's clit as she came. Jolts of rapture shot up her spine, and the tension in her belly evaporated as a warm glow of pleasure washed over her.

She kept her mouth locked over Jo's clit as she came, sucking hard. Gradually, her taut muscles softened and her pussy contracted gently with little aftershocks of orgasm. Jo's mouth was no longer on her, and Katie felt the girl shifting her weight. Jo lifted herself up on her hands, until she was on all fours like a dog, her dripping fanny pressed hard into Katie's face. She swayed her hips, rhythmically rubbing her crotch against Katie's mouth.

Lovingly, Katie mouthed her partner's taut clit. Jo exhaled sharply, each hissing breath seeming to take her closer to orgasm. She arched her back and moaned softly, her hips moving quickly. Katie extended her tongue and allowed it to brush against Jo's clit as she slid back and forth. Her body stiffened and she sat down hard on Katie's face. She let out a series of staccato moans, sobs almost, then circled her hips, crushing her spasming quim into Katie's mouth.

'Oh, that was incredible,' Jo said weakly, when it was over. 'I've missed you.' She rolled off Katie's face and slithered round on the bed until she was upright. She wrapped her arms around her lover and nestled in to her, resting her head on Katie's chest.

'I missed you too,' said Katie, stroking Jo's hair. 'I can't believe I was so stupid. I almost lost you! I promise I won't be so foolish again.' She kissed Jo's sweat-damp head.

'But I bet you will. That's the point, isn't it? We don't mean to be stupid, but we are. Because we're human and we can't help it. Sooner or later, we're bound to do something silly. I don't expect you to be perfect and I know I can't be. Promise me you'll do your best and that you'll always be honest with me, in future. That's good enough for me.' She lifted her head and kissed Katie gently on the mouth. She smiled at her lover. 'Now, come here. I've got a lot more apologising to do . . .'

FOURTEEN

Sally let herself out of the flat and headed for her car. Things had gone well. That was a relief. Katie and Jo were made for each other: it was obvious to anyone who saw them together. She was so glad she had managed to get them speaking again.

And now it was her turn. She unlocked the car and settled herself behind the wheel. It was almost lunchtime; Liz would be at the pub. Or, at least, she hoped so. Please don't let it be her day off. She started the engine and manoeuvred her way out of the gravelled parking area. Out on the main road, she flipped the switch activating the electric sunroof. It slid open, letting light and warmth flood into the car. The smell of ripening corn reached her from the fields that skirted the narrow road. Here and there, scarlet poppies peeped out from between the golden stalks of grain. She spotted a wild rabbit quietly cropping the grass verge. It rose up on its hind legs and looked at her quizzically as she drove by.

Traffic was light. A mud-splattered tractor rattled out of a farm gate and trundled along the road. She overtook. She was minutes away from Hailsham Edge, now. Her heart danced an anxious quickstep in her chest. Please, let Liz be in. She wanted to get this over and done with.

She drove past the pond, where ducks quacked and waddled around the grassy edge. She rounded a curve and the village came into view. The church spire soared above the huddled stone houses. At the top of the hill sat The Moonraker, its white plaster façade banded by blackened beams. She parked in the small public car park next to the church and rummaged in her handbag for a mirror. She combed her hair. She wasn't wearing make-up, but she would have to do.

As she stepped out of the car, the church bells began to peal, a rapturous tumble of sound that seemed to brighten the day. A wedding party emerged through the wooden porch of the church. The bride and groom held hands and smiled under a blizzard of confetti. The bells continued to proclaim the joy of the occasion. An omen, she thought.

She took a deep breath and went into the pub. She spotted Liz immediately, pulling pints for a couple of thirsty hikers. What should she do, now? She had not thought that far. She had been so concerned that Liz would not be there that she had not actually thought about what she might say. She hovered near the bar, feeling slightly ridiculous. She would buy a drink; then she would ask if they could have a talk.

'Hello, stranger.' Liz had beaten her to it. 'I thought you'd forgotten us.'

Sally felt even more ridiculous, now. Was she imagining it, or was Liz peeved? She had every right to be. Sally had swanned off to sort herself out, without even giving a thought to how Liz might be feeling. She was probably hurt and upset. She might even have rung Sally at the cottage and got no answer. And now here was Sally, expecting to be welcomed back into the fold. Just how selfish could she be?

'I've been away,' she began. 'I went to Arundel and spent a couple of days in the pub my book is about. I didn't plan it; it was a spontaneous thing. I'm sorry I didn't tell you I was going away. I imagine you're feeling pretty pissed off with me.'

'I'll live. What can I get you?' Liz was friendly, yet business-like. Sally couldn't tell if she was upset or not.

In for a penny, in for a pound, she thought. 'Actually, I came here to see you. I hoped we might have a chat. If you're free.' Sally smiled weakly. She scrutinised the landlady's beautiful face, looking for any clue that might betray her feelings.

Liz smiled broadly. 'Sure. But I can't get away until after the lunchtime rush. We're short-staffed today. Tell you what – why don't you go and have lunch in the restaurant, on me? We can go upstairs for a chat when things quieten down.'

'I'd love to. That's very kind of you,' said Sally.

'Go through and take a seat. I'll send a waitress straight over to you.'

Sally enjoyed a pleasant lunch. She drank two glasses of wine to calm her nerves. Now, she was on her second cup of coffee. There had been a steady flow of customers in the restaurant, but it was slowing down now. The two waitresses had certainly had their work cut out. They had been attentive and competent, no matter how busy they were. She took her hat off to Liz. The Moonraker was an efficient operation and the food was divine. Here in the restaurant, the menu was a little more formal than in the bar, but it was still good value. And she offered bed and breakfast, too. With a little bit of luck, Liz would soon be raking it in. And she deserved it. She had worked hard.

One of the things that had first attracted her to Liz was her energy and enthusiasm for her work. Liz's eyes shone with excitement when she talked about her plans for the pub and Sally had been able to empathise. She had recognised Liz's passion because she shared it. When her own work was going well, there was nothing she would rather be doing. Well, almost nothing, she smiled to herself. But even she recognised that she had to take time off from sex occasionally. She was lucky, as

Liz was, to have a job that she enjoyed. A job which filled her with excitement and provided her with a sense of worthiness as well as an income. But there she was, putting things down to luck again. It wasn't chance or fate that had led her here: it was choice. Liz had chosen to leave London and sink her savings into the pub. And Sally had chosen to channel her energy and urge to communicate into writing, rather than taking on the boring but worthy research job everyone had expected her to.

A series of choices had led her here and now she was facing another choice. Perhaps the most important choice of her life. But, if she knew nothing else, she knew that she wanted Liz. And she was not leaving here until she had made Liz understand how she felt. It was quite exciting actually. She recognised the familiar tingle of anticipation growing in her chest and she welcomed it. Funny, she should have been scared, but she wasn't. After all, she was about to declare herself to the woman she loved and she risked losing everything. Surely that justified a little bit of anxiety? But instead, her heart was filled with joy and hope and anticipation. A world of limitless possibilities was spread in front of her and, for the first time, it did not seem to be beyond her grasp.

Liz appeared from the bar next door and beckoned to Sally with a crooked finger.

'Panic over,' she said. 'I've got a couple of bottles of decent wine upstairs. How about joining me for a glass? I need to unwind.'

'I'd love to,' said Sally. She got up and followed Liz across the bar and through a door which led to her private domain. Liz walked up the stairs. Sally followed, her eyes trained on Liz's ample arse, wiggling invitingly, only inches away.

Unlike the traditional brass-and-beam décor of the pub itself, Liz's private rooms were light and modern. She led Sally into her living room, a restful symphony of pale greens. The walls below the dado rail had been hung with a dusky sage textured paper. Above it, they were a toning, paler shade. Even the ceiling was green. Liz was obviously a fan of Charles Rennie Macintosh; a tall, black, ladder-back chair stood against one wall. Two elegant console tables stood on either side of the art-deco fireplace. One table held a sculpture of a girl, her short hair carved into the complicated waves popular in the 1930s. Her limbs and face were carved from ivory and her short shift dress was cast from a piece of bronze. She stood on a marble plinth, feet apart, her left hand behind her supporting a bronze hoop.

The other table held a lamp with a svelte bronze nymph, her delicate arms held aloft and her hands seemingly supporting the glass tiffany shade.

'I love Art Deco,' Sally said. 'This is gorgeous.'

'Glad you like it,' said Liz, smiling. 'This place is my retreat from the chaos downstairs. Sit yourself down: I'll get the wine.'

Sally looked at the rest of the room. A round walnut display case stood between the two sash windows, opposite the fireplace. Its shelves held 1930s china and glass. There were even a couple of pieces which Sally recognised as Clarice Cliff. Two dark green Deco-style armchairs sat either side of a three-seat sofa.

She sat down and Liz returned, carrying a bottle and two full glasses. Liz set the bottle down on a side table and passed Sally one of the glasses, before sitting down.

'Don't you have a TV or stereo?' Sally asked, looking around the room.

'I'm afraid I do. Over there, in the cupboard in the corner. They seemed out of place so I had the cupboard made.' She surveyed Sally coolly. 'Anyway. You didn't come here to talk about my viewing habits. To what do I owe the honour of your company?'

'First of all,' said Sally, 'I wanted to apologise. I didn't mean to go away without letting you know where I had gone. I just went out for a drive, found myself in Arundel and decided to stay for a couple of nights. I had some thinking to do, if I'm honest. And somehow I found the place helped me sort things out. A lot of my thinking was about you, actually. But, in retrospect, it was rather selfish of me to swan off "to find myself", without even letting you know where I was.' She looked at Liz, hoping for a sign of how her words were being received. But there was nothing. Liz sat impassively, sipping at her wine. She wasn't going to make it easy, Sally reflected. And Sally didn't blame her.

'Anyway,' she went on, 'there's no easy way to say this, so I'm just going to say it. I might not be able to express myself very eloquently or very clearly, but I want you to know that, if nothing else, I mean every word.' She took a deep breath. 'I haven't been able to get you out of my mind since we met. I think you're so beautiful. And you're funny and you're strong, and you're fun to be with. And you're great in bed. And then we found out that we're both interested in bondage. That we both want to explore our inner natures. It was incredible to me to find someone I could share that part of myself with. It made me feel really close to you, really . . . really known – does that make sense?' She paused.

Liz nodded, indicating that she understood.

Sally continued. 'And I hoped you felt the same. But I wasn't sure. Next morning, you dashed off without so much as a cuddle. Then you suggested we get into a threesome. Which, I admit, I loved. But, surely, you don't do that if you're interested in a relationship? Anyway, I couldn't work out whether you liked me or not and I wanted you to. But I was too nervous to show my own hand, in case you rejected me. So, I guess, I ran away to Arundel. But I've finally realised that I love you. It's a bit late, I know, but having realised, I have to act on it. In a sense, it doesn't matter to me if you care about me or not. Obviously I'd like you to; but if you don't, it isn't the end of the world. Somehow, it's more important for me to finally tell someone how I feel, to go for what I want, than for you to love me back.'

She'd run out of steam. The words had just tumbled out; she wasn't even sure if she had made sense. And now she felt drained. Exhausted, but good. She was glad she had got it all off her chest. She looked at Liz, scrutinising her face for a sign, any sign that her feelings were reciprocated.

Liz smiled. 'I can't tell you how relieved I am,' she said finally. 'I liked you from the beginning, but I must admit I couldn't seem to pin you down. One minute, you were hot for me; the next, you were giving me the cold shoulder. I couldn't tell if you liked me or not, either.' She laughed. 'So I guess what you were picking up was my reaction to your behaviour. What a pair we are. I like you a lot and I'd like to spend some time getting to know you better. Exploring my fantasies in a loving relationship with someone who's on my wavelength was special to me. I hope we do a lot more of it. And I hope that, from now on, you'll tell me what's on your mind and not swan off across the county every time you're feeling confused.'

'I promise.' Sally couldn't take her eyes off Liz's gentle face. Her lover's dark eyes were sparkling, her full mouth curved into a smile. She took a sip from her glass. The berry-dark liquid stained her lips.

'I bought you something,' Liz said finally. 'I'll fetch it.' She got up and left the room. A moment later she was back, a long, flat, gold box grasped between her delicate fingers.

'I bought it the other day,' she said, 'after we spent the night with Ros. I thought you'd like it.' She handed the box to Sally.

'Thank you,' said Sally. She put the box down on her knees and lifted the lid. She gasped. 'Oh, my God . . .'

'Do you like it?' asked Liz anxiously.

'Oh yes, I love it.' It was a dog collar. A very elegant one, but a dog collar nonetheless. A thin black leather strap, less than half an inch wide, which was fastened with a delicate silver buckle. She picked it up and held it between her fingers. It was beautiful. Beside the buckle was a D ring, sewn into the leather. She pulled on the ring experimentally.

'That's where I fit your lead,' Liz explained, tongue in cheek.

'You bought a lead, too?' Sally asked excitedly.

'One step at a time, sweetheart.' Liz laughed. 'Why don't you put it on?'

'I think you should put it on me.'

'Yes, I should, shouldn't I? Come here.' Sally handed the collar to Liz. Deftly, Liz undid the silver buckle. She put the collar around Sally's neck and fastened it. Sally could hardly breathe, she was so excited. The sensation of the soft leather on her neck was incredible. She liked the weight of it, the feel of the buckle resting against the base of her throat. She was tingling all over.

'I'm waiting for you to thank me,' said Liz simply.

Sally looked at her. The hint of a smile played around Liz's lips. A jolt of excitement shot up Sally's spine, and the short hairs on the back of her neck stood up. 'Thank you for my collar, mistress,' she said, her voice quavering with excitement.

'You're welcome. How about taking the rest of this wine into the bedroom?' Liz's voice was husky with arousal. Without waiting for an answer, she drained her glass and picked the bottle up off the table. 'Follow me.'

Sally stood up and obediently followed Liz across the room and through the door. They went along the short entrance corridor and through another door. Liz's bedroom was as cool and restful as her sitting room. Pale shades of peach adorned the walls and several Klimt prints hung from the picture rail. Liz's bed was huge, with head and footboards of blonde wood. A raspberry red throw was spread over the bed. It looked warm and inviting.

Liz closed the door behind them and took Sally's hand. She pulled her lover over to the bed and began stripping her clothes off. 'I know I should be doing this more delicately,' she said, 'but I can't wait. I want you naked. Now!' She pulled Sally's T-shirt over her head, unhooked her bra and peeled it off. She unbuttoned Sally's wrap-over skirt and tossed it aside. Finally, she slid Sally's knickers down her legs. 'You're shaved!'

'Yes. Do you like it? I went back to the club on my own and met Ros's mistress. She made Ros shave me.'

'I love it. And I only wish I had thought of it first. You have been a busy girl, haven't you? Come here, let me touch you.' She pulled Sally close and kissed her.

Sally surrendered to Liz's invading tongue, allowing her to possess her mouth. She wrapped her arms around her lover and held her tight.

'Are you sure you're dressed appropriately for the occasion?' Sally asked finally.

'You're right,' Liz agreed. She broke away from the embrace and undressed quickly, clothes flying everywhere. When she was naked, she climbed on to the bed and pulled Sally down beside her.

'Now, where were we?' she asked huskily. She rolled on top of Sally. Her ample body was soft and warm. They kissed.

Sally closed her eyes and wrapped her arms around her lover's waist. Liz's hot mouth felt like home.

Liz brushed Sally's hair back from her brow and showered her face with butterfly kisses. She kissed each closed eyelid, the temples, the point of her chin. She nibbled Sally's ear-lobe and nuzzled her face into Sally's hair, drinking in the perfume.

She wetted the flesh of Sally's neck with her tongue, then nipped it with her teeth. She trailed her tongue along Sally's collarbone, down her cleavage, then grasped Sally's wrists and pushed her hands above her head, holding them there. Liz teased her breasts, sucking and nibbling on the soft flesh, licking it. She stuck out her tongue and circled each of Sally's areolae in turn. She flicked her tongue across the surface of each taut nipple until Sally let out a long, hissing breath.

'That's so good,' she murmured.

Liz caught one erect nipple in her mouth and sucked on it hard. She used her teeth to nip and nibble. Sally writhed under

Liz, thrashing against the bed. Liz's strong hands held her arms above her head, and Sally relished the sensation of confinement. It was so exciting being at Liz's mercy.

Her beautiful companion moved her attention to the other nipple. She was biting it – and biting it increasingly hard. Sally was in heaven. The distinction between pleasure and pain was completely blurred. She didn't know if it hurt or not. All that she knew was that it felt good. So good that she could hardly bear it. She kicked her legs against the mattress.

'For God's sake, touch my cunt. I can't bear it any more.' She was surprised by the ferocity of her own words, by the brazen and naked lust she was articulating. But she couldn't help herself.

'Keep still. I can't hold you! I think I'll have to tie your wrists so I've got my hands free,' said Liz. She rolled off Sally and reached down to the floor. Among the tangle of abandoned clothes, she found her shirt. She wrapped the sleeves around both of Sally's wrists and tied it tightly to one of the bedposts, then pulled on Sally's wrists, making sure she was securely bound. Panting and sweaty from exertion, she slithered back down on top of Sally, using her substantial weight to pin Sally down.

She sucked one of Sally's erect and still sensitive nipples into her mouth. She licked and nibbled it, teasing Sally to the edge of ecstasy. With her fingers, she squeezed and pinched her lover's other swollen teat.

'Please, I want you to touch my pussy,' Sally begged urgently.

'I think I'm going to have to gag you, too, until you can learn to be patient. I'll decide when you're ready.' Liz leant down to the floor and scooped up Sally's panties.

'These will do,' she said. She rolled them into a ball and stuffed them into Sally's mouth. 'Can you breathe OK, sweetheart?' she asked anxiously.

Sally nodded.

Liz went back to Sally's nipples, working her eloquent magic on them. Sally thought she might die of pleasure. She pulled on the shirt that bound her hands and discovered that she was held tight, unable to resist. She breathed in deeply through her nose. Her mouth was crammed full with her own knickers: how wicked. Only a fortnight ago, she would never have dreamed this was possible. Now here she was, bound and gagged and being teased into a frenzy of desire. She was in heaven.

Liz bit each of Sally's nipples in turn, drawing her teeth along the length of the swollen nub and nibbling at the tip. Denied of any other means of expression, Sally squirmed, so Liz gripped one nipple in each hand and pinched hard. She pulled on them, stretching them, twisting them, and Sally watched as Liz manipulated her elongated nipples. It felt so good. She pressed her legs together for relief; she was so juicy she could hear herself squelching.

Liz ran her nails hard down Sally's abdomen. Sally's body glowed where Liz had touched her, burning trails of red, which stood out against her pale skin. But there was no blood; Liz hadn't broken her skin. She felt Liz's fingernails again, this time running up the underside of her thighs. She waited for the heat, the tingle. It felt so good. She didn't understand it, but she didn't care.

Then Liz touched her cunt.

Sally thrust out her hips, and Liz's fingers trailed up the length of her wet slit and down again. She plunged them inside the aching hole, circled them. Sally let out a muffled moan and Liz slid two fingers slowly in and out of her partner's slippery cunt. With her other hand, she spread Sally's buttocks and slipped one juice-moistened finger into her nether hole. The puckered opening yielded easily to the invading digit, sucking it inside. Sally rocked her hips, trying to establish a rhythm.

Liz slid down the bed and lay flat on her belly. She dipped her head and tasted Sally's naked pussy, then stuck out her tongue and ran it up the slick red slit. She licked each shaven labia, rubbed her lips against the smooth, bare flesh. Her face felt soft against Sally's skin. She opened her mouth wide and covered Sally's clit. She licked the swollen bud, sucked on it. Sally exhaled deeply; the hot mouth felt incredible against her skin.

Liz's fingers slid in and out of her lover's tight holes. She curled her fingers upwards and massaged her G-spot. Sally moaned as the pressure set off a delicious cascade of pleasure inside her. She was on the edge. She ground her crotch against Liz's face, lifting her arse up off the bed. She wrapped her hands around the shirt which bound her to the bed and pulled hard.

Liz's mouth worked her clit rhythmically. Sally's quim contracted around her lover's fingers. Moisture flowed freely; a dark stain was spreading on the bedspread beneath her. She rocked her hips urgently, keeping pace with Liz's squirming tongue. Her body was alive with sensation. The brush of the bedspread against her skin felt like a caress and the tickle of Liz's hair falling over her thighs and belly was like a velvet kiss. Her lover's breath against her shaved pussy seemed like a shower of love.

She was panting now, biting down hard on the knickers in her mouth. Her back was arched, her tight nipples thrust upwards. Sweat sheened her body; tension drummed in her belly, rose to a peak and dissolved in a thundering crescendo of pleasure.

She was coming. She pressed her heels down into the mattress and pulled hard on the shirt that tied her to the bedpost. Her bottom was in mid-air, tense thighs twitching from the effort. She pressed her throbbing cunt against Liz's mouth and grunted, breath snorting down her nose as she bit on her gag. She was shaking all over as waves of incredible pleasure ricocheted around her body.

Sally straightened the sheaf of paper she had just taken out of the printer. She tapped its edge on the table, neatening the edges. She clipped them together and slipped them into the envelope she had just addressed. She would take the package down to the local post office in the morning and post it off to Margaret. Her three chapters were finished at last.

She smiled to herself, remembering how confused and overwhelmed she had felt by the project, only a few weeks ago. It was hard to imagine, now, that she could ever have felt so impotent with anxiety. But she had. Her notes and interviews had sat on her top shelf for months, like a malignant presence waiting to ambush her. Just looking at them had terrified her. But it wasn't just her work that she had been hiding on the top of her bookcase, she realised – it was her life. She had stuffed everything up there, out of sight. Everything she was afraid of, everything she didn't feel able to face – real or imagined. She laughed out loud at the image.

When she had lifted them down and blown the cobwebs away, she had discovered that there was nothing to be afraid of after all. Far from it. The secrets she had been hiding at the back of her dusty shelves were good ones, not bad. And by taking them down and opening them up, she had freed her spirit. Not only had she finished Margaret's three chapters ahead of schedule, she was well on course with the rest. And finding the courage to face her true sexual nature had liberated her. Most importantly of all, she had got Liz. She was so lucky.

Sally frowned. It was twenty to eleven. She had left the pub just before six, when Liz had had to go back to work. In their excitement, they hadn't remembered to make an arrangement about meeting tonight. Her body ached for Liz. She could still smell her lover's perfume on her own skin. She didn't want to sleep alone tonight. But she didn't even know Liz's phone number! Somehow, she'd never got round to asking for it. She could put her jacket on and stroll down to the pub; it would only take five minutes. But there was a gentle rain falling and she didn't really fancy getting wet.

She went over to the sideboard and picked up the phone

book. She carried it back to the table and opened it. Did she look up The Moonraker, or Liz's surname? She had never looked up a pub before. She would look for Liz's name first – Godfrey. She licked her finger and turned over pages until she found the Gs. She put her glasses on and scanned the names.

A tap at the front door disturbed her concentration. Liz? She wasn't expecting anyone else. She tossed her reading glasses on to the table, trotted over to the front door and put her eye against the spy hole. Yes, it was her lover, looking chilly and sheltering under an umbrella. Quickly, she slid back the bolts and unlocked the door.

'Hi, I was just looking up your phone number,' she said. 'This is a pleasant surprise.'

'I realised we hadn't talked about tonight, and I wanted to see you. So I thought I'd walk over. I got a bit wet, though.' She shook her umbrella and stood it up against the outside wall. She came in and grabbed Sally, gathering her up into her arms. They kissed.

'Did you get much work done?' Liz asked

'I got my three chapters done. I've packed them up ready for the post tomorrow.' Sally smiled.

'Well done. I think that calls for a celebration, don't you? How about we open this bottle of bubbly that's tearing a hole in my jacket pocket?' She pulled a bottle of champagne out of her pocket with a flourish, like a magician producing a rabbit.

'And I brought glasses, in case you don't have any,' she said, bringing two champagne flutes out of her other pocket.

'Don't tell me you've got a bunch of flowers and a rubber chicken in there, too!'

They laughed.

'Let's open this upstairs,' suggested Sally.

'You read my mind.'

Sally ran her fingers through Liz's damp hair. She cupped the nape of Liz's neck and pulled her face close. They kissed; their tongues moved together in a ritual dance of love. Sally pulled away and smiled. She took the champagne from Liz and gripped her hand, then led her lover across the small living room and up the narrow stairs to bed.

FIFTEEN

Sally propped herself up against her pillows and poured herself another cup of black coffee from the tray on the bed. She leant over and kissed Liz, then lazily reached for another croissant.

'This is lovely,' said Liz, spooning marmalade onto her croissant. 'Breakfast for me is usually a hurried slice of toast before I deal with the deliveries. Most days, I don't even get time for that. And sharing it with you makes it all the more enjoyable, of course.' She leant over and gave Sally a sticky kiss.

'I don't do this every day – just special occasions. Or I'd be as big as a house'

'Well, this certainly qualifies as a special day, doesn't it? I assure you, it isn't every day that a gorgeous, talented writer asks me if she can be my sex slave.' Liz smiled wickedly.

Sally burst into laughter. 'That makes me sound deliciously wicked,' she said.

'What made you bite the bullet, in the end?' Liz asked. 'If you were so unsure about how I'd respond, how did you find the courage to approach me?'

'You'll laugh,' said Sally, colouring with embarrassment. 'It sounds silly.'

'I promise I won't laugh, but you've got to tell me, now; you've piqued my interest.'

Sally set her plate and coffee cup down on the tray. She wiped some crumbs away from her lips and took a deep breath. 'Actually, it was a combination of things. Getting in touch with my submissive nature helped. And partly, it was just being here, away from London. After I went back to the club on my own and got involved with Simone and Ros, I felt incredible. It was like having my blinkers taken off. Everything suddenly made sense. But I was still scared that you would reject me if I declared my feelings. I couldn't get you out of my mind, but I was too scared to approach you, so I went for a drive and finally found myself in Arundel and decided to stay.' Quietly, Sally told Liz about her experience in The Green Man. About sleeping with Anna Lee, about Anna coming to her in a dream, and turning out not to be Anna after all. She told Liz all of it, how both Annas had given her the same message and how it was that message which had helped her to find the courage she needed.

'I can't believe the "dream" Anna was actually a ghost, but I can't explain it, either. I told myself it was my subconscious – that I had forgotten that the ghost and the Lees' daughter shared the same name. But I'm still not sure I believe that. Anna put it down to her highly developed sense of empathy and that makes more sense to me. Whatever it was though, I'm sure there was more than a little bit of magic involved. And I kind of like that explanation.'

'And so do I,' said Liz, nodding.

'You do surprise me. You're so practical and down to earth. Believing in magic – well, it seems a bit out of character.'

'You forget, I live in an ancient inn myself. I can understand how the spirit of past residents can inhabit a building. They aren't ghosts, exactly – at least, I can't believe they are ghosts –

but they are definitely there. A sort of benign presence – more like atmosphere. They are part of the building's history, if you like. At The Moonraker, there always seemed to be a welcoming friendly atmosphere. Ever since I was a child, I always felt safe and protected there. And I've never felt more . . . centred, grounded, than when I am there. That's why I didn't think twice about taking the place over when my parents died. In fact, being at the pub was the only thing that made sense in those terrible few months after the accident. It was almost as if the building were comforting me, sharing my loss. But I'd better shut up or you'll start thinking I am a vegetarian, crystal-waving, aura-worshipping weirdo.'

'Not at all,' said Sally, shaking her head. 'I know what you mean, I think. Some buildings and places do speak to you. Sometimes you just know when you are home.'

'That's it exactly,' agreed Liz. 'The Moonraker is home. I belong there. You studied The Green Man, you are writing about it – why shouldn't you feel some special bond with the place and its history?'

'Well, whatever the explanation is, I'm glad I did find the courage to tell you how I felt about you. Because if I hadn't, you wouldn't be here with me now. And I wouldn't have missed this for anything in the world.'

'Me neither,' enthused Liz. 'It's not every day I get breakfast in bed.'

Sally guffawed. She picked up the tray of crockery from the bed between them and put it down on the floor. She picked up her pillow and threw it at Liz. It bounced off and landed on the floor and then Sally launched herself at her lover, throwing herself on top of her. They giggled like schoolgirls as they wrestled on the bed. Liz pushed her heels down into the mattress and raised one shoulder off the bed. She put her weight behind it and pushed her body against Sally. Sally rolled off Liz and slid off the edge of the bed. She fell on to the floor, landing with a bump. Liz toppled after her and landed on Sally's chest; knocking the wind out of her.

'I submit!' said Sally, slapping the floor in mock submission.

'I know you do,' agreed Liz, 'and that's why I love you.'

'Come up, food's nearly done,' said Katie. The electronic door catch buzzed and they entered. They hurried up the stairs.

'Hi,' said Katie, greeting them both with a hug.

'We've brought supplies,' said Liz, holding up two bottles of Bollinger she had brought from the pub. 'They're already chilled.'

'Lovely,' said Katie. 'Let me get an ice bucket for them. Jo's in the sitting room; go in.' She bustled into the kitchen.

They went into the living room. Jo hugged them both. Katie came in with a tray of glasses and an ice bucket. She set them down on the table.

'Why don't you be mother?' she asked Liz. 'I always end up spilling half of it, like a Formula One driver who's just won the race. I'm sure you've got the professional touch.'

Liz expertly eased the champagne cork out of the bottle. She poured the fizzing golden liquid into four glasses and Sally passed full glasses to Katie and Jo and took one for herself.

'Happy first anniversary, Katie and Jo,' said Liz.

The four friends clinked glasses and drank a toast to their joint anniversary.

'Actually,' said Sally, 'this is a double celebration. I finally exchanged contracts on my flat today. So that means I'll be moving in with Liz next month!' She hugged Liz.

'Congratulations, that's wonderful news,' said Katie. 'It'll be really lovely to have you living so close.'

'I'll say it will,' said Liz. 'It's been hell, this past year, only being together at weekends. I can hardly wait to have Sally living with me full time. Although we are going to have to do some reorganisation to fit all her stuff in. We might convert one of the B&B rooms into a study. Sally must have somewhere of her own to work.'

'I thought that now you'd had two best sellers, you didn't need to work any more,' teased Jo.

'I wish,' said Sally. 'But I'm still worried that no one will buy my new book. After all, I've never written a novel before.'

'They'll love it,' said Katie. 'From what I've read of your work in progress, it's great. It's funny and original and sexy. Just like you.' She beamed at Sally.

Sally blushed scarlet. 'In that case, I'd better get on and finish it,' she said. 'A lot's happened in the last year, hasn't it?'

'Well, it has for me,' said Jo. 'A year ago I was just a schoolgirl, living at home with my parents. They didn't even know I was gay! Now I'm a university student living with my lover, who I adore. And the best bit about it is that my parents love her, too. They don't mind a bit that I'm a lesbian and they treat Katie like a second daughter.'

'Yes, they do,' agreed Katie, 'and I love it. I didn't realise how much I missed my own parents. It's nice to have Jo's as a substitute.'

'We've got something else to celebrate,' announced Sally. 'We didn't tell you before, because we were waiting for it to be confirmed. But Liz has just found out that The Moonraker has won a food award. The Food Critics' Circle have given it a Gold Chevron as the best pub restaurant in the South East.' She grabbed Liz and hugged her proudly. Liz blushed.

'Liz! That's wonderful,' said Katie. 'You've worked so hard. You really deserve it.' She threw her arms around Liz's neck and kissed her.

'That's amazing,' said Jo, pouring more champagne. 'It just goes to show what you can achieve if you focus on your goal and work hard for it.'

'I'll drink to that,' said Sally, raising her glass.

★

Later that evening, Liz and Sally undressed in Katie's spare bedroom. Sally stepped out of her shoes and lifted her dress over her head as Liz sat in front of the dressing table, putting moisturiser on her face. Sally took off her underwear and sat down on the bed. She looked over at Liz and smiled.

'Have I told you recently that I love you?' she asked

'About fifty times today, I think.' Liz turned and smiled at her.

'I'm sorry, but I can't help it. I just look at you and my heart sort of fills up and I have to tell you. It's your fault. You're so beautiful. Inside and out.'

'I'm glad you think so,' said Liz, standing up, 'because the feeling is most definitely mutual.' She walked over to the bed and bent to kiss Sally. She cupped Sally's face with both hands and kissed her gently on the mouth. She fingered Sally's dog collar, running one finger along the delicate band of leather, and smiled.

'I can't keep my hands off you,' she said. 'Let me get my clothes off, too, and we can give this mattress a thorough testing.' Liz unbuttoned her blouse and let it fall to the ground. She hooked her thumbs under the elasticated waistband of her skirt, pushed it down her legs and stepped out of it. She stood before Sally in only her underwear. Her ample body was smooth and tanned, from spending much of her free time sunbathing in her private roof garden. Her ripe breasts seemed to be straining against the delicate fabric of her lacy bra. She reached behind her and unhooked it, releasing her gorgeous tits. They tumbled out invitingly, tempting Sally with their fat chocolate nipples.

As Liz slid her silky knickers down her thighs, Sally watched, fascinated. Her lover stepped out of her panties and she licked her lips.

'Come here,' she whispered, reaching a hand out to Liz.

Liz scrambled on the bed and lay down beside Sally. She wrapped her arms around her lover and pulled her close. Her body was soft and warm. Sally nuzzled against Liz's neck, burying her nose in the shiny, dark hair. She inhaled deeply, filling her nostrils with the scent of rosemary shampoo.

Liz was biting her, her teeth gently nibbling along her shoulder. It made Sally tingle. She drew in air through her teeth. Liz had reached her neck now and she was kissing her. Sucking and licking her throat, just above her leather collar. Sally threw her head back, stretching her neck taut. It was delicious. She gasped as she felt Liz begin to nibble the sensitive flesh of her throat.

She stroked Liz's back, sliding her hands up and down her silky skin. She reached down and cupped her partner's buttocks, pulling her closer. She held tight and rolled over on her back, pulling Liz on top of her. Liz's weight felt good, pressing down on her.

Liz's mouth was moving downwards. She licked along Sally's collarbone. She squirmed her tongue into each armpit and nibbled the soft flesh that flared out at the margin of her breasts. Liz's hot mouth was travelling down her cleavage now, wetting the skin. She teased Sally's left nipple with her tongue; circling the sensitive flesh until it crinkled and stiffened. She sucked the swollen nub between her lips, warming it, and her teeth nipped at the reddened teat, teasing it.

Sally began to pant. She gripped Liz hard. Her pussy throbbed, and she pressed her heels down into the mattress and rocked her hips. Liz moved to the other nipple and lavished it with the same loving attention she had bestowed on its partner. Sally thought she might explode. She stroked Liz's hair, cupped the nape of her neck.

Liz looked up and smiled. She shuffled down the bed and used her strong hands to part Sally's legs. She pressed Sally's thighs apart urgently. She ducked her head and kissed the inside of one knee, then planted a trail of soft, wet kisses along the inside of Sally's thigh. When she did the same to the other leg, Sally shivered.

Liz's face was poised above Sally's moist crotch. She buried her face in the blonde curls and inhaled the scent rising from her lover's warm skin. The primitive odour of arousal, a tang of fresh sweat, and freesias. She closed her eyes, losing herself in the scented haven. Liz lapped along the groove between pussy and thigh, then circled her tongue around the rim of Sally's tight opening, pushing it inside.

Sally opened her legs wider. Her pulse raced. Liz's mouth felt so hot against her skin. She never felt so alive, so complete, as when she and Liz were making love. It meant everything to her. She looked down at her lover's face moving between her legs and sighed.

Liz was working her taut clit now, licking and sucking on the reddened bud, bringing her ever closer to fulfilment. Liz's thumbs circled at the entrance to her hole, teasing her. Blood pounded under her skin. Her pussy throbbed and she arched her back. She reached above her head and grabbed the rails of the brass bed, wrapping her hands around the cold metal bars and gripping them until her knuckles turned white.

Expertly, Liz manipulated the clit she knew so well. She sucked hard on the slick bead as she circled her thumbs at Sally's opening. Her mouth slid easily over the slippery surface. Rhythmically, she sucked on Sally's engorged clit, drawing it into her mouth and flicking her tongue across its sensitive tip.

Sally gasped. The muscles of her upper arms stood out as she pulled hard on the bedstead. She tossed her head from side to side, matting her hair. Her eyes moved beneath closed lids. She licked her lips. Her hips were moving, rocking back and forth, in synchronised rhythm with Liz's mouth. She ground her cunt into Liz's eager face, her skin feeling as though it was on fire. Her whole body was alert and sensitive, and the breeze from the open window felt like angel's fingers on her skin.

Liz sucked harder, knowing that Sally was close to orgasm. Sally began to murmur a complicated, wordless chant of ecstasy. Her body stiffened. She lifted her arse off the bed and thrust her hips forward, pressing her cunt into Liz's mouth. Sweat dripped off her chin.

Gradually, her body softened. She let go of the bed rails, relaxed the muscles in her legs. Her breathing returned to normal. She reached down to Liz and beckoned. Liz crawled up the bed and lay down in her arms.

A sound reached them through the bedroom wall: a high-pitched sobbing, a sort of keening.

'Mm,' said Liz, 'you don't have to be Sherlock Holmes to work out what our hosts are up to.' They listened. The sound was louder now and increasing in urgency and speed. A second, deeper voice took up the melody; low moans and gasps, which signalled imminent orgasm.

'I think they're both going to come together,' said Sally. They listened as the duet of love reached them through the bedroom wall. Both voices rose to dramatic crescendo, then subsided into silence.

'I don't know about you,' said Liz, 'but I can't help feeling that we ought to see if we can do better than that.'

'I agree,' said Sally, stroking her lover's cheek. 'It would be rude not to . . .'

SAPPHIRE NEW BOOKS

SWEET VIOLET
☐ *Published in September 1999*   Ruby Vise

Violet is young, butch and new in town, looking for a way to get over her childhood sweetheart Katherine. And there are plenty of distractions in 1980s London, as the rarefied big-city dyke scene is both sexually and politically charged – full of everything from cosmic mother-earth worshippers to sexy girls in leather.

£6.99   ISBN 0 352 33458 4

GETAWAY
☐ *Published in October 1999*   Suzanne Blaylock

Brilliantly talented Polly Sayers has had her first affair with a woman, stolen the code of an important new piece of software and done a runner all the way to a peaceful English coastal community. But things aren't as tranquil as they appear in this quiet haven, as Polly realises when she becomes immersed in an insular group of mysterious but very attractive women.

£6.99   ISBN 0 352 33443 6

NO ANGEL
☐ *Published in November 1999*   Marian Malone

Leather. Fetishes. SM. The words conjure up a multitude of feelings for erotic fiction writer Sally Avery, for Sally has a secret. Despite her explicitly written prose, she is relatively inexperienced when it comes to forbidden pleasures. Frightened by the depth of her yearnings, she starts to explore her darker side with other women. Her journey of self-discovery begins in the sleazy, sexy fetish clubs of Brighton . . .

£6.99   ISBN 0 352 33462 2

PREVIOUSLY PUBLISHED

BIG DEAL
☐ *Published in May 1999*   Helen Sandler

Lane and Carol have a deal that lets them play around with other partners. But things get out of hand when Lane takes to cruising gay men, while her femme girlfriend has secretly become the mistress of an ongoing all-girl student orgy. The fine print in the deal they've agreed on means things can only get hotter. It's time for a different set of rules – and forfeits.

£6.99   ISBN 0 352 33365 0

'The deal of a lifetime' – *The Guardian*

RIKA'S JEWEL
☐ *Published in June 1999*   Astrid Fox

Norway, AD 1066. A group of female Viking warriors – Ingrid's Crew – have set sail to fight the Saxons in Britain, and Ingrid's young lover Rika is determined to follow them. But, urged on by dark-haired oarswoman Pia, Rika soon penetrates Ingrid's secret erotic cult back home in Norway. Will Rika overcome Ingrid's psychic hold, or will she succumb to the intoxicating rituals of the cult? Thrilling sword-and-sorcery in the style of Xena and Red Sonja!

£6.99   ISBN 0 352 33367 7

'Splendid stuff' – *Diva Magazine*

MILLENNIUM FEVER
☐ *Published in July 1999*   Julia Wood

The millennium is approaching and so is Nikki's fortieth birthday. Married for twenty years, she is tired of playing the trophy wife in a small town where she can't adequately pursue her lofty career ambitions. In contrast, young writer Georgie has always been out and proud. But there's one thing they have in common – in the midst of millennial fever, they both want action and satisfaction. When they meet, the combination is explosive.

£6.99   ISBN 0 352 33368 5

ALL THAT GLITTERS
☐ *Published in August 1999*   Franca Nera

Marta Broderick: beautiful, successful art dealer; London lesbian. Marta inherits an art empire from the man who managed to spirit her out of East Berlin in the 1960s, Manny Schweitz. She's intent on completing Manny's unfinished business: recovering pieces of art stolen by the Nazis. Meanwhile, she's met the gorgeous but mysterious Judith Compton, and Marta's dark sexual addiction to Judith – along with her quest to return the treasures to the rightful owners – is taking her to dangerous places.

£6.99   ISBN 0 352 33426 6

------------✂------------------------

Please send me the books I have ticked above.

Name ....

Address ....

....

....

.... Post Code ....

Send to: **Cash Sales, Sapphire Books, Thames Wharf Studios, Rainville Road, London W6 9HA.**

US customers: for prices and details of how to order books for delivery by mail, call 1-800-805-1083.

Please enclose a cheque or postal order, made payable to **Virgin Publishing Ltd**, to the value of the books you have ordered plus postage and packing costs as follows:

UK and BFPO – £1.00 for the first book, 50p for each subsequent book.

Overseas (including Republic of Ireland) – £2.00 for the first book, £1.00 for each subsequent book.

We accept all major credit cards, including VISA, ACCESS/MASTERCARD, DINERS CLUB, AMEX and SWITCH.

Please write your card number and expiry date here:

....

Please allow up to 28 days for delivery.

Signature ....

------------✂------------------------

WE NEED YOUR HELP . . .

to plan the future of Sapphire books –

Yours are the only opinions that matter. Sapphire is a new and exciting venture: the first British series of books devoted to lesbian erotic fiction written by and for women.

We're going to do our best to provide the sexiest books you can buy. And we'd like you to help in these early stages. Tell us what you want to read. There's a freepost address for your filled-in questionnaires, so you won't even need to buy a stamp.

THE SAPPHIRE QUESTIONNAIRE

SECTION ONE: ABOUT YOU

1.1 Sex (*we presume you are female, but just in case*)
Are you?
Female ☐
Male ☐

1.2 Age
under 21 ☐ 21–30 ☐
31–40 ☐ 41–50 ☐
51–60 ☐ over 60 ☐

1.3 At what age did you leave full-time education?
still in education ☐ 16 or younger ☐
17–19 ☐ 20 or older ☐

1.4 Occupation _____

1.5 Annual household income _____

1.6 We are perfectly happy for you to remain anonymous; but if you would like us to send you a free booklist of Sapphire books, please insert your name and address

_____

_____

_____

_____

SECTION TWO: ABOUT BUYING SAPPHIRE BOOKS

2.1 Where did you get this copy of *No Angel*?
- Bought at chain book shop ☐
- Bought at independent book shop ☐
- Bought at supermarket ☐
- Bought at book exchange or used book shop ☐
- I borrowed it/found it ☐
- My partner bought it ☐

2.2 How did you find out about Sapphire books?
- I saw them in a shop ☐
- I saw them advertised in a magazine ☐
- A friend told me about them ☐
- I read about them in _____ ☐
- Other _____

2.3 Please tick the following statements you agree with:
- I would be less embarrassed about buying Sapphire books if the cover pictures were less explicit ☐
- I think that in general the pictures on Sapphire books are about right ☐
- I think Sapphire cover pictures should be as explicit as possible ☐

2.4 Would you read a Sapphire book in a public place – on a train for instance?
Yes ☐   No ☐

SECTION THREE: ABOUT THIS SAPPHIRE BOOK

3.1 Do you think the sex content in this book is:
Too much ☐   About right ☐
Not enough ☐

3.2 Do you think the writing style in this book is:
- Too unreal/escapist ☐
- About right ☐
- Too down to earth ☐

3.3 Do you think the story in this book is:
- Too complicated ☐
- About right ☐
- Too boring/simple ☐

3.4 Do you think the cover of this book is:
- Too explicit ☐
- About right ☐
- Not explicit enough ☐

Here's a space for any other comments:

SECTION FOUR: ABOUT OTHER SAPPHIRE BOOKS

4.1 How many Sapphire books have you read?

4.2 If more than one, which one did you prefer?

4.3 Why?

SECTION FIVE: ABOUT YOUR IDEAL EROTIC NOVEL

We want to publish the books you want to read – so this is your chance to tell us exactly what your ideal erotic novel would be like.

5.1 Using a scale of 1 to 5 (1 = no interest at all, 5 = your ideal), please rate the following possible settings for an erotic novel:

- Roman/Ancient World ☐
- Medieval/barbarian/sword 'n' sorcery ☐
- Renaissance/Elizabethan/Restoration ☐
- Victorian/Edwardian ☐
- 1920s & 1930s ☐
- Present day ☐
- Future/Science Fiction ☐

5.2 Using the same scale of 1 to 5, please rate the following themes you may find in an erotic novel:

Bondage/fetishism	☐
Romantic love	☐
SM/corporal punishment	☐
Bisexuality	☐
Gay male sex	☐
Group sex	☐
Watersports	☐
Rent/sex for money	☐

5.3 Using the same scale of 1 to 5, please rate the following styles in which an erotic novel could be written:

Gritty realism, down to earth	☐
Set in real life but ignoring its more unpleasant aspects	☐
Escapist fantasy, but just about believable	☐
Complete escapism, totally unrealistic	☐

5.4 In a book that features power differentials or sexual initiation, would you prefer the writing to be from the viewpoint of the dominant/experienced or submissive/inexperienced characters:

Dominant/Experienced	☐
Submissive/Inexperienced	☐
Both	☐

5.5 We'd like to include characters close to your ideal lover. What characteristics would your ideal lover have? Tick as many as you want:

Dominant	☐	Cruel	☐
Slim	☐	Young	☐
Big	☐	Naïve	☐
Voluptuous	☐	Caring	☐
Extroverted	☐	Rugged	☐
Bisexual	☐	Romantic	☐
Working Class	☐	Old	☐
Introverted	☐	Intellectual	☐
Butch	☐	Professional	☐
Femme	☐	Pervy	☐
Androgynous	☐	Ordinary	☐
Submissive	☐	Muscular	☐

Anything else? _____

5.6 Is there one particular setting or subject matter that your ideal erotic novel would contain:

SECTION SIX: LAST WORDS

6.1 What do you like best about Sapphire books?

6.2 What do you most dislike about Sapphire books?

6.3 In what way, if any, would you like to change Sapphire covers?

6.4 Here's a space for any other comments:

Thanks for completing this questionnaire. Now either tear it out, or photocopy it, then put it in an envelope and send it to:

**Sapphire/Virgin Publishing
FREEPOST LON3566
London
W6 9BR**

You don't need a stamp if you're in the UK, but you'll need one if you're posting from overseas.